E.L. BATES

Glamours and Gunshots

First published by StarDance Press 2024

Second edition

ISBN: 979-8-9858009-7-5

This book was professionally typeset on Reedsy.
Find out more at reedsy.com

Contents

1	Dead Man Walking	1
2	A Shot on the Street	22
3	A Plan of Action	45
4	Books and More Death	60
5	Shadows and Light	82
6	Speculations	108
7	Maia Uses Her Head	124
8	Shadow Spell Again	142
9	The Pieces Start to Fit	160
10	A Suspicious Invitation	178
11	Stars in Their Courses	196
12	All is Well …	215
13	… That Ends Well	231
Acknowledgments & Author's Note		240
About the Author		242
Also by E.L. Bates		244

1

Dead Man Walking

Merry birdsong filled the air on that bright April morning when the dead man stumbled into Aunt Amelia's front hall.

Technically, he was dying, not dead, else he couldn't have stumbled anywhere; corpses in general being no longer animate. There was just enough time for Maia, passing through the hall on her way to the Rose Parlor for a magic lesson with Aunt Amelia, to drop her books and papers and dash forward, catching the man in her arms beneath the butler's outraged nose.

"Call a doctor!" she cried, but it was too late. The man's eyelids fluttered and he breathed a single word:

"Beware."

Then he sighed and expired.

It was so ridiculously like something out of a dime novel that Maia couldn't believe it was real. She looked up, half expecting a beautiful foreign adventuress in furs and jewels to next appear in the hall, followed by a leering, greasy-haired scoundrel waving a gun.

All she saw, however, was the sagging jaw and round eyes of Mr. Lorde, her aunt's ever-so-dignified butler. That, and the limp weight in her arms, convinced her this was no hoax. She'd seen dead bodies before—held men as they died, in her time in France—and recognized the reality of the situation, however absurd it seemed.

"Mr. Lorde," she said in a soft voice most unusual for her. "I believe you should fetch my aunt. At once." She set the man down on the polished floor, careful not to disturb him more than necessary. Her decorous side wished to close his staring eyes; her practical side warned her the scene should be as little disturbed as possible.

"Yes, miss," the butler said, closing his mouth and swallowing hard. "And the doctor, miss?"

"No need for one anymore," she said, not taking her eyes from the dead man's face. "The police are more likely—or Domestic Protection—but Aunt Amelia first."

The butler positively scurried out of the room, a sight which would have delighted Maia at any other time, and Maia set to work. The light was poor in the entryway, thanks to the stained-glass windows above the door preventing sunlight from properly entering, so she murmured a spell to assist her task. Aunt Amelia did not approve of apprentices using magic unsupervised, but Maia had mastered this particular spell before she had even begun her apprenticeship. Besides, this was an emergency.

"*Lux fiat,*" she said, and a ball of steady silver light sprang to life above her open palm. Maia directed it to hover over the body while she began her examination. Aunt Amelia wouldn't approve of this either, but some tasks Maia preferred not to entrust to others.

With steady hands, she patted him down, checking his pockets and examining his body. It didn't take long; he was a short, sturdy man, dressed in middle-class clothing consisting of unkempt trousers and a collared shirt, though missing a coat and tie. No identification on him, no incriminating papers, nothing helpful at all. After she had finished, she sat back on her heels, frowning.

"*Finiatur*," she said absently, and the silver light vanished.

In her experience, people who died of illness were not usually waltzing around London immediately before so doing, and there were usually telltale signs of said illness left behind. On the other hand, people who died from violence generally bore the traces of their wound. This man was unmarked and appeared in perfect health, aside from the fact that he was dead.

Maia did not believe in jumping to conclusions. Still, she thought it a reasonable assumption that magic was most likely behind this. After all, he had come to Aunt Amelia's house to die. Amelia Rawlings was well known throughout Europe—the magical population thereof, at least—as one of the finest magicians of her generation.

The front door swung, causing Maia to jump and search her mind for a defensive spell. She relaxed when the newcomer proved to be a young lady of African descent dressed in the very latest spring fashions, her dark curly hair covered with a *chic* cloche and her black eyes sparkling.

"Hope you don't mind," she called as she sashayed through the doorway. "It was open ..." The words died in her throat as she took in the incongruous tableau.

It must have been an absurd sight. The brown-and-gold papered walls of the entryway, Maia in her plain but practical working costume of blue cotton dress with pleated skirt, the second housemaid frozen in the background with her mouth open in a silent scream, and the dead body on the spotless floor.

"Good morning, Helen," Maia said.

Aunt Amelia, trailed by a still-shaken Lorde, popped out of the Rose Parlor at that exact moment. Old woman and young both opened their mouths and said,

"Maia Whitney, what have you done now?"

It was the "now" that really irritated Maia. It wasn't as if she made a habit of collecting dead bodies and stirring up general mayhem. True, there had been that one occasion, but that was nearly four years ago, and none of it had been her fault. Well, maybe one or two bits of it, but …

"This is none of my doing," she said, rising to her feet and striving to keep her voice from sounding petulant. She wasn't certain she entirely succeeded. "He came in and dropped dead at my feet. Aunt, it's your house. Do you recognize him?"

Aunt Amelia came closer and peered down at him. "No," she said. "Mr. Lorde?"

The butler didn't move. "Madam?" he said. Maia detected a note of pleading under that stiff word.

"Oh, don't be such a coward, Lorde," Aunt Amelia said. "Come here and look at the fellow and tell me if you know him. He's dead, he's not going to jump up and bite your nose off."

When Lorde had reluctantly obeyed and disclaimed any knowledge of him, to be thankfully dismissed, Helen approached to take her turn as well.

"You're not likely to know him," Aunt Amelia objected.

"You never know," Helen said. "I made no secret of my intentions to spend the morning with Maia. Maybe it was me he was trying to reach!" She stood next to Maia and looked down. "Is he really dead? He looks so peaceful." She sighed. "No, I don't recognize him, either. What do we do now?"

"I think he might have died of a magic spell," Maia said. "There's no sign of injury or illness on him."

Aunt Amelia pursed her lips. "Checked that already, did you?"

"I did," Maia returned.

Her aunt did not speak, but Maia thought she saw some approval beneath the surface frown. Though it might have been wishful thinking. Her aunt seemed to approve of independent thought and deed in everyone but her niece-apprentice.

Helen backed away from the body a few steps and made a faint noise in the back of her throat. The sparkle in her eyes dimmed. "Sorry," she said weakly when the other two looked at her. "Don't mind me. I just … it suddenly struck me that this is real."

"I know," Maia said, smiling at her friend with sympathy. Helen was twenty-one, four years younger than Maia, who had lied about her age to get into the VADs when she was seventeen. This was likely the first time her energetic, effervescent friend had ever seen a dead body outside the cinema. "It seemed unbelievable to me at first, too."

Aunt Amelia turned her frown on Helen. "Why are you here anyway, Miss Radcliffe?"

"The Magicians' Ball is at the end of the week, remember, Miss Rawlings? Maia and I were going to go shopping for new gowns today."

When the two ladies had met for tea last week, Helen had said, "Oh Maia, we must get new frocks for the Magicians'

Ball," and Maia had said, "I don't think so, Helen," and Helen had said, "Good, I'll pick you up Friday morning and we can visit Mme. Julie's." Maia had protested that she had lessons with Aunt Amelia every morning, and Helen had waved that objection aside as breezily as she did everything else.

It wasn't that Maia despised the thought of a new gown, by any means. It was rather that she had entered her fourth year of magical apprenticeship to her aunt and was determined to not let it go into a fifth. She had discovered her magical ability much later in life than most, and while she was deeply thankful to have use of this extra sense at all, she was beginning to chafe under her aunt's rules and restrictions, especially while people younger and—she had to say it, even if it sounded vain—less talented than she were already journeymen or independent magicians. Somehow, gown shopping for her fourth Magicians' Ball as an apprentice did not appeal. Helen, however, was determined to keep Maia from "depression of spirits," as she airily put it, and therefore insisted on regular outings and excursions. Maia appreciated her efforts and at the same time found them maddening.

Aunt Amelia, who never ceased to criticize the fashions of the day and insisted on still dressing as though Queen Victoria sat on the throne, waved her hand. "Yes, yes," she said. "Excellent idea. Lessons canceled for today, Maia. You girls run along and have fun."

Maia stared. Aunt Amelia seemed unaware of her niece's scrutiny as she bent closer to the dead man, but the set of her shoulders told Maia a different story. "Excuse me, Aunt."

Aunt Amelia looked up, a faint line appearing between her eyebrows. "Maia, I am preparing to cast a highly delicate spell in order to find out what killed this unfortunate man, do you mind not making me lose the threads?"

"Terribly sorry," said Maia, not feeling particularly sorry at all. "But don't you think this is the sort of thing your apprentice ought to assist with?"

"Or … I'm sorry, but should we be doing anything about this at all?" interrupted Helen. She did sound apologetic. "Shouldn't we call Domestic Protection?"

"That useless excuse for a magical police force?" Aunt Amelia said, her bosom shaking with outrage. "In my house?"

Maia was reluctant to hand such a juicy mystery over to the authorities, but she had to admit Helen had a point. "She might be right, Aunt."

To do her justice, Aunt Amelia was stubborn and set in her ways, but she wasn't stupid. "Allow me to diagnose what killed him first. That will give us a better idea of who we need to bring in." She held up a finger. "And you girls may watch, but do not interfere. Especially you, Maia! I have no desire to add a house fire to the list of this day's calamities."

It took all Maia's self-control to keep from blushing. Just because her powers tended to … explode out of her control at times was no call for Aunt Amelia to make a crack like that. It wasn't as if Maia was continually setting fire to the furniture, after all. She hadn't had an accident in at least three and a half months.

It was especially galling to have her master poke at her in front of another magician, even one with whom Maia was so friendly as Helen. Masters were supposed to brag about and defend their apprentices from others' ridicule, not expose them.

Thankfully, Helen ignored Aunt Amelia's comment except to move a step or two closer to Maia's side, as if to show she had no fear of Maia letting loose with an explosion. Aunt Amelia turned her back to both of them, raised her hands above her head, and spoke clearly and crisply in Latin.

"*Quid occursum est.*"

A wave of revulsion so strong it nearly drove her to her knees hit Maia like a fist. Beside her, Helen gagged and doubled over, hands clasped to her mouth. Aunt Amelia stumbled back, face ashen.

"*Finiatur!*" she boomed.

As though someone had flipped a switch, the revulsion vanished. Helen slowly straightened and pulled her hands back down to her sides.

"What … what was that?" she managed to choke out.

Aunt Amelia examined her own hands, as though checking for contamination. Maia realized that she herself had not only touched that body, but had held it in her lap. Her skin crawled, and she had to resist the urge to scrub at her arms.

"That man died of one of the vilest forms of sorcery I've ever come across, and that's saying something," Aunt Amelia said. "That body needs to be burned at once."

"No, we mustn't," Maia said, then bit her lip. If it was bad form for a master to criticize her apprentice in front of others, it was even worse for an apprentice to contradict her master.

Aunt Amelia was never predictable. Instead of scolding Maia, she folded her arms across her ample bosom. "And why not? Why should I leave a body leaking the vilest of magics lying in my front hall?"

"We must know where it came from, what happened, who he is," Maia said. "What if it's not a spell, but rather a magical plague? Or if it is a spell, surely we must find out who cast it, and why, and bring him or her to justice. We cannot do that if we burn the body and lose all the clues it might contain."

"Looking for an excuse to play detective, child?" Aunt Amelia said, the sarcasm in her voice sharp enough to cut.

Maia clenched her fist, driving her nails into her palm until the desire to scream faded. She was twenty-five years old, hardly a child. And while Aunt Amelia scorned her fondness for detective novels and occasional ventures into solving puzzles in real life, Maia was proud of her deductive abilities. She and her friend Lennox Davies spent many a happy half hour going over newspaper accounts of various crimes and trying to solve them. Len, an undercover agent for Magical Intelligence, had vastly more experience, but Maia's attention to detail and logical approach to criminology kept the honors about even between them.

Not that Aunt Amelia knew about those clandestine meetings. Len was perfectly respectable, but Aunt Amelia had a personal dislike toward him and considered him a distraction to her niece's studies. Their occasional tea at Lyons had to be carried out with ridiculous secrecy.

Maia refused to let her aunt dictate her personal relationships. Apprenticeship only went so far.

Before Maia lost her temper and self-control entirely, Aunt Amelia spoke again.

"Very well, I suppose we'd better call in the authorities." She heaved an enormous sigh. "I shall never live this down—common investigators, in my house!"

"Miss Rawlings, you know my brother Matthew has just started with Domestic Protection," Helen said. "If you like, I can summon him. He might be able to arrange things so that your privacy is protected."

Aunt Amelia eyed her with surprise and rare approval. "That

is most thoughtful, Helen, thank you."

Helen nodded and withdrew into the Rose Parlor to cast the summoning spell which would let her brother know he was needed urgently at this location. Maia and her aunt were left alone.

"This is quite inconvenient," Aunt Amelia said, staring at the body.

Maia raised her eyebrows. Death and black magic were hardly what she would call "inconvenient." Deadly, dangerous, and disastrous, yes. A minor irritant, no.

"There is trouble brewing between France and England," Aunt Amelia continued, answering the unspoken question. "A scandal involving an English magician and a French non-magical nobleman … the Circle and the French *Société* are at each other's throats over this. The Circle has been threatening to send me over to discipline our magician lest the French take it into their heads to do it for us, though given the provocation I find my sympathies are entirely with him."

"That is all very interesting, no doubt, but hardly to be compared with a mysterious dead body leaking some sort of vile spell in your hallway, Aunt!"

"My dear child, it is matters such as this that can lead to wars. Should the French governing body of magicians attempt to imprison or punish an English magician, it would be a breach of agreement between all the magical governments of the world and could splinter us into factions, bringing up long-buried grievances and leading to individual alliances. It could be another worldwide war, only this time between magicians. Compared to that, a dead body in my hallway is indeed a sordid inconvenience."

Put like that, Maia could understand her aunt's point of

view. On the other hand, as she looked at the crumpled figure and recalled the weight of it in her arms in that moment of change between a living human being and an empty corpse, she couldn't help but think that though his death might not spark a war, he too was important, and he deserved more.

* * *

Within a short time of Helen's summons to her brother—either he was highly protective of his sister or her summons had had an extra edge of urgency about it—England's magical police force had arrived at Aunt Amelia's residence in all its glory. "All its glory," in this case, consisted of a worried-looking Matthew Radcliffe and a grey-haired elderly woman with tired eyes who was introduced as Mrs. Taylor, their curse expert.

Matthew was tall and sturdily built, not resembling his sister much beyond the curly hair he tried and failed to tame under a hat, and a shared determination around both their mouths. Where her dark eyes sparkled, his were clouded and grim, and where she seemed to shed light wherever she walked, he seemed under a darkness. Maia suspected it was the nature of his work that did that to him, though he was old enough he might have had a year in the war, as well.

Matthew and Mrs. Taylor gaped in mutual dismay at the corpse. Whatever latent curse Aunt Amelia's diagnostic spell had triggered had only grown stronger in the time since it had been set off; no one could now bear to go within a five-foot radius of the man.

"This is beyond my abilities," Mrs. Taylor admitted in a shaken voice.

"Fortunately for you, it is not beyond ours," said a sharp, ice-cold voice from the front door.

All heads turned as a short, thin man with a pinched face and a tall woman stepped into the hall. Behind them, a man so insignificant as to be almost unnoticeable carefully closed the door.

"Agent Barry, Agent Marsh," the man said, introducing themselves with a careless wave of the hand. "Magical Intelligence."

Aunt Amelia shot a glare at Maia, who spread her hands in innocence. If she had contacted Intelligence, which she hadn't, she would have gone straight to Len. Not this man.

"I don't recall inviting Intelligence to look into this affair," Aunt Amelia said, her bosom swelling with offended dignity.

"You didn't, yet here we are." Agent Barry glanced around the room, looked down at the corpse, over at Matthew and Mrs. Taylor, and sniffed, the edge of his upper lip curling. "This curse is far beyond the abilities or jurisdiction of Domestic Protection. Clearly this is no petty curse-caster. A spell of this nature could have implications for national security, or could even be part of an international plot."

"Though we are happy to have the assistance of Domestic Protection," the third, unnamed agent added. He stood behind Barry and Marsh, his face shadowed. "After all, we are all on the same side."

Matthew looked unhappy, but he did not resist. The truth was that very few of England's magicians took Domestic Protection, or Deep, as it was frequently referred to, seriously. For crimes of a non-magical nature, the ordinary police force served the community's needs, the same as any other citizen. For crimes of national importance or international intrigue,

Intelligence rooted them out and enacted justice. If a magical crime succeeded in also breaking England's laws, Magical Intelligence would send in one of their agents disguised as part of Scotland Yard to "help" solve the case while covering up any evidence of magic from the true authorities.

Domestic Protection was, as Agent Barry had sneered, left to handle the smallest of offenses—someone carelessly using magic where non-magical persons might see it, or casting an unpleasant-but-not-fatal curse against another magician. Grey magic, as Lennox Davies called it. Not serious enough to be evil, but not pure enough to be good.

Maia knew, through Helen, that Matthew was hoping to work with Intelligence at some point, and considered Domestic Protection a first step along that path. He would not want to do anything now to damage his chances later on.

"We'll take the body to the Deep morgue, as that's closest, there to be examined by our best curse experts," Agent Marsh said. "Driver, will you see to it they are informed of where to go and how virulent this curse is?" The other agent nodded and slipped back out the door. "Our special cleansing team is now on the way to purify these premises. If you take the witness statements, Radcliffe, I'll collect them once you've finished."

"Right," said Matthew, seeming relieved at being given something to do.

"I suggest you start with me," Maia said. "Since I was the first on the scene. Helen and Aunt Amelia came in after."

Matthew opened his mouth, but Agent Barry raised his eyebrows. "Do you generally take orders from civilians, Radcliffe?" he asked in a soft voice. He flicked a quick, dismissive glance at Maia. "Perhaps this apprentice is unaware of protocol, but in MI, at least, we start at the top and work our way down."

"In any case, I was here only moments after Maia, and my butler saw it all," Aunt Amelia interrupted. "There is no need to question these young ladies at all."

Maia pinched her lips together to keep from venting her anger in front of all these people. Did Aunt Amelia think she was going to throw her career away and join Intelligence as soon as she qualified as a magician simply by talking to an agent?

It seemed she did. That was the reason she jabbed Maia so frequently for her role in that four-years'-past affair, and why she strove so urgently to keep her apart from Len. Aunt Amelia insisted Maia's magical talent was enough to make her a regional governor, or even Head Magician of the Circle, and she had no intention of letting her niece "waste" that talent on something so mundane as Intelligence, nor to let her be even tempted by it through talking with an agent.

"But that's nonsense, we were right here for the entire thing, and we might have seen something Miss Rawlings missed!" Helen burst out.

Barry ignored her and turned back to the body. "Radcliffe, can't you even control your sister?" he tossed over his shoulder.

"You aren't helping things, Helen," Matthew hissed. He cleared his throat. "Right you are, Barry, Miss Rawlings. Ladies, this is not a fit scene for the two of you. I am sure you are most distressed by the, er, distressing death you witnessed …" The words died in his throat at the identical steely glares the young ladies in question were giving him. Anything less distressed could hardly be imagined. He took a deep breath and tried again. "You can best assist the investigation by going about your business as though nothing were wrong. Er, Helen, weren't you and Maia going to do some shopping today …?"

"Mr. Radcliffe and Agent Barry are perfectly right," said Aunt Amelia with a smug expression. "As I told you girls earlier, this is no place for you. Off you go now, shoo." She flapped her hands at them as though they were chickens, only she was shooing them outside the coop instead of in.

Within moments, Maia found herself with coat, hat, and gloves on, and the two were shut out—literally—from the action.

"Well," said Helen, straightening her hat and turning away from the closed front door. "I call that positively unfair."

Maia glanced down at her hands. A magician's aura—the traces left behind after working a spell or when one's magic was leaking out of control—was generally invisible to everyone but the said magician. Right now, the glimmers of silver shining through her tan kid gloves were bright enough she was surprised Helen could be unaware of her struggle to keep the magic from bursting free of her control.

If she wasn't careful, she was going to set Aunt Amelia's spiraea on fire right here on the front steps for all the neighbors to see.

It wasn't merely the indignity of being treated as a child—she, who had been running her family's home since she was fourteen and her sisters had driven away their first housekeeper, who had been a nurse in France during the war, who had stopped a magical conspiracy which would have destroyed England four years ago when she had barely even learned of her abilities.

It was that this Barry seemed to have his own agenda apart from the case. It was that Agent Marsh had something chilling about her, something that unsettled Maia without her being able to articulate why. As for Matthew—well, she couldn't be too hard on Matthew, he was in rather an impossible position, though she did wish he'd shown more backbone. But Aunt Amelia …!

Did no one involved in this case care at all about the man who now lay dead? They wanted the curse contained, the culprit caught, the world back as it should be. All laudable goals, but none of the people involved seemed to care that a man had been alive and was now dead.

Maia slowly clenched and opened her hands, breathing in through her nose and out through her mouth, focusing on stuffing her magic back down within its proper bonds. It felt, as always, like wrestling a feather mattress back into its tick, and even after it was safely confined, there were a few puffs and feathers of power left floating. Nothing too dangerous, though—nothing that would explode anything or anyone.

Helen, unaware of Maia's struggle, made her way down to the street and looked both ways. "Shall we do our shopping, then, since we aren't allowed anything more exciting?"

Maia narrowed her eyes. Ever since she was a child, being told she was not permitted to do something was the surest way to pique her interest in that very thing. "You may, if you wish," she said. "I have other plans."

Helen looked back at her and laughed. "You have something devilish in mind, I can tell," she said. "Whatever it is, count me in."

Maia's eyes were generally blue, but under certain light or the influence of certain emotions they shone green. She did not have a mirror handy, but she was fairly certain, given how she felt at this moment, that they were as green as a cat's eyes. She had spent too many years weighted down with the responsibility of her careless and highly dramatic family, believing she was too dull and staid to ever have an interesting life. Ever since discovering her magic and coming to London to train with Aunt Amelia, she had delighted in proving herself wrong.

"I merely thought I might chat with some of the neighbors, see if any of them saw or heard anything interesting," Maia said. "That can't be considered interfering—we are merely gossiping and being neighborly, correct?"

"Just as young women ought to do," Helen said, fluttering her long eyelashes. She eyed Maia's clothing. "It is unfortunate that you are wearing that," she said. "You don't look at all appropriate for chatting with the neighbors in that ancient skirt and those shoes. I'd glamour you something different—" glamours were Helen's specialty— "But non-magical eyes can't see glamours, so it would be wasted effort."

Maia barely listened to this. She had gotten into the habit of tuning Helen out whenever she dragged glamours into the conversation. They might be fascinating to the other girl, but they held little interest for her. "Never mind, old thing," she said vaguely. "There's not much point in talking to the owners of the nearby houses, anyway. Most of them wouldn't notice an interesting occurrence if it leapt up and bit them on the nose." Rather like Aunt Amelia. "The servants, however, always know everything. And they won't care if I am less than impeccably dressed."

Helen laughed again and sighed. "Oh dear, you really don't know anything at all about servants, do you?"

"I was on very good terms with all our servants at Stanbury, thank you very much," Maia said. The ones Mother, Ellie and Merry hadn't scared off.

Helen waved a hand. "Oh, country servants, old retainers, families who all know each other and all that. Of course they wouldn't care how you were dressed. I'm sure you were 'the eldest Whitney daughter' no matter where you went within the village, and shopkeepers always tipped their hat to you and saved you the best cuts of meat without you even asking."

Maia couldn't deny any of it.

"But London servants, my dear! If they think you are dressing beneath your station, they won't give you the time of day."

It was Maia's turn to sigh. Helen was London born and bred and kept her finger unerringly on the social pulse of the city. There was nothing for it.

"*Abscondo meum in manifestis conspectu.*" She had never revealed to anyone else that she knew this spell. It was one of Len's favorites, and she'd learned it from him, which alone was a good reason to keep it secret from Aunt Amelia. It did not turn her invisible, but allowed her to blend in with her surroundings. Len called it his chameleon spell, and Maia found it quite useful.

Helen stared, and blinked. She reached out a tentative finger and poked at Maia's arm, looking relieved to make contact. "I say," she said in a hushed voice. "Do teach me that! It would be splendid for sneaking out of the house without Mother knowing."

Maia ignored this. "Wait for me at the corner," she said. "I'll sneak in the back door, run upstairs and change, and then join you."

"Wear that navy suit with the silver embroidery," Helen ordered. "And heels!"

Maia loathed heels—she was tall enough as it was, and heels

made her wobble when she walked—but if she thought of it as a disguise, something Sherlock Holmes would put on in order to hunt down clues, she could just about bear them.

* * *

None of the servants on either side of Aunt Amelia's had heard or seen anything, or at least would not admit it to Maia and Helen. Maia found herself wishing for Len's manservant Becket. He was shy but kind-hearted, and servants would be far more likely to talk freely to him than to ladies of gentility. No matter! She had heard nothing from Len to indicate he was off on another mission, so she assumed they would meet for their monthly tea tomorrow as planned. If she and Helen had no luck here, she would ask to borrow Becket and see if he came up with more results.

However, the house across the street yielded her something. The scullery maid, a girl with flaming red hair that made Maia's look positively muddy, had stepped outside "for a spot of fresh air," she said, though from her breath Maia suspected she'd gone out to smoke a cigarette, and had seen the entire thing through the railings.

"Saw 'im plain as day, I did," said the girl, who went by the improbable name of Angelina. "Swaggered right up to the front door all prim an' proper, pressed the doorbell, and then 'e froze, like that," snapping her finger, "an' when the door opened, 'e just keeled over inside. 'Gent's got a stomach pain,' I said to meself, but then Cook called me back inside and I didn't see no more. Is 'e dead then, miss?"

"Yes, I'm afraid so," Maia said. "The, ah, undertaker is taking him away now." She and Angelina watched as Barry and three

19

other men brought out the tightly wrapped body on a stretcher.

"Poor chap. Were 'e a friend of the family?"

"Distant relative," Maia improvised wildly. "Very distant. Thank you for your time." She pressed a coin into Angelina's hand and hurried away to where Helen was frantically motioning to her from the street.

"We'll be seen!" she hissed. "Matthew is coming now. Do that, that *not-visible* spell you did earlier, quick!"

"Very well, but you'll have to hold quite still," Maia said, swallowing her nerves. She'd never done this to cover anyone but herself before. She closed her eyes and sketched a quick shape in the air with her forefinger, something that, if drawn by pencil, might have looked like a child's rendering of a lizard. Hand motions were not necessary, but they did help focus one's concentration. Aunt Amelia despised such concessions, naturally, but for this, Maia thought she needed all the help she could get.

"*Abscondo meum in manifestis conspectu*," she whispered, and felt the spell tug and take hold. Out of the corner of her eye, she saw that Helen was slowly fading from sight. Maia released her breath.

Matthew and the lesser agents assigned to him scattered and converged upon the neighboring houses, no doubt in search of the same information Maia and Helen had just scrounged. As soon as their attention was engaged, Maia let the spell slowly dissipate as she and Helen backed away and slipped around the corner. Judging they were safe enough now, Maia relayed Angelina's story to Helen.

The shorter girl nodded. "That's what the housemaid of the place next to that one said, too. I think she and your Angelina were out smoking together, actually." Helen waved a hand in front of her face, wrinkling her nose.

Nobody was entirely certain why, but nicotine and magic did not react well to each other, and most magicians avoided cigarette smoke as much as possible.

"What now? It seems as though we've few options open to us," Helen continued. "We can try to hunt down the victim's identity, but I've no idea how to do that. We can try to research the spell that was cast on him, but I don't exactly know how to investigate curses without setting off quite a number of people's alarms, including my mother's. Or," she finished, brightening. "We can go shopping as we were told to do, and rack our brains for ideas at the same time as we find smashing frocks for the Ball."

2

A Shot on the Street

Len had been shot at more times than he cared to remember. It came with the territory of a field agent for Magical Intelligence. Never before, though, had he been shot at in broad daylight while walking down Piccadilly toward the Thamuaturges Club.

To add to his embarrassment, he didn't even see his assailant—he, Lennox Davies, legendary among agents for his finely honed instincts and sense of danger. The first he knew of it was the sudden blossoming of red on his left coat sleeve, followed by a burning pain in that arm. A lady strolling toward him stopped short, screamed, and swooned into her escort's arms, and everything turned to chaos.

"You've been shot, mate!" announced Gus, the doorkeeper at the club, running to Len and staring in awe at his arm. Len clamped his hand over the wound. It wasn't bad—the shot had nearly missed him altogether, barely creasing the skin. "I seen it all!"

"Did you happen to see who did it?" Len asked through clenched teeth. He looked around at the rapidly thickening crowd and raised his voice. "Did anyone see who did it?"

No one, it seemed, had. For a moment, Len considered giving chase. But given that he had no idea who he was looking for or what the devil was going on, he abandoned that plan.

The club doctor and a policeman arrived at the same time. The doctor hustled Len inside the club, accompanied by a clearly delighted Gus, while the policeman stayed outside to question the onlookers and search for clues. Len wished him luck.

This was appalling. He had survived working behind enemy lines during the war, had chased down countless enemies of Britain, had outwitted criminal masterminds and foiled their deadly schemes. He had not only been an agent for Magical Intelligence since he was seventeen but also did occasional non-magical work for the Secret Service, now to be brought low by a potshot he hadn't even seen coming on his home turf.

The policeman took his statement while the doctor examined the injury. Len only wished he had more to offer.

"It's the rummest case I ever saw, I must say," the policeman said, tipping his helmet back to scratch at his head. "Can't seem to get a straight story from anyone. One person says they saw a woman holding a pistol, another says it were a man, another says it weren't no gunman at all, just someone throwing something at you, and one bloke says everyone's gone loony and there was no gunman, no shot, and no injury, neither."

"I can contradict the latter, at least," said the doctor, finishing off the bandage with a neat flourish.

Len could have told the policeman that five witnesses watching the same scene would have seen five different things, but since this bobby was not known to him—and not one of the magicians on the force, to Len's best judgment—he simply shook his head. "I know you'll do your best, officer," he said.

"And you've no idea who would want to shoot you?" the policeman asked for the third time.

Len could think of several people, but none he could say out loud. "It's a mystery to me," he said, putting on his best rueful face. "Dashed irritating, all this." He considered complaining that it would throw off his cricket game, but decided he didn't need to carry it that far.

"Your arm will be fine in a day or so," the doctor said, washing his hands and shrugging back into his coat. "Afraid this shirt is done for, though." He shook his head sadly at the torn and stained sleeve. "The jacket as well, I shouldn't wonder."

"You'd be surprised at what can be done with baking soda and a needle and thread, sir," said a diffident voice.

Len looked up in relief at the small, neat figure of his valet. "Becket, there you are!"

With the arrival of Becket, things sorted themselves out quickly. The policeman left, the doctor gave a few instructions for cleaning the wound, the crowd of club members all eager to hear the tale melted away, and before he knew it, Len was ensconced in the most comfortable chair in the lounge, with his feet up and no one else around.

"Becket," he said. "Remind me to give you a raise."

Becket merely smiled and fetched another pillow. Len settled it behind his back more comfortably.

"So," he said. "To repeat what our poor bobby kept asking, who do we think wants to kill me?"

"Shall I fetch the list, sir?"

Len hesitated. He could never quite tell when Becket was being humorous. It seemed like a joke, but on the other hand, he wouldn't put it past his valet to keep such a list.

"More importantly," he went on, deciding to ignore the question for the moment, "who hates me so much as to attempt to murder me in broad daylight, in public, yet did such a poor job of it? The bullet barely scratched my arm. The shooter was lucky he didn't hit someone else by mistake, really."

"The other possibility is that nobody wants you dead, but they want you thinking they do," Becket said.

"A trick?" Len frowned. "But what would be the point?"

"I confess, I cannot think of one. But it was, as you said, a remarkably poor attempt at assassination."

Len began to wish he didn't have such a low tolerance for alcohol. A neat whisky would be just the ticket right about now. The cup of tea Becket had placed by his elbow didn't have quite the same feel.

"It doesn't make sense, dash it," he said.

"No sir, it doesn't," Becket acknowledged.

Something about this whole thing felt off, but Len couldn't put his finger on what or why.

A man entered the lounge, took one look at Len, and snorted. "Davies, you idiot, what sort of trouble are you stirring up now?"

Len sat up a little straighter. "You know me, sir, anything for a few days' rest."

Harrison Eastwood was well known in London and beyond as the head of Eastwood & Stevenson, general merchants and one of the largest purveyors of goods and products throughout the Empire. Tea, spices, cloth … Eastwood & Stevenson's ships brought them to London and then sent them out again. Harrison Eastwood was a shrewd yet fair businessman, respected by all who knew him.

Only a handful of people knew he was a magician, a highly placed Intelligence operative, overseeing Len's department among others. He also happened to be married to Len's cousin Joanna, but though they might be "Harrison" and "Len" to each other at family gatherings, when it came to Intelligence work it was strictly "Sir" and "Davies."

"How did you hear about this?" asked Len, motioning to his arm. He knew Harrison was good, but it hadn't even been a full hour since it happened.

Becket drew up a chair across from Len's and set a decanter, siphon, and tumbler on the table beside it. Harrison lowered himself into the seat with a grunt and a nod of thanks. "Doctor Shaw," he said.

Len knew the doctor was a magician. No one could be a member of the Thamuaturges Club if they weren't. He hadn't realized the man was one of Harrison's contacts.

"So, who did it and why?" Harrison asked.

"Honestly, sir, I've no idea," Len said. "It is utterly bizarre."

"That could be said of much of our business," Harrison said. He took a mouthful of whisky. "Good quality stuff here. Nothing to do with your last case, then?"

"I don't think so, sir," Len said. That had been an open-and-shut business, some stupid young magician trying to sell spells to a fellow from India, despite the no-profit laws governing international trade of magic. He'd slapped the chap with a fine, returned the fee to the Indian magician (who took one look at the spells he'd paid for and demanded his money back in disgust anyway, saying they were so elementary a child of ten could figure them out), and returned home by the next boat. A case so simple he'd almost wondered why he'd been put on it instead of some first-year agent needing a gentle introduction into the world of Magical Intelligence.

"Nobody you've particularly irritated lately?"

"Not more so than usual."

Harrison snorted a laugh. "Damn strange day all the way around," he said, taking another drink. "First the dead fellow at the Rawlings place, now this … what's going to be the third, I wonder? If I'm lucky, someone will shoot at me and then I'll finally get to take a holiday and go fishing up in Scotland. Your sister and her husband accepting guests right now?"

Len hadn't heard any of this past "the Rawlings place." "What dead fellow?" he demanded, sitting bolt upright. "Amelia Rawlings? What happened?"

"Not your case, Davies," Harrison reeled off the standard line. He relented at Len's stricken face. "All right. Some fellow wandered into Amelia Rawlings' front hall and dropped dead in her apprentice's lap. Some deadly curse, according to Barry, but if you ask me he died of one of Miss Rawlings' lectures."

Her apprentice—Maia! The rest of the words slowly caught up to Len. "Did you say Barry?"

"Mm, he happened to be hanging about when Driver brought me the report from Miss Rawlings, and volunteered to go out and take a look. Considering that most folk usually run the opposite direction from the woman, I gave him the task." Harrison raised his eyebrows at Len, daring him to speak.

Len swallowed his words. Edwin Barry was everything he loathed in an agent and a magician. His magical abilities were weak, as with most agents, but his arrogance and ruthlessness knew no bounds. His superiors approved of him because he always got the job done; Len despised him because of how he did it.

It was a dangerous luxury, having a conscience as an Intelligence agent. Len knew that. Many of his colleagues considered him soft for the times he put individual persons ahead of the greater cause. That didn't particularly bother him. He might not be as efficient as Barry or some of the others, but he'd never failed an assignment yet.

The cordial dislike between Len and Barry had come to a head several months ago, when Barry's ruthlessness and determination to get the job done at all costs had brought about the death of another agent on the case. The man hadn't been a friend of Len's, but Len had felt strongly enough about Barry's skewed priorities that he'd confronted him afterward, and the two had nearly traded blows and spells—would have, had not Harrison and a few others intervened.

It was Len who'd been reprimanded for that, not Barry, as he was the provocateur. It was considered exceedingly bad taste to criticize another agent publicly, "especially," as Harrison chided him afterward, "when that agent has a success rate like Barry's!"

"Do you consider leaving behind a fellow agent to be killed by a rogue Russian *volshebnik* just so he could escape with the papers a success?" Len had snapped.

"You know I don't," Harrison had answered, his quiet gravity calming Len's rage. "But others do. Speaking out against him like that isn't going to help your career, you know."

Yes, Len knew, but he'd been too angry to care. Come to think of it, ever since then he'd been put on simple missions, like the one he'd just completed. Dash it all, was that why … Len caught himself. None of that mattered at the moment. Even his own shooting receded in the distance.

"Was M—the apprentice all right?"

Harrison shrugged. "Seemed to be. Barry hadn't yet come in

when I got word about you. He is showing his usual diligence over this, which is a good thing, considering it is Amelia Rawlings." Once again he paused for Len to insert a comment, and once again Len held his tongue. "But there was no call for healers, so I would think the young lady is fine." He eyed Len. "Oh yes—you know her, don't you? Didn't she get herself involved in that business a few years back, with the Austrian agent?"

"Miss Whitney was of great assistance in that case, yes," Len answered stiffly. He would have bet a year's income that Harrison had looked up his connection with Maia before even sending Barry out on the case, as well as every other detail of her involvement with the case. "She is a talented magician as well as quite sharp-witted."

"As long as she isn't as sharp-tongued as her aunt," Harrison said. He heaved himself up out of the chair. "Well, I'd best be getting back to the office. Do you want me to put someone on your case, Davies? I think Amy Marsh is available. She went to the Rawlings residence with Barry and Driver, but Barry said they didn't need three senior agents on the case, so she's currently free."

Agent Amy Marsh was as ambitious as Barry, though Len didn't think she quite shared his ruthlessness. At least, not yet. She was a few years junior to the two men. Give her enough time, Len thought with unusual pessimism, and she could turn out even worse. She didn't like Len very much, either.

He struggled to his feet out of respect to the standing older man. "No, thank you. I don't think it's worth the time."

"Very well," said Harrison. He eyed Len. "Davies—I know you have tea with the Whitney girl every so often. That's not my business. This dead body, though, that is. Don't interfere.

It's Barry's case, not yours. That's an order."

Len bit his tongue. "Yes sir," he said.

What else could he say?

* * *

Promptly at three o'clock Saturday afternoon, Len entered the Lyons Tea Shop on Coventry Street. He told himself it was ridiculous to feel nervous, but he still couldn't stop himself from adjusting his tie and smoothing his hair as he removed his hat upon entering. Just like a gawky schoolboy wanting to make a good first impression, he scoffed.

Maia's actual first impression of him, he still wasn't certain of. He had been attempting to present himself as the careless, empty-headed, man-about-town sort he had played so well for so long, but it hadn't taken her any time at all to learn who he truly was. It was still somewhat unnerving when he thought about how easily she pierced his defenses.

He'd thought her splendid from the first moment they met, and nothing that had happened since had changed that impression, only deepened it.

By the time they had successfully completed that first case, he'd known Maia to be one of the bravest, cleverest, loveliest people of his acquaintance, with a magical ability which far outstripped his own. Their friendship since that time had only grown, though their acquaintance was sporadic and, thanks to Miss Rawlings' dislike of Intelligence agents and her own poor opinion of Len, absurdly clandestine.

He didn't much care for Miss Rawlings, either. She considered MI a home for magicians who were either unscrupulous in how they used their magic or poor enough magicians that it didn't matter if they crossed the occasional line. He considered her a hidebound traditionalist whose refusal to consider different approaches to magic was choking the very life out of Britain's magicians. As for personalities … it was fair to say they clashed there, as well.

Thankfully, Maia was not one to let anyone else's prejudices influence her, and she'd made it clear to Len that she had no intention of letting Aunt Amelia dictate who her friends could and could not be.

He saw her now, seated at a corner table and waving to him, looking none the worse for her misadventure yesterday. She wore a suit in a dark, rich blue, with a brown hat tilted back over her long bob, allowing him to see her blue-green eyes and wide smile.

He smiled back as he wove through the maze of customers to take the seat across from her. "Dashed good to see you again, Maia."

"You as well," she said. Her smile turned to a frown as she took in his appearance. "What on earth has happened to your arm?"

He'd forgotten the bandages, and the fact that they would make a lump beneath his sleeves. Trust Maia to pick up on them. "Nothing to fret about. Some idiot took a potshot at me yesterday, but he barely even drew any blood." He saw the alarm and determination grow in her eyes, and hurried to head her off. "I'm more concerned about what happened to you yesterday. I trust you aren't feeling any ill effects?"

She shook her head. Len delighted in the small reddish-brown curl that escaped its hairpin and whisked across her cheek as she did so. "None in the least, unless you count enduring countless tests from Aunt Amelia afterward to ensure

I wasn't corrupted."

They were interrupted by a Nippy who took their order for a pot of tea and a plate of scones. Once she was safely on her way, Maia picked up the thread of conversation.

"How did you—oh, of course. Mr. Barry is your colleague."

Len tried not to snort, but his face gave him away.

Maia brightened. "Oh good, you don't like him either. Honestly, Len, he seems utterly incompetent. He didn't even ask Helen or me any questions! Matthew was going to take our statements, but Aunt Amelia told him not to bother, that we couldn't possibly have anything of value to say, and Barry went along with it, the spineless coward."

"He's not really incompetent," honesty compelled Len to say. "Just indifferent toward any people he considers unimportant to his cases or his career. Who are Matthew and Helen?"

"Matthew and Helen Radcliffe. Helen is a friend of mine, and Matthew is her brother. He recently entered Domestic Protection."

Len looked up as the waitress brought them their tea and scones. "Thank you," he said, smiling at her.

She smiled back, blushing a little, and darted along to her next table, moving as "nippily" as the nicknames for Lyons' servers implied. Maia lifted the teapot to pour.

"Poor chap. Deep—" the slang for Domestic Protection— "is a necessary function of our magical society, but try convincing the average magician that the people who work there are anything but second-rate."

Maia's sigh had an unusual wistful sound to it. "If only I could convince magicians of anything," she said.

"Buck up, old bean," he said sympathetically. "You'll make it to journeyman soon enough. Even Miss Rawlings can't keep you an apprentice forever."

"I know I should be grateful," Maia conceded. "Once I do fulfill her requirements for journeyman, I'll be as qualified as most independent magicians. It is galling, though, when most magicians my age are miles ahead of me."

"Five-year apprenticeships are the most common, and you're only in year four," Len reminded her. "It's just your bad luck that you started that much later than most."

"I know." Maia took a sip of tea and returned to her usual brisk manner. "Enough about me," she said. "What about your arm? You can't simply mention someone shot at you and then expect me to let it go!"

"It was nothing, I'm sure. Some young idiot burst out of the crowd and took a potshot at me, managed to wing my arm more by luck than by skill, then vanished before anyone could grab him. The doctor bandaged me up, and that's the end of it. Did you get any sense of what sort of a curse was used on the dead man, and do you have any idea who he—" He stopped himself short. Dash it, Harrison had given him specific instructions to stay out of this case. He couldn't go nosing in now.

But this was *Maia*, someone might have hurt her, someone might be after her, she could be in danger, and Barry was not remotely fit to keep her safe or catch the culprit. Granted, Maia was more than capable of keeping herself safe in general, but despite her skill she was still only an apprentice, and one couldn't expect her to go up against a curse-caster of this depth.

Thankfully, Maia ignored his questions all together. "The man who shot you must have been a magician, don't you think? How else could he have taken you by surprise, or vanished so quickly?"

"I did think of that," he said. "But even so, he's a poor shot and not too quick on the uptake, to make an attempt like that. I really don't think we need fret."

"But what if next time he decides to forego the gun and use magic to do away with you?"

"Can't imagine that happening. Magic used directly against another person in that way is pretty dark, you know. Most magicians would do almost anything to avoid that. That kind of magic … it leaves its mark on you. You're never the same again."

Maia raised her eyebrows. "Yet yesterday, only a short time before you were shot, someone used a curse against another human being so potent my aunt spent all this morning personally cleaning her front hall to remove all traces of it."

"Look here, you don't think these two affairs are connected," Len protested. He stopped. "Do you?"

"It would be a coincidence," Maia admitted. "Still, I don't like it. What if there's someone out there targeting magicians?"

"Do we know if your dead man was a magician?"

"No," she said. She briefly clenched her fists. "We need more information!"

Len twisted his mouth wryly. "The cry of every investigator on every case since the beginning of time. I suppose there's a chance, even if your dead man were not a magician, that he was the messenger. The curse could have been meant for your aunt, only it was too potent and killed him first."

"If someone is going after magicians, he's thoroughly incompetent," Maia sniffed. "He missed his chance with Aunt Amelia and with you." A shadow crossed her face. "That doesn't mean he won't succeed next time."

Len stroked his chin, thinking it over. "Technically I'm not supposed to get involved in your case, but if they are connected and indicative of a larger threat, someone ought to know."

Maia pinched her lips together. "Technically I'm not supposed to get involved either, despite the man literally dying in my arms." Her eyes lightened with a flash of mischief. "I don't intend to let that stop me, however!"

"Good for you," he said, thinking it over. He couldn't mention their theory—if it even was strong enough to be called such—to Barry or Harrison, both of whom would think he was merely looking for a chance to interfere. "I'll mention the notion to Driver, see if they have any evidence to support it."

"Excellent," Maia said. "If I said anything to him, he'd think I was jumping to conclusions."

Len grinned. "Are you sure we aren't?"

Maia narrowed her eyes. "We have not jumped anywhere. We have propounded one possible explanation based on the limited information we have available to us. Should that explanation prove incorrect, we will move on to the next."

Len held up his hands. "Right, sorry. Should not have phrased it so poorly."

"In the meantime," Maia continued. "Since there is not much we can do about my case without stepping on official toes, should we look into your would-be assassin for now, until and unless such a time as the two cases are proved to be one?"

Len didn't think it was likely, nor did he think much of their chances of finding the individual who shot at him, but he would have gone to far greater lengths to spend time with Maia again. "Absolutely."

Her next words shattered the hopes he was starting to build. "I'll let Helen know."

Len choked on his tea. "Ah—er—Helen?"

Maia handed him a napkin. "Bite of scone go down the wrong way? Most irritating when that happens, especially in public. Helen Radcliffe, Matthew's sister, of course. The one who came along right after the Mysterious Stranger died, and who was also ignored by the proper authorities, including her own brother. She assisted me in interviewing the few servants along the road we could get to before Matthew came along, and she would be most put out to be left out of things now. It wouldn't be at all right not to include her!"

"Must we let a stranger know about my job?" he asked, trying not to sound too plaintive.

"You wouldn't guess it at first glance, but she can be most discreet."

The last thing Len wanted was an extra female trotting along after them, interfering and giggling and distracting Maia from more important things. He couldn't figure out a gracious way to rid themselves of her, though. He let it go for now. "Speaking of siblings, how is your family?"

The talk turned to more general topics, and they parted shortly after with plans to meet the next day, along with Helen if she were available, to begin their investigation.

* * *

"Mr. Davies, I am so pleased to make your acquaintance," Helen said, looking up at him through dark, curly lashes. "I've heard great things of you."

"Oh?" said Len, with a sideways glance at Maia.

"Not from me," she disclaimed hastily, her dismayed expression showing a moment too late that she hadn't meant that as it sounded.

Len's face crimsoned with suppressed laughter, and Helen giggled.

"My family had dinner with your cousins the Eastwoods the other evening," she explained. "Mrs. Eastwood shared some of your childhood exploits with us."

"Oh lord," Len said.

Helen laughed merrily.

"My cousin Joanna is married to Harrison Eastwood, of Eastwood and Stevenson's," Len explained to Maia. "She was a Lennox before marriage—a cousin on my mother's side. We, ah, share many of the same family traits."

A spark lit her eyes and she nodded.

From his father, Len had inherited an estate near the Welsh border, a love for the land, and his broad shoulders. From his mother came his love for puzzles, his wanderlust, and his knack for magic. Neither his father nor his sister were magicians, but nearly everyone on his mother's side had at least a smattering of magic ability.

He shifted the subject away from the Lennox family magicians—there was a memory there that still hurt, even after all these years. "As I understand it, you two ladies are willing to help me look into my little contretemps from the other day," he said, motioning to his arm.

"Yes, since we are forbidden from investigating Maia's," Helen said with a scowl that in no way detracted from the prettiness of her face.

"We do think there might be a connection," Maia reminded her. "And that is one of the things we hope to discover from our investigation."

"I've never been a detective before," Helen said brightly. "Do we need magnifying glasses? Pipes and violins? Deerstalkers?"

Len laughed. "Let's start with our wits, shall we?"

"If we must," Helen said.

"I want to find the bullet and perform an, er, examination on it, to tell us its origins and something about the shooter," he said, glancing at the passers-by and hoping his companions would understand he meant a magical examination without his having to be explicit.

"How do we find it, since it didn't lodge in your arm?" asked Maia.

"Logic," said Len. "And mathematics. How are you two ladies at higher arithmetic?"

Helen beamed. "As a matter of fact, I'm something of an expert."

Though he would have preferred spending time with Maia alone, Len had to like Helen. She was bright and eager, and if half of what he'd learned in looking up her magical specialty and abilities was true, had a formidable intelligence (habit of an Intelligence officer—one never made a new acquaintance without first learning all one could about him or her).

When they reached Piccadilly, they set about recreating what Helen enthusiastically called "the scene of the crime." They could not attempt a chameleon or any other sort of distraction spell in the middle of London, in the middle of the day, so they had to endure the odd looks of the passers-by as they re-enacted the shooting.

"Let's see, I was standing about … here," Len said, taking Helen by the shoulders and steering her into place. She endured this puppet-mastery with only a few giggles.

"And the shooter was here, or close to it," he said, setting Maia in place. "I can't be exactly sure, as I didn't see him or her. But it seems about right. We'll try it, anyway." He stepped back and looked at the two of them, chewing on his lower lip. Pulling out a small notebook, he scribbled for a few moments, scratched his head, crossed out several calculations, and scribbled again. "Given trajectory and speed, the bullet ought to be over there." He pointed with his pencil.

Helen broke position, waving her hand at the pavement so a faint yellowish-green "x" shimmered where she had been. A glamour, Len realized, put down to mark her spot. Rather clever, that. Non-magic users couldn't see it, and it allowed them to move about freely.

"Let me see that," Helen said, crossing to where Len was standing and squinting into the distance. She took the notebook with scant ceremony, studied it, and shook her head. "No, you've calculated this bit wrong. The angle should go like *this*, see, where it glances off you, and so that means the bullet would be *there*."

Len peered down at her adjusted lines and figures. "So it should."

Helen glamoured the spot where Maia stood, in case they needed it again, and they spread out to search the indicated area, finding nothing: no bullet, no hole, not even a scratch in the pavement.

Helen stole Len's pencil and scribbled down a few more angles and figures to determine other possible places the shooter could have stood given where the bullet had hit.

"It seems a miracle nobody else got hit, given how crowded the street is," Maia said, glancing up and down the busy pavement.

A cold feeling trickled down the back of Len's neck.

"Let's search again based on the new figures," he said to distract himself.

He thought Maia cast him a curious glance, but he forced himself to move forward as though nothing were wrong. This was probably all his imagination. They would find the bullet and then—

"Nothing," Helen said, throwing up her hands in frustration. "I don't understand! It has to be here."

"Perhaps it did hit someone else?" Maia asked.

Len shook his head, the cold feeling settling somewhere in his stomach. "Not likely. The person who was hit would have made a fuss, wouldn't they? They would stand there going, 'ho-hum, appears I've got a bullet in the old tum, wot wot.' They'd raise a hue and cry over it."

Maia gestured angrily at the space around them—full of people and paving stones and buildings, but empty of the one tiny thing they needed to further their investigation. "Then where is it? Bullets don't just vanish!"

"They do if they aren't bullets," said Len. "Here is a good lesson for you ladies—when sorcery is involved, never take things as they appear. Check everything and suspect everyone," he intoned. "Something I forgot."

If there was no bullet, he'd been hit by something else. He remembered the mixed accounts the policeman had received of the incident, the fact that no non-magical person had seen the wound, and that even a doctor could be fooled by a good enough glamour.

A curse disguised as a bullet, and it had been in his system long enough now to do goodness-knew-what. Perhaps even cause him to drop down dead like the poor chap at Miss Rawlings' house.

Perhaps something worse.

"I need to get to my laboratory," he said.

Maia had clearly reached the same conclusions he had. Her lips set in a thin line. "I'm coming too."

* * *

Under other circumstances, Len would have been delighted to show his flat to Maia. Not for any improper reasons, but to see if she approved of his taste in decorating and style of living. Even as it was, he couldn't help but hope she'd notice and like the sage-and-brown color scheme, the squashy leather chairs in the sitting room, the full bookcases and modern conveniences around every corner.

Helen had not been able to join them for this, as she had an appointment with her mother to take tea. Len unlocked and opened the door, and Becket appeared a moment later.

"Sir? Hello, Miss Whitney," he said, stepping aside to let them enter and taking their hats and coats.

"We might have an emergency situation, Becket," Len explained tersely. "I hope to God it's not—but we need to check my arm. In the lab."

"Oh," said Becket. Then, "*Oh*."

Without wasting any more words, Becket finished with their outdoor things and turned to lead the way to the laboratory.

The laboratory was a large, brightly lit room with plenty of windows, bookshelves lining the walls, and a plain wooden table in the middle with a few chairs gathered around it.

"Boring, isn't it?" said Len. He grinned, hoping to disguise how worried he was. "It used to be the library, and I've a good disguise spell on it—the opposite of a glamour—which still makes it look that way to non-magical eyes."

"Well-lit and spacious," Maia said. "All any good magician

needs in his or her workshop."

"Well," said Len after a moment more's hesitation. "Let's get this over with."

He removed his jacket and sat down in one of the chairs while Becket rolled his shirt sleeve up above the bandage.

"Is that still the bandage the doctor put on?" Maia asked, her VAD training coming to the fore. "It should be changed today regardless." She picked up a pair of scissors off the table and made a neat slit in the white wrapping before gently peeling it back from Len's muscular arm.

"Len…"

"There is no injury, sir," Becket filled in when her voice faded.

Len twisted his head to see the unblemished skin on his upper arm. "What, none?"

"No sign of even a healed wound," Maia said. "I don't understand."

"It means I wasn't shot," Len said. His stomach twisted.

"But you felt pain," Maia said. "And the doctor—people on the street—other people saw the wound."

"Certain curses can cause physical pain upon contact with the victim," Len said, his face set in stone, his words a dull monotone. "And if it was a curse and a glamour cast at me at the same time, the glamour would have made it appear I had an actual flesh wound to those with eyes to see it. If the doctor had had to do more than swab my arm clean and wrap a bandage around it, he might have noticed something off, but …" He swallowed. "There is no point in reciting 'ifs' now."

"One moment, sir," Becket said before exiting the workroom. He returned moments later with white fabric folded in his hands, shaking his head. "No hole, no blood," he said.

"The shirt I was wearing yesterday?" Len asked, receiving a

nod of confirmation.

"I was going to repair it this afternoon," Becket said. "But there is no need."

"What now?" Maia asked.

"Now I will cast a seeking spell, miss," said Becket. "This will tell me if there is any trace of magic other than his own residing in Mr. Davies. Once that is determined, we can move to the next step."

"If there is other magic, it should be obvious whether it is benign or vicious," Len elaborated. "If it is vicious, we will have to try to extract it without damaging me or my own magic in the process. That's the tricky part."

"If you are ready, sir, I shall begin," said Becket.

Len steeled himself. "Go ahead."

Becket held his hands above the injury and said, *"Inveniatur ars magica."*

They all waited, and then Becket's shoulders slumped. "I can't find anything, sir. I must have done the spell wrong; I can't even sense your own magic."

Maia frowned. "It seemed a perfectly good spell to me. Do you mind if I try?"

"Please do," said Becket, and Len nodded.

Maia positioned her hands in the same manner Becket had and repeated the invocation, the air taking on a silver shimmer above them as Len watched.

She shook her head. "It's not you, Becket. I can't sense any magic either."

"The spell worked, I could see it. You should have at least been able to sense my magic. You mean you couldn't sense any outside magic." Len frowned. It wasn't like Maia to be sloppy in anything, including her use of language.

Her eyes widened. "I—couldn't," she almost whispered. "Oh, Len—there was no magic at all."

Len sat bolt upright. No, no, no. It couldn't be—it wasn't possible—he would have felt it. It was true he hadn't cast any spells since getting shot—but that wasn't unusual, he only used magic as he needed it, not for everyday tasks. He wasn't on a mission, he was recuperating—he hadn't had any call to cast a spell. He could still see magic, as he had seen the glamours Helen had cast earlier, and Maia's magic just now.

He steadied himself and stretched out his mind and energy while at the same time rooting himself more deeply in his core. He set the parameters in his mind's eye and opened his mouth to cast the most basic spell of all, the one every magician worth his or her salt could do without even thinking.

"*Lux fiat!*"

Nothing happened. He couldn't even sense the light he was trying to gather into the spell.

His magic was … *gone*.

3

A Plan of Action

Maia returned to St. James's Street with her head spinning. Len had bolted out of his laboratory as soon as he'd failed to cast the *lux* spell, saying something about a parasite and danger and needing to contact Harrison right away. Becket, his face grey and drawn, had escorted her to the door, murmured in an unconvincing voice that all this would be cleared up soon, and left the flat hard on her heels, heading in the same direction as Len.

Maia would have liked to have followed him, but it wouldn't have done to butt in where she wasn't wanted—just like that silly nanny goat her mother had purchased years back, always shoving her way between people and getting stuck in hedges when she tried and couldn't force her way through. No thank you!

Besides, Aunt Amelia would be furious if she were home too late for her evening work. There was a shield spell Maia was supposed to learn, to prevent curses or other dark magic from getting into the house. It had to be cast at dawn and renewed each morning at the same time, so Maia needed to memorize the incantation and practice the right focus of will this evening.

When she entered the foyer at St. James's Street, all was chaos.

This was not unusual for Aunt Amelia's household, but what was unusual was Aunt Amelia's disheveled appearance. Generally her aunt stood aloof from all the disruptions she caused, looking down upon them with a faint Jovian frown, as though wondering why mere mortals had to scurry to do things that were perfectly simple to one of her mind.

Not today. Today her usually impeccable coiffure was coming loose, untidy strands straggling down her forehead and cheeks as she bustled from one place to the next, her shirtwaist had pulled loose from the tight belt of her skirt, and her face bore a smudge of dirt. Shocking!

"Whatever has happened, Aunt?" Maia said, standing just inside the doorway, gazing about.

Aunt Amelia stopped short in her rushing about, causing Lorde to stumble in his tracks in an attempt to not run her over. He did not seem to blame Aunt Amelia for this loss of dignity, but he cast Maia a dirty look.

"Maia! There you are. Where have you been, girl? Never mind. I am off to France by the next train, and you will have to stay here under the supervision of the servants."

Maia swallowed her first instinctive words and changed them to a mild, "Excuse me?"

Aunt Amelia waved an impatient hand. "That French scandal, I told you about it—no no, you stupid girl, not that hatbox, the one on the left side of the wardrobe shelf!"

Servants who cringed under harsh words rarely lasted long in Amelia Rawlings' employ. Elsie, the newest and youngest of the housemaids, bobbed a quick curtsey and carried the scorned hatbox back toward the upstairs without so much as a flinch. Only Maia, from her perspective by the door, could see the slight eye-roll as she went.

"I must tend the matter in person. It's far too delicate to take an apprentice along …" Aunt Amelia's eyes slid sideways suddenly, and she passed a hand over her unkempt hair. "That is … yes. I don't want your studies interrupted, or for you to miss the Magicians' Ball. However, with someone out there running around casting curses and whatnot, not to mention the volatile nature of your magic, I don't feel comfortable leaving you here unsupervised. Lorde and the rest are all perfectly competent magicians in their own right. They will make sure you stay safe and follow instructions."

For heaven's sake, she wasn't a child. This was *mortifying*. Being left in the charge of the servants?

She didn't have to put up with this. She could turn around and walk right out that door, return to Stanbury. With her small allowance from her father, she could even get a flat of her own somewhere far away from both her parents and her aunt. No other magician would take her on as an apprentice once she'd reneged on her agreement with Aunt Amelia, but she could go to that new college for magicians hidden inside Cambridge. Or Len could teach her unofficially—

Len.

Maia's fevered soul steadied as though she had plunged her head into a cold pond. Of course she couldn't leave. No matter how humiliating this way, she couldn't walk out on Len. Nor on the other case, the poor dead man whom nobody seemed to care much about, not even the agents assigned to his case.

"Yes, Aunt," she said.

She would stay, and she would follow Aunt Amelia's instructions to the letter. In the meantime she would follow her own investigations, both into the vanishing of Len's magic and the death of the unknown man.

She had wanted to ask Aunt Amelia about magical parasites, but now did not seem the time. Nor did she want to give her aunt any indication of Len's troubles. That was his business, no one else's.

"And you can go to the dance with the Radcliffe family," Aunt Amelia said. She smiled in a condescending fashion. "I know how much you and Helen were looking forward to attending in your new frocks."

Maia seized advantage of the opening. "Oh, yes—I will have to go out with Helen a few more times. We couldn't settle on a particular gown when we went out before, and then there's all the other furbelows that must accompany such things. Rather too much for me, but Helen insists."

Aunt Amelia vanished into the Rose Parlor. "Yes, yes," her voice trailed back. "That should be perfectly acceptable. Lorde! Where are my dratted spectacles?"

As the butler hastened after her, a gentle knock sounded on the door. Since she was right there, Maia opened it herself rather than waiting for the servants to take notice.

She found herself face-to-face with a strange man—no, his face was vaguely familiar. Where had she seen him before?

"Oh!" he said, stammering a little. "Ex-excuse me. I-I didn't mean to in-intrude."

Something clicked inside Maia's head. Of course, he was the third agent who had come to the house to investigate the mysterious death. She didn't think she'd heard his name at all. The other two agents had barely taken notice of him, any more than they had of her. A spark of fellow feeling caused her to smile warmly and hold out her hand.

"Not at all," she said. "I'm afraid I can't remember your name, sir. I am Maia Whitney."

He shook her hand, his own damp and clammy within her grasp. "Jasper Driver, Miss Whitney. I had a few questions for Miss Rawlings about the, um, incident the other day. Is she in?"

Maia was not going to waste this opportunity. "I'm afraid my aunt is unable to receive callers of any sort at the moment. However, I would be more than happy to assist you with any questions you might have." She glanced over her shoulder. Lorde or her aunt might emerge from the parlor at any moment, and her chance would be lost. "This is terribly poor manners, but would you care to step into the kitchen? As you can see, we're in considerable disorder in the rest of the house."

Driver meekly followed her into the large, airy kitchen at the back of the house. The only people occupying it at the moment were Mrs. Oates, the cook, and little Betsy Aikin, the scullery maid and Mrs. Oates's apprentice in cooking magic.

"Don't mind us," Maia said, sitting down at the big wooden table. "Mr. Driver has some business related to the unpleasantness of the other day and we thought it best to conduct it here so as not to disturb the rest of the household."

Mrs. Oates was not as warm and loving as the cook at Stanbury, but neither was she as stand-offish as Lorde. "Right you are, miss," she said, and set the kettle on for tea before turning back to her pastry dough while Betsy watched wide-eyed.

Maia folded her hands together atop the table. "So, Mr. Driver. What can you tell me about the man who died? Has he been identified? Do you know the curse that killed him?"

He blinked. "Agent Barry said not to … er, that is, no, miss. Not yet."

"I see." Maia relented. The poor man was positively perspiring. She didn't envy him, working under the power-hungry Agent Barry and the sharply cold Agent Marsh. "You had some questions for us?"

"Um," he said, scrambling to reorient his thoughts. "Yes. Um …"

Maia waited patiently while he pulled some papers out of his coat pocket, scanned them, and tucked them back away. "Yes," he said, focusing on her again. "When the man spoke to you, did you notice any distinguishing accent or manner of speaking?"

"He said only one word," Maia said. "And it was very faint. I can be fairly sure he did not have a French or German accent, nor Russian. Other than that, I can't tell you anything. I am sorry."

"I see," he said, shrugging his shoulders. "I suspected as much. And you are sure neither you nor your aunt has remembered anything that might have slipped your mind at first, something you overlooked in the hyst—er, the excitement of the moment?"

It was a fair question, though neither Maia nor Aunt Amelia were prone to overlooking things, nor to hysteria. If it hadn't been that Agent Driver was clearly trying to smooth out Agent Barry's words, Maia might have had some sharp comments for him. As it was, she answered the question simply and straightforwardly.

"I'm afraid not," she said.

"And there was no trace of any magic on him until your aunt

cast her diagnostic spell?"

"That is correct. No magic on him or from him—that is, he was not in the process of casting a spell when he died, as best I could tell."

Driver sighed and seemed to deflate. "Very good. Thank you, miss." He started as Mrs. Oates set a cup of tea down at his elbow. "Er, thank you, ma'am."

Maia beamed at the cook as she received her own cup. "Lovely, Mrs. Oates, thank you ever so much." She turned her attention back to Driver. "Tell me, Mr. Driver, are you making any progress on the case at all? Judging by your questions, it seems not."

He looked down at the table, gulping his tea in an indecent haste to be gone. "I'm really not supposed to talk about it," he mumbled.

Reluctantly, Maia dropped him as a possible source of information. He did not have the other agents' arrogance, but neither did he seem to have backbone enough to go against them. A pity.

It was possible he might give her other useful information, however.

"Mr. Driver, can you tell me if there are such things as magical parasites?"

He looked up sharply, setting the teacup down with a clatter. "Where did you hear of such a thing?" he asked, his voice taking on a new edge.

Maia was taken aback. It seemed this was a more touchy subject than she'd realized. She was thankful she'd chosen to ask it of Driver, who presumably could be diverted, rather than the sharp-witted Aunt Amelia.

"I heard someone mention it once," she said with as casual

an air as she could manage. "And I wondered if it was true or merely a myth. Are they real, then?"

Driver's face was ashen. "One only h-hopes not," he said. "Miss Whitney, am I correct in understanding that you have not long been, er, acquainted with magic?"

"Yes," she had to answer.

"Then you would have no way of knowing, a p-parasite is one of those things of which we do not speak. A parasite curse drains one person's magic and gives it to the curse-caster. It is … un-unspeakably vile magic. Whoever spoke to you of it?"

Maia couldn't answer at first. That … *that* was what Len thought had happened to him? "But it comes back?" she demanded, ignoring Driver's question.

It had to come back. Magic was a sense like any other, albeit one few had the ability to use. One couldn't lose it like one could a limb. Could one?

"No such occurrence has ever been recorded, miss," Driver said. "There are few enough records of a p-parasite curse happening at all, and in each of those few, the magic was, ah, gone for good. I'm sorry, miss, I really must know. Who spoke of this to you?'

Maia swallowed her nausea and tried to think straight. She didn't want to reveal Len's affliction, but nor did she want to name someone else and get them in trouble. "Are you acquainted with Lennox Davies?" she asked. "I don't remember the occasion, but I think it must have been him, ages ago. I had asked about unusual magical ailments, and he mentioned parasites and then quickly changed the subject. I hadn't thought about it since, but since the mysterious death it popped into my mind that perhaps there were actual real creatures who could drain the magic from a person, and perhaps even their life …" she trailed off.

She was not as gifted at dissembling as Len, but her explanation seemed to reassure Driver, who relaxed back into his chair.

"Ah. No, our experts examined the body before we took it to Deep's morgue, and I can assure you that while we do not know exactly what the curse on him is, it is not a parasite spell." He paused, then changed the subject. "I was not aware you were acquainted with Davies. One of the best, he is. Saved my life, you know."

Maia allowed herself to be distracted from the new horror she had just learned. Len … magic-less … *forever*. It was impossible. Therefore she would not think of it.

"No! I had not heard that tale."

"Six months ago it was. I was tasked with tracking down a rogue magician. I thought I had the fellow cornered, but he was onto me the whole time. Set a trap for me. Would have had me, too, save for Davies. He jumped in without thought for his own danger, shattered the trap, hauled me to safety, and captured the rogue magician without even half trying." Smiling shyly, Driver met Maia's eyes for the first time. His own were a startlingly bright blue. "I owe him more than I can ever repay."

* * *

After both Driver and Aunt Amelia had left, one quietly departing out the back door, the other leaving in a flurry of pomp and circumstance through the front, Maia spent a quiet evening working on her spells and trying to keep her mind off what had happened to Len. It couldn't be a parasite spell, not really. He was an agent, so naturally his mind would jump to the worst possible conclusions.

Before bed, he sent her a brief note through enspelled pen and paper, stating that his superior agreed the matter was concerning but couldn't confirm the type of curse or his total loss of magic. A healer would examine him more thoroughly the next day, and he would keep her informed.

It wasn't much, but Maia held on to that slim hope even as she fell asleep, through her awakening at dawn and laying of the shield spell (wobbly, but not bad for a first solo attempt), through breakfast, and right up until Helen came to fetch her to finish their shopping for the Ball. Helen's chatter was enough to distract her, and for that Maia was grateful. The last thing she needed was to sit around chewing her nails and trying to be optimistic while waiting to hear back from Len about the healer's report.

"Oh, Maia, you do look smart," Helen said admiringly, stepping inside the front hall. "With your hair, you shouldn't be able to do any shade of red at all, but somehow you make that deep crimson look ever so elegant. I don't know how you do it. Is it a spell?"

Maia laughed. She had slept poorly, plagued with nightmares about giant parasitic bugs fastening on the backs of all her friends and loved ones and sucking the life out of them, leaving them grey husks which then withered into dust and blew away in the breeze.

Helen always brought a fresh energy into any room she entered, and already Maia felt better. "I would hardly waste my energy on something so frivolous."

Helen scowled. "Oh, you sound like Mother. She gets so irritated when I say anything about fashion and magic.

'Now Helen, our family has not been among England's best magicians since Queen Elizabeth's day only for you to go dabbling about making fripperies and furbelows for other people!'"

Maia sympathized with Mrs. Radcliffe—despite the egalitarian claims of the magical community, prejudices died hard, and a young lady of African descent, as Helen was, had to work twice as hard to earn respect from her peers as someone like Maia. There were still those who would sneer at Maia for being a woman, but that was nothing compared to what Helen must endure.

On the other hand, it was monstrously unfair that Helen should have to give up her dream simply because of society's assumptions. More injustice!

Sometimes Maia got so angry with the world she wanted to sweep it all away and start fresh. The one thing holding her back from falling headlong into the kind of evil magery inspired by such grandiose schemes was seeing how poorly Bolshevism and anarchy actually worked in the everyday world, and a prim dislike of anything smacking of unchecked emotionalism.

"I shouldn't have disparaged your interests," was all she said. "I do apologize."

Helen nodded graciously. "Fashion is a neglected field of magic," she said as Maia threw a lightweight coat on over her silk tunic and skirt suit. "We have our magical tailors and dressmakers, such as Mme. Julie whom we are going to see now, but they use magic only in small ways—to conjure up a glamour of the finished dress on an image of yourself, so you can see how it is going to look, for example. Or, if working with natural materials, to speed up the sewing process. But nobody uses magic as part of the design itself! Imagine, Maia, a gown which changes color based on how one wants to appear—if you were cheerful, for example, you could make it yellow, and if you wanted to be more somber you could switch it to navy blue with a simple word. Or one that enhances your natural charms. Or, well, anything! A dress with embroidered birds on it who really sing, or trees and vines," motioning to the design on the hem of Maia's skirt, "that show fruit in autumn, bare in winter, flowers in spring, and leaves in summer. The possibilities are endless."

"You've given this considerable thought," Maia said. The passion in Helen's voice sparked wistfulness in her. Would the day ever come when she would have one aspect of magic she cared this deeply about?

"You have no idea," said Helen. "Oh, I've even thought of having clothing that tells a story only to other magicians, with a glamour—an overlay in the color of one's own magical aura, showing significant events in one's life or symbols of one's magical specialty."

"That's brilliant, Helen. Why on earth are you wasting your time with small glamours when you have such marvelous ideas of your own? Why, every magician in England would come to you for clothing if you implemented even half of these notions. And it isn't as though they are simple magics, either—a mood-changing fabric? I can't even begin to think how many spells that would take."

Helen cast her eyes down modestly. "Oh well—Mother, you know. I can't disappoint her. Though I sometimes think, if I could just show her, if I could show everyone, just once, some of my ideas, she wouldn't mind so much. It's the idea of it that bothers her so." She stopped and stared, apparently struck by the same idea that had just come to Maia.

"The Magicians' Ball," Maia said.

"You didn't buy a gown yesterday," Helen said.

"If it's done between friends, and not a business transaction—"

"If I am not setting myself up as a common dressmaker, but showing this as art—"

"Can you do it in the time we have left before the ball?"

Helen's eyes flashed. "Just try to stop me!" She broke into an enormous smile. "Are you sure, though?"

Maia disliked having all eyes on her, but for Helen's sake, she would endure far worse. People wouldn't be staring at her, anyway—she would merely be the backdrop for Helen's creation. And she knew her friend well enough to know said creation would be glorious. "I will be the envy of every magician there," she said with a laugh. "I should be asking you if you are sure you want to use me for your model!"

"We'll go to Mme. Julie's for the base of the gown this morning," Helen said, catching Maia's arm and half dragging her out the door. "Then we can get started right away. Oh— bother it. Some of the books I need are in my old master's library. I don't see how I can borrow them without telling her the whole scheme." She frowned. "I want this to be a surprise to *everyone*."

Maia brightened. "I know! We'll go to Whegg's Antique Books. He's sure to have something useful."

She might even find a book there to help her understand what had happened to Len, and how to reverse it.

Mr. Whegg had, along with the ordinary old books filling his shelves, the largest collection of magic books in England. Few of these were for sale; rather, Mr. Whegg worked as a lending library, allowing those who needed one book or another to borrow them for a month or so at a time. His only stipulation was that books were returned in the same condition as they were taken, and that any interesting magic books one found and didn't need for oneself were offered to him before any other dealer.

Aunt Amelia didn't want Maia reading any books she didn't approve of, but Maia had no more idea of following her aunt's whims in that regard than she did as regarded her friendship with Len. She never dared bring any books back to the house, but frequently went in to browse when she was out and about on her own. Mr. Whegg was a short, plump, bald-headed man with a kindly, if vague, smile, and wise eyes. He rarely spoke unless spoken to, but he also never interfered with Maia's perusal of his books, so she was predisposed to like him.

"Oh!" said Helen. "Haven't you heard? No, I suppose you wouldn't have, I only know because Matthew spoke of it at breakfast this morning. Mr. Whegg has gone missing!"

"What?"

"The bookstore has been closed the last few days. He's never taken a day off in anyone's memory, not even when he was ill with the Spanish flu. Right now Deep is not too worried, as it's possible all that working without pause got to be too much for him and he took an impromptu holiday, but they're keeping an eye on the matter. Either way, we can't go there." She sighed. "I suppose I'll have to bring Mrs. Henry in on it. I suppose it is best to have her approval for it after all. It will look better to the magicians who judge whether or not this is a fitting master's project."

Maia barely heard this, as she was still mulling over the news about Mr. Whegg. She couldn't see how this related to the mysterious dead man or Len's loss of magic, but it was another Odd Thing. At some point, some of these had to start connecting.

4

Books and More Death

Len hadn't slept at all that night. When dawn broke, he quit even trying, rising from the rumpled sheets and blankets covering his bed to wrap himself in his dressing gown and stare out the window at the foggy London morning. He was not particularly surprised when Becket brought him a cup of tea, early though the hour was.

"Breakfast, sir?" his man asked in a voice even quieter than usual.

Len shook his head. He didn't think he could stomach more than tea right now. Becket had brewed it to perfection, strong and milky, with a hint of lemon.

Even that wasn't enough to undo the cold pit in the middle of Len's stomach, right where his magic used to dwell.

"What time are Mr. Eastwood and the healer arriving, sir?" Becket asked, though Len was sure he knew perfectly well.

"Nine o'clock," he answered.

There was a pause. There didn't seem to be anything else to say. Becket left the bedroom as unobtrusively as he had entered.

Harrison's face when Len had told him of the loss of his magic floated to the front of Len's memory. In all their years of knowing each other, since Len had started working under him and he and Jo had begun courting, Len had never seen the man look so stunned. Not even when Len had had to tell him about Alec—shock, rage, heartbreak, all those, but not stunned. Harrison had known better than they what Alec, Len, and Jamie, the third agent in that affair, were getting into when they left on that mission.

Nobody, not even Harrison Eastwood, could have anticipated this turn of events.

Len stood at his window, lost in thought, until Becket came back and insisted he get dressed. Len complied, thankful that his valet wasn't the sort to use empty platitudes or useless reassurances—"I am sure the healer will fix you right up" or some such nonsense. They went about the usual routine in grim silence, and Len was presentable by the time Harrison and the healer entered the house.

"Not the time to fuss about secret meeting places and whatnot, eh, Davies?" Harrison said as he came in.

"Don't believe you've met Miss Fisher before," Harrison continued, motioning to the tall, weedy lady standing beside him. "Fisher, this is Davies."

Len recognized the name, if not the individual. This dreary-looking person was Angela Fisher, Magical Intelligence's top healer. Up to this point in his career, he'd never needed to meet her.

"We need a diagnostic first," Miss Fisher said. "Where is your workroom? That will do nicely."

"Lead the way, Becket," Harrison said.

Len trailed after the other three into his laboratory. At this hour, it was filled with watery spring sunshine, welcoming and practical.

Out of habit, Len attempted to check his wards around the room, to make sure they were still stable. The blankness that met his reach sent him staggering against the doorframe, like stretching up high to pick an apple off a bough only to find one's fingers closing on air.

"Better—" His throat closed. He cleared it and tried again. "Better stabilize the wards, Becket."

Becket's face was unreadable. "Yes, sir."

Miss Fisher stripped off her gloves and tossed them on the table. "This will take a while," she said, no apology in her voice. "I wish to take into account every possibility before stating a definite diagnosis."

"Yes," said Len. "That seems an excellent idea."

Miss Fisher did not seem inclined toward idle chit-chat, her eyes half-closed in concentration as the spell progressed. Harrison turned his back to the entire endeavor, perhaps in an attempt to spare Len. Becket hovered near the door, only just succeeding in not wringing his hands. The wait stretched on … and on … until Len thought he'd scream like a banshee if he had to endure the silence another moment.

Twenty minutes after casting the spell, Miss Fisher broke the silence. "I'm so sorry. I must confirm that your magic is gone entirely, and through a leech spell. Unbelievable as it seems, you were attacked by a parasite."

"But I can still see … spell residue, and glamours, and …" Len's protest trailed off as Miss Fisher shook her head.

"That is what we call a phantom effect, and will fade as time passes. In a week, maybe two, even that will go away. According to the books," she added. "Obviously there is no healer in England today who has had personal experience with this."

In less than two weeks, he would be as magic-less as the person who lived his or her entire life without knowing of magicians, spells, or any of it. It was what he had braced himself for from the start, but having it confirmed hurt worse than he'd expected.

"Can we undo it?" Harrison asked sharply, while Len's stomach lurched its way down toward his toes.

Miss Fisher shook her head. "As I said, we have little information on leech spells, but there is no known way to reverse its effects. It's not an illness, so we cannot cure it. It is not strictly a curse, so we cannot counter it. It has simply drained away his magic."

"Giving it to somebody else instead," Len said hoarsely. Miss Fisher nodded.

"If we find the culprit, can we take Mr. Davies' magic out of him and return it to Mr. Davies?" Becket asked from the doorway. His face and voice were as properly expressionless as ever, but his hands shook.

Miss Fisher blinked. "Not unless you wanted to kill the other magician. And possibly Mr. Davies as well. Not to mention I know of no way to take magic from an unwilling person except through a curse, and while such an act might be considered justified in such a case as this …"

"It's still illegal. And unethical. And opens the caster to the temptation of doing it again, to an innocent person next time," Harrison filled in. It was his turn to shake his head. "I'm sorry, old chap."

Len swallowed. "Thank you, Miss Fisher," he said to the healer. "I am glad to know for certain what has happened.

Always better to know the worst than live with false hope, what? Appreciate your efforts on my behalf. Becket, would you be so kind as to show Miss Fisher out?"

The two left the lab, leaving Len alone with Harrison.

"Filthy luck, Len," Harrison said. The use of Len's first name rather than his surname hit like a blow. Harrison was treating him like—well, like his wife's cousin, not his subordinate.

Len pulled himself upright and squared his shoulders. "We'll catch the parasite, sir. I don't need magic to hunt down a criminal."

"Out of the question, Davies," Harrison barked. Len felt a surge of relief. He was back on solid ground. "Take some sick leave—if ever a man needed it, you do. We will take care of this parasite problem. Seems it must be connected to the curse at the Rawlings place. Can't imagine two separate magicians choosing the same day to unleash deadly curses, one of which is practically unknown and one of which we still can't identify … I'll put Marsh back on the case with Barry and Driver, maybe a few junior agents as well, enough to get the job done."

"You're going to let Barry hunt down the man who stole my magic? And Marsh?"

Harrison's face set. "I know you don't like them, but—"

It wasn't a matter of like or dislike. Len didn't trust them to find the parasite. Frankly, he trusted no one in MI aside from himself and Becket. There was a reason these sorts of missions usually fell to them.

"Sir, I wouldn't mention this if I didn't think it important. You know that Barry hates me." Amy Marsh's dislike was personal, and therefore less obvious, but Len supposed Harrison knew about that as well.

"I told you it was a bad idea to publicly accuse him of being, what was it? 'As good as a murderer?'"

"I couldn't—" Len caught himself. This was not the time to defend his actions. "Maybe it was," he said. "But whatever the cause of his hate, do you honestly think he'll be able to devote himself fully to catching the man who put me out of action?" He swallowed hard again as he finished that sentence. Out of action—he'd have to take the time later to work out everything that entailed. Right now, stopping the parasite was his first priority.

"Frankly, Davies, I expect him to work twice as hard on it for that very reason," Harrison said. "I expect he'll leap at the chance to prove himself a better magician and agent than you—that he is able to catch the person who undid you."

Len flinched. He had asked for that.

Harrison's reasoning was brutal, but that candid, cold logic was one of the reasons the man was in such a high position at MI, just as Len's own impulsiveness and occasional hot-headedness were factors in his role as field agent.

Had been factors. Now there were others.

"Besides, you know Marsh and Driver will also work with all they've got, once they hear it's you."

No question but that Jasper Driver would leap at the chance to pay back his debt to Len. Amy Marsh … well, if Harrison thought the woman Len had rejected romantically eight months ago would want to do him a favor, he must be right, but for Len's part, he couldn't see it.

He couldn't explain that to his chief, though.

"Listen, why not go up to Scotland for a few weeks, visit Philippa and her husband. Jo told me something about them expecting their first? I'm sure they'd welcome a visit from soon-to-be Uncle Len. Once we get the parasite captured, you can come back and … and we'll go from there."

Meaning, at that point Len would be reconciled to his loss, and Harrison wouldn't have to deal with it. They could write him off, promote a new agent to fill his shoes, and he would fade into obscurity as an object lesson to be dragged out in training.

"Thank you for your advice," he bit out. "I'll take it into consideration." He moved to the door. "Becket!" he shouted. "Mr. Eastwood is ready to leave."

"Davies!" Harrison said.

Habit and training made him turn to face his superior.

"Don't do anything stupid."

Len gave a short, humorless laugh. "I'll do my best, sir."

Becket appeared, and Len left it to his valet to see his chief out the door.

* * *

There were people he had to tell. Mother, for one. Len shuddered away from the thought of that conversation. Not that the mater would cry, or faint, or anything so *déclassé*. She wasn't that sort. Nor would she insist on him immediately marrying a lady of strong magical abilities, so the family talent might not be lost. Thank heavens, she wasn't *that* sort, either.

Never in all their childhood had Len felt he had some sort of special status that his sister Philippa had not. Though his lessons included aspects neither Phil nor their father knew about, his mother had always made it plain that magic did not make him better than anyone else.

"It's character that matters most," she had said to him more than once. "I'd rather see you a poor magician and a good man than the other way around."

So no, Mother wouldn't be crushed by this news. Yet he couldn't face telling her all the same. Telling Mother—telling anyone—would make it real, make it irrevocable.

Len decided he would wait until the last vestiges of his magic had gone, until he could no longer see or sense anyone's magic. Then he would start telling people, not before. Then, maybe, he would be able to believe it himself.

There was one person who needed to know right now. Len absentmindedly reached for his notepad, preparing to cast the spell to allow him to transfer his words instantly to Maia's notepad. He stopped with his fingertips an inch from the paper, his heart thudding against his chest, his breath coming in short gasps.

No more spells performed without thought. No more magic making his life richer and fuller. No more connection to other magicians.

He could wait for Becket to return, ask him to cast the spell for him. This would be his life from now on, always needing others to help and guide him where once he could act alone, or assist others when needed.

No! He couldn't bear it. He would come to that eventually—and if he needed constant assistance, Becket was a better helper to have than anyone else he could think of—but just now he couldn't stand it.

Len turned on his heel, stormed out of the lab, flung on coat and hat, and threw open the front door preparatory to going for a walk—somewhere—anywhere.

He came nose-to-nose with Maia, who stopped, hand raised to knock, blue-green eyes wide with surprise.

"Oh," she said. "I was—I wondered how—that is, I think I

have a lead."

"A lead," Len repeated.

"Yes, I, that is—Mr. Whegg of Whegg's Antique Books is missing, and I think it might be connected."

"We'd best investigate it then, hadn't we?" said Len. "Becket!" he called over his shoulder. "We're looking into a potential lead at Whegg's Antique Books!"

"Yes, sir," came the inevitable response. "Coming, sir."

They set out, Len walking beside Maia, Becket a few paces behind. Len could feel Maia's curiosity—he knew she had come for more than aid in investigating the bookstore—but now that the moment had come, he wasn't sure how to break the news to her.

They paced in silence for a few streets before Maia finally snapped,

"Oh, for heaven's sake, this is ridiculous. I daresay I'm prying and if you don't wish to speak of it by all means say so and I'll ask Becket later, but Len, I must know: what is the state of your magic?"

Some of the pressure inside him eased at the frankness of the question, but that didn't make it any easier to say: "Gone. Permanently. It was a leech spell from a parasite, as I suspected."

Maia didn't gasp in horror. She didn't cover her mouth, or whisper, "Oh Len, I'm so sorry." She didn't burst into tears, or fall into a panic at the thought of a parasite loose in London, or withdraw from him in sudden repugnance, as though magic loss was somehow catching.

Her lips pressed together in a thin line, her eyes flashed green fire, her gloved hands clenched briefly into fists and then relaxed.

"I see," was all she said.

Nobody spoke the rest of the way to the bookstore.

Far away from the fashionable stores of Regent and Oxford Streets, Whegg's Antique Books was tucked away in a dusty side street off the Strand, found only if one was looking for it. Right now the blinds were pulled and the door locked, the "closed" sign plain to see.

By unspoken consent, the three investigators spoke and acted as though the revelation of Len's loss of magic was old news, accepted and dealt with in a matter-of-fact manner. Len would have to face up to it at some point, but for now, the case took precedence.

Becket concealed them; Len used his picklocks to undo the padlock holding the door closed; Maia insisted on doing a sweep for defensive magic before any of them set foot inside.

Maia's spell revealed no danger, so they entered the small, dim shop.

There were a few bookcases standing around, all filled and double- or triple-stacked, but mostly it was just stacks of books. Books on tables. Books under tables. Piles of books on the floor. Books covering most of the windows, blocking what little light the blinds let in. Freestanding stacks towering so high they relied on nearby stacks to keep them upright, leaving one with the fear that removing one book would send the entire place crashing down around one's ears.

Somewhere in the back were the magical books, unseen to non-magical eyes. Unlike some libraries Len had seen— his mother's among them—these books would not change to show a non-magical title and text if an ordinary person held them. No, these were literally invisible to any but magicians. Invisibility was a dashed difficult spell, even on inanimate objects (it was nearly impossible on people and animals); Len had never been able to study Whegg's spell properly to see how it was woven together. He supposed there was no point now.

Everything was covered with a thin layer of dust, further proof, if any was needed, that Whegg was gone. He never let a single day pass without conscientiously dusting all the books—though Len was never able to understand how he did it without knocking them all to pieces.

"Oh dear," said Maia, sounding more than a little overwhelmed. "How are we ever going to find anything?"

Insensibly, this cheered Len. He might be worthless as a magician now, but he could still conduct a proper investigation.

"We make a few observations right away," he said, taking her arm and pointing. "For example, no footprints in the dust covering the floor."

"So that tells us no one has been here since Mr. Whegg last closed the shop," Maia said, catching on right away.

"Exactly. You see *and* observe, Watson."

Maia sniffed. "I am *not* the idiot friend, Mr. Holmes."

Len grinned. "Not even close. No collapsed piles of books, or broken tables, or anything of that sort, which tells us no violence happened in the front of the shop."

"So he likely wasn't abducted or attacked here."

"Which doesn't preclude abduction or attack, but lets us know it didn't happen here," Becket said, venturing further into the shop and peering into its corners. "Miss Whitney, would you be so kind as to shed some light on this subject?"

Maia beamed and happily performed her *lux* spell. Len looked around in the new light from Maia's silver globe hanging in the air above their heads. Sherlock Holmes or

Hercule Poirot might have been able to pick up more clues from the threshold alone, but Len couldn't see anything else that appeared useful. "So now that we have gained all we can tell from here, we follow Becket's valiant footsteps and cross the threshold. If I were doing this alone, I'd do a quick check of the place first, followed by an exhaustive examination of the counter and desk area. Since Becket's with me, I'll leave the checking to him and go straight for the counter."

"What should I do?" Maia asked, following him and coughing slightly as their feet stirred up the dust.

"A shadow spell would be useful," Len said. "Give us some idea of the last thing that happened here, don't you know."

"I *don't* know," said Maia. "What's a shadow spell?"

"A shadow spell," Len said, rocking back on his heels and clasping his hands behind his back in his best imitation of his pompous boyhood tutor, "catches the traces left behind by magicians and reconstructs their movements. It won't reveal details, but it could give us an idea of the last activity done in this shop. You have to be careful to give it proper parameters, though, or it will capture shadows from months back—both useless and exhausting to the spellcaster. It's quite the useful little spell in investigative work."

"Well then," said Maia, pretending to push up her sleeves. "You'd better teach it to me."

"Aunt Amelia won't like it," he teased. "She would find it beneath you."

"All the more reason for me to learn it," Maia retorted.

Len's laugh held sympathy rather than mockery. "Still a battle between the two of you, eh?"

Maia shook her head. "Do all apprentices have such struggles to make their own place? Helen's mother refuses to accept what Helen wants to do with her life, but I don't know, maybe that's mothers. But here I have Aunt Amelia trying to mold me into her idea of the perfect magician, and sometimes I feel as though the magic inside me is going to explode out of my pores if I don't find some better way of channeling it!" She caught her breath. "And sometimes it does," she ended grimly.

Len noted that with concern, but addressed the immediate question first. "It's a mixed bag, I suppose," he said with a shrug. "No different from ordinary people's struggles with their teachers, tutors, and parents. Each generation always wants something different from the previous."

"How wise you are," Maia said mockingly, but with a glint of appreciation in her eye. "Now. Teach me that shadow spell."

Before Len could do so, they were interrupted by a call from Becket, at the back of the shop. "Mr. Davies, Miss Whitney! You'll want to come see this, if you please!"

With one accord, the two rushed toward the sound of his voice, stopping short at the scene which confronted them.

Becket stood in what had been the magical book section. It had been ransacked: books were thrown everywhere, pages torn out of many, some lying on the floor broken-backed from being flung against the wall, some shredded from being stomped on. Maia made a noise low in her throat.

"Such violence," she almost-whispered.

"I think it is safe to say we have come across a clue," said Becket.

"Hold off on the shadow spell for now, Maia," Len said. "Let's see what we can find through conventional means first."

She looked disappointed. "Why not use magic, if it will make things easier?"

"Because sometime you might not be able to, and if you are

too used to relying on it, then you'll be stuck," Len responded.

Maia flushed. "Sorry," she said.

The spectacle of Maia apologizing was rare enough to startle Len. "I didn't mean—" he started.

He hadn't been thinking about the loss of his magic, in fact; he'd remembered the numerous missions where using magic was impractical or even dangerous, revealing one as a magician when it needed to remain a secret.

He didn't explain this. Even the fact that Maia had apologized twisted the dagger more deeply. She *pitied* him—that was why she'd jumped so quickly to say she was sorry.

He didn't want her pity. Couldn't bear it, in fact. If even Maia saw him as an object of pity ...

"The first thing to do is sort through the books and see if any are missing," Becket told her.

Len snapped out of his haze. At least he still had Becket.

"How shall we tell?" Maia asked, then answered her own question. "Of course, a catalog."

Becket hunted behind the counter until he found the catalog—it was crammed into the back of a drawer, not noticeable until he pulled the entire drawer out and the catalog unstuck from behind it. "Good thing I've had plenty of practice, sir," he murmured to Len, who cleared his throat sheepishly. He didn't know how it was he always managed to jam papers into drawers—certainly he never tried.

Len and Maia picked up and sorted the books, calling out their titles while Becket checked them against the thankfully alphabetized catalog. When they finally had the entire mess in several neat stacks, there was only one discrepancy between the books present and the list.

Parasite to Predator, Spells to Strengthen One's Gift.

"I'd say we've found the reason our Whegg is missing," Len said. He ruffled his hair with his hand, realizing too late that he had probably just smeared dirt through it.

Maia, lovely even when dust-smudged and worried, touched the books lightly. "You think he is the parasite, then?"

"This book was a recent acquisition," Becket said, looking at the catalog. "Likely as he read it, he fell prey to the lure of easy power."

"So he cast a death spell on that poor man who came to Aunt Amelia's—we really must do something about identifying him, your Agent Barry has made no progress there, according to Agent Driver—and then cast the leech spell on Len, and is now wandering around London glutted with life and power? Why hasn't he come back? And why such wanton destruction of all these other books?"

"Excellent questions," Len said. "He must be afraid of being suspected. Either that or he is out looking for more victims."

"Or he could be using his newfound power to do things he's always wanted to do but never could," Becket added.

"Either way, there are plenty of reasons why he wouldn't come back. As for the books …"

"To make it look like a robbery," Becket suggested.

"Or to keep people from guessing which book was missing, should anyone come looking," Len concluded.

Maia tucked a loosened strand of hair behind her ear. "But … that's so illogical. If he's out because he's glutted with power, he wouldn't be thinking clearly enough to make it look like he'd been robbed, or even care. And if he's afraid of being suspected, why wouldn't he come up with a reasonable explanation for his disappearance, so that people wouldn't even come here looking for him in the first place?"

Len opened his mouth, then shut it without saying anything. She was right. They had Whegg acting too stupidly on one side and too cleverly on the other.

"Besides," she continued. "If he didn't want anyone to know about this, he would have destroyed the catalog, not the books. I cannot think that anyone who cares so much for books as Mr. Whegg did could have wrecked these for anything, even his own safety." She gestured to the battered tomes stacked around them.

"Your logic is impeccable," Len said. "What is your theory, then?"

She gestured wildly, hands flying through the air. "How can I theorize without more facts? At first glance this looks like a straightforward robbery: the parasite stole the book and then destroyed the rest to hide it. That still leaves so many unanswered questions. How did he—or she—find out about the book? Why steal, when one can borrow or buy? How does our mysterious dead body tie into everything? Where is Whegg, if he is not the parasite? Above all, of course, who is the parasite and what is he—or she—after?" She scowled. "I need to make a list, get everything sorted. Then I can properly theorize."

They separated after that, Maia returning to the Rawlings residence to reassure her keepers she was being responsible instead of gadding about, Len and Becket to wend their way back to the flat, where Len was surprised to find a summons from Harrison. He was to report to his superior at the Eastwood warehouses at once.

The hair on the back of Len's neck prickled. This wasn't unprecedented, but it was unusual. Meetings at Harrison's legitimate place of business did not generally happen, as people might start to get suspicious of a more-than-family connection between the two men. Besides, Harrison had told him to go to Scotland. Why did he now want to see Len?

Len trusted Harrison and Jo more than any others in MI. There was no reason for him to feel uneasy about this. For all he knew, it could be good news. Maybe Barry had surpassed himself and solved the case and Harrison wanted to inform Len personally.

On the other hand …

Ten years ago, Len and his mate Jamie had volunteered for a desperately dangerous wartime mission to prevent a power-mad magician from turning the tide of war toward Germany. To Len's dismay, his young cousin Alec—Jo's much younger and much-loved brother—had also volunteered. He was newly come to MI, far too inexperienced to participate in a mission of that sort. Len had argued strenuously against his inclusion, but the Circle members in charge, Amelia Rawlings among them, had decided to let him go.

Alec and Jamie had died in Germany, and while the heartbreak of losing both of them had been bad enough, even worse was Len having to come back to tell Jo and Harrison about Alec. The goal had been worth the sacrifice, Jo had stoically said, while Harrison blamed himself for letting Alec join MI in the first place. Neither of them had blamed Len, nor seemed to harbor the secret resentment he bore against Amelia Rawlings and the rest who had allowed it to happen.

Len couldn't believe what he was thinking. There was no chance either Harrison or Jo would harbor a secret desire for revenge for ten years and then stoop to such despicable lengths to get it. It wasn't in their characters.

His loss was playing tricks on his brain. He would meet

Harrison at the warehouses and hear whatever he had to say, and he would do so without fear of walking into any sort of trap.

He would, however, use Becket as backup, just in case. That was only prudent.

* * *

Eastwood Warehouses nestled between several of its brethren on Thames Street, processing tea, sugar, and other goods to be sold in London and beyond. Len was an infrequent enough visitor that he didn't recognize the guard at the front gate. The man had apparently been told to watch for him; he gave Len a brief nod and stepped back to allow him to enter.

On a Sunday afternoon, the place was mostly empty of people, the space taken up with bales, crates, and sacks. Len wended his way between them to the large, well-lit office in the back.

Harrison was seated behind his monstrous desk, swearing softly and clutching at his head as he scanned papers and jotted notes. For the first time, Len wondered how he balanced his legitimate business with his MI work.

With an enormous amount of help from Jo, he answered almost in the same moment.

Harrison looked up, irritation creasing his face. "Who—oh, Len! Good man, come in and shut the door."

Len did so, instinctively feeling with his inner sense for that *click* which would indicate a muffling spell around the room had activated. When it came, it was nearly intangible, sending a jolt through his gut.

The fading of his ability to sense magic had begun.

He wrenched his attention back to Harrison.

"I shouldn't be doing this," the older man began without preamble.

Len held his breath. Was Harrison going to include him in the official investigation after all?

"I can't include you in the official investigation," Harrison continued, dashing Len's hopes. "But I have a task for you, if you're interested."

"Of course," Len said automatically. "What happened to 'go to Scotland, Len'?"

Harrison rubbed his mostly bald head. "I had to report this to my own superiors at MI, you know, and as happens, word spread like wildfire and the rumors began."

In only a few hours? That was quick even for Len's colleagues.

"Some have started saying … well, parasites and leech spells are far-fetched even for our division, you know. Some are suggesting this is nothing of the sort."

Realization sank in, leaving Len cold. "They think I took advantage of the curse at the Rawlings place to justify a lack of skill on my part."

"A lack of dedication," Harrison corrected. "It's partially my fault. The less exacting missions I've been sending you on recently, and now sick leave because of a supposed leech spell …"

"Sir," said Len, curiosity overcoming good sense (*as usual*, Becket would probably say). "Why *did* you start sending me out on those elementary missions?"

Harrison straightened in his chair, steepling his fingers together. "A few different reasons, my boy. One, I was starting to see signs of strain in you from all the high-pressure missions you'd been on, yet you refused to take a holiday. Two, even the best agent is going to have bad luck eventually, and I didn't fancy having to tell my wife I let her cousin get killed because I overused him. Three, your handling of the Barry affair seemed to indicate an arrogance and setting yourself above your fellow agents I found alarming and I needed to know you would still do as you were told."

"Oh." Len couldn't think of much else to say to this. After a few moments, he added, "Signs of strain?"

"It happens to all of us," Harrison said. "For me, that's when I transferred from field agent to supervisor. Some agents end up cracking, going rogue, or getting themselves killed. I didn't want the latter to happen, and I didn't think you were ready for the former. So I thought I could ease the pressure and give you a longer lifespan in the field."

Len would have to think about this. Later. Right now, he needed to stay focused. "Well, what about this investigation? Since it seems it will be my last no matter what," he added bitterly.

"Don't think I'm not sorry about that," Harrison said in a soft voice. "Even aside from what it means to you, I'm damn unhappy about losing my best agent." He cleared his throat and pulled one paper out from under the others on the desk. "This turned up this morning—death of a hedgewitch out in Basingstoke."

Len blinked. "That's unfortunate, of course, but not exactly cause for us to investigate."

It was a harsh but true fact that hedgewitches and -wizards—the untrained magical people of England—did die frequently, from uncontrolled power or a homemade spell gone wrong. It was one reason why magicians like Amelia

Rawlings were so insistent on strict rules and structures to the magical system. Len wasn't convinced it was the best response, but this was hardly the time to get into that.

"Yes, well, this one was murdered. Shot through the heart and left just inside her front door."

"That is odd," Len agreed. The usual way hedgewitches died was unmistakable, as their magic escaped their control and consumed them, leaving behind a withered husk. There was an entire division of Deep dedicated to cleaning up such deaths before the ordinary authorities noticed them. "What makes you think it might be connected to the parasite, sir? If she wasn't drained of magic or life, that is." Either Harrison was sending him on a wild goose chase, or there was more to the story than met the eye.

"It's a small detail," Harrison admitted. "I did mention it to Barry, but he insisted there was more than enough work to do here on the case without chasing down every tiny will-o-the-wisp."

Len tried without success to keep from grimacing. He always chased the will-o-the-wisps. In his experience, they were often the crucial clues that led to the truth. Not Agent Barry, though. He focused so narrowly on his main goal that he couldn't be distracted by a freight train, much less a chimera. It was one reason so many in the agency fawned on him as an expert agent and simultaneously despised Len as too easily distracted. Never mind that Len had almost as many successes to his name as Barry ...

"The curse that hit you was disguised with a strong glamour to make it look like a bullet wound," Harrison said. "That's how you, the doctor, and Becket were all fooled. This Basingstoke hedgewitch, now, she specialized in glamour potions. It might not mean anything, there are plenty of trained magicians who can do a glamour without a potion, but there's the smallest chance she might be connected to your case." Harrison folded his hands and looked steadily across the desk at Len. "It's up to you. Will you go down and look into it, or should I let it go?"

Len considered it. Harrison was right—the chance that this was connected to Len's case and the parasite was slimmer than slim. On the other hand, it was folly to let even the slimmest chance escape.

"I'll take it," he said.

5

Shadows and Light

Maia was exhausted by the time the housemaid Elsie helped her prepare for bed. This day had felt a hundred years long, from her spell-casting at dawn to learning of Len's leech spell to the violence in evidence at Whegg's, to now. Her stop by Helen's to see how the glamour for her gown was coming along had been the lone bright spot in the day. Even meals had been draining, with Lorde glaring at her from the side of the room with every course.

Perhaps she could arrange to take meals on a tray in her workroom for the rest of the time Aunt Amelia was away. No one could complain if she was putting in extra effort on her studies and practice, could they?

She had a sinking feeling Lorde—and by proxy, Aunt Amelia—could and would.

She saw in the mirror that Elsie had finished hanging up her clothing, and rose from the her seat at the dressing table to dismiss and thank the maid.

"It's my pleasure, miss," said the younger girl. On her way out the door, Elsie hesitated.

"Do you think we're likely to see any more cor—corp—dead bodies on our doorstep, miss?"

Maia smiled in what she hoped was a reassuring fashion. "Oh, I shouldn't think so, Elsie. I have the shield around the house now. There's nothing to worry about."

"Oh." To Maia's surprise, Elsie's face fell. "That's good, miss."

"Is it?" Maia asked, amused.

Elsie shuffled her feet on the carpet. "Only … it was ever so exciting, that morning, wasn't it, miss?'

"I … suppose. In a way," Maia said.

Elsie sighed. "Well, good night, miss."

Smiling, Maia closed the door behind Elsie and moved toward her bed, stopping when the whisper of a spell filled the room.

She recognized it as the activation of the send-and-receive spell on her notepaper in the middle of her desk. Curious as to whether it was further instructions from Aunt Amelia, an update on her dress from Helen, or something else entirely, she swiftly walked to the desk and sat down to read the words as they came through.

Hullo, old thing. Care for a spot of detecting in Basingstoke tomorrow? It's most likely a wild-goose chase, but the Old Man seems to think there might be something in it so I'm toddling off there bright and early in the morning. Becket has his own inquiries to make here, and I wondered if you would tear yourself away from your studies to accompany me. -Len.

Curious. Maia did not need more than a moment to make up her mind. If Len was investigating a lead, no matter how slim, she was not going to sit around Aunt Amelia's practicing cantrips and enduring Lorde's disapproval.

I'll meet you at the station in the morning, unless you prefer to motor down.

She could almost hear the ruefulness in his reply: *Afraid the confounded thing is refusing to run properly again. I almost think an automobile is more trouble than it's worth these days.*

The station it is, then, she wrote back. *I look forward to hearing all the details. Goodnight.*

The spell faded. Maia stared at the paper, wondering what it must be like for Len to have to rely on Becket to set up and end these simple spells for him now. A task Len could have done last week with as much ease as tying his shoes or brushing his hair was now beyond his reach—forever, if the healers were right.

Maia forced her fists to unclench before she snapped the pencil she still held in her tightened grip. She set the writing implement down beside the notepad, now as blank as it had been before her conversation with Len. No record remained of things said this way unless one copied them down on a separate piece of paper as soon as the words appeared.

She shivered. Thoughts on the shortness of human life and futility of human endeavor, mankind's inability to make a lasting mark for good on the world, drifted across her mind.

"Enough of this!" she scolded herself aloud.

Indulging in morbid and morose thoughts wouldn't solve this case any sooner, nor would it help Len. Action was what was required here.

Maia would have to battle Lorde tomorrow morning for the right to leave the house again. A sparkle lit her eye.

Perhaps a little aggressive action against a self-important butler was just what she needed.

* * *

Len gave Maia the bare outlines of the lead in the morning while they waited for the train to come in. She would have preferred discussing it more fully, but after boarding they found themselves in a carriage with several other people. Since they could discuss neither magic nor the case in such a public setting, they instead spent the time discussing books, plays, and the latest news from India.

Maia was sure Len knew more about the battle against militant tribes and the efforts of Wing Commander Pink and the RAF than he was able to tell, but from the newspaper articles alone they managed a reasonably intelligent discussion of it.

"I should like to fly," Maia said, gazing out the window at the blurred landscape. "Airplanes must be frightfully thrilling."

"Or thrillingly frightening," Len said.

"Have you ever been in one?"

"No, thank heavens, and I've no desire to correct that."

"Just once," she said. "Once, and then I'd be satisfied. To soar above the ground, to see everything dropping away below you, to get up amid the clouds …"

Len held up a hand. "No more, I beg of you."

He did look a little green. Maia smiled. "Sorry."

He changed the subject to mystery novels—Len's secret addiction, one to which he had introduced Maia a few years back. He preferred Sherlock Holmes; Maia had a sneaking fondness for Christie's Hercule Poirot.

"My dear Maia, Holmes is a classic! No one will ever come close to matching him."

"There have only been two books featuring Monsieur Poirot as of yet, it's far too early to dismiss him," Maia countered.

Len conceded the point with an open hand. "Have you read

that story by Miss Sayers, *What Body* or some such?"

"*Whose Body*? Yes, I ordered it as soon as it came out a couple years back. There're rumors of a sequel, but alas, nothing yet." Maia sighed. "Aunt Amelia calls all detective stories poor trash, but I think they are splendid."

"You and your chums fancied yourselves detectives when you were young, didn't you?" Len asked.

She was surprised he remembered—she'd mentioned it only once, long ago. "Yes, thankfully we went from wanting to be gentlemen burglars like Raffles to gentlemen detectives!" Maia laughed. "I suppose in some ways I've never quite outgrown that desire." She took note of the other occupants of the car, many unabashedly listening, and hastened to add an explanatory footnote. "I still enjoy puzzles, turning my mind to try to make sense of something that seems completely irrational and nonsensical." That was true enough, even if it wasn't jigsaw puzzles she was referring to.

"When there's one nagging piece that doesn't quite fit, and then suddenly you put it in its place and—everything is clear!" Len nodded, the twinkle in his eye showing he understood perfectly well her meaning. "Of course," he added casually. "The adventure part of being a detective wouldn't be so bad, either."

Maia adopted his joking tone. "Chasing after criminals, risking life and limb to bring about justice … no, not so bad." Maia tapped her fingers on the windowpane. "The trouble with us, Len, is that we've not quite grown up yet."

"If by that you mean we haven't gotten stodgy and dull, then I hope we never do."

She looked at him and smiled, truly smiled for the first time since they'd found out about his magic. "Hear, hear."

So much had changed in just a couple of days, but Len was still Len.

Len's mysterious Old Man had arranged for them to meet with the magician assigned to attend the hedgewitch's death, and the young lady considerately met them at the station. She was a Chinese girl looking barely out of school, smartly dressed in a pleated peacock-blue skirt and matching blazer, a knotted tie peeking out from beneath the collar of her blouse. A cloche was pulled down tightly around her ears, leaving only the slightest hint of a black bob to show beneath its brim. Maia instantly felt dowdy, dull, and old-maidish beside the chic young lady.

"Mr. Davies and Miss Whitney? I am Gwen Zhang." Her voice was low and rich, with a hint of Welsh musicality rolling through the otherwise public-school-trained clipped syllables.

First Len, then Maia shook her hand, and the trio set off walking in the direction of the hedgewitch's house, a mile outside the town proper.

"Glad to have you here," Gwen said. "This is my first case to take all on my own—I've been graduated from Saint Dorothea's for a year next month, and I'm still in training at Deep. Mostly I was handed this assignment because nobody else wanted it but still, I'd hate to muck it up. It's possible that it's a non-magical affair entirely, but it would be dreadful to make that assumption and then have it proven wrong. Are you able to tell me anything about your case back in London, that you think the two might be connected?"

Good heavens, but the child was eager. Maia added "ancient" to her list of how the girl made her feel.

"It isn't so much of a case as it is a personal interest," Len said smoothly. "This is more of a private investigation."

Maia mentally applauded that discreet answer.

"Oh," said Gwen, looking downcast. "But I thought—they said you were sent by the head of the London Branch of MI."

"So I am, but in a private capacity," Len said. "Technically I'm on sick leave. This is …"

"This is mostly for my benefit," Maia said briskly. "I am still an apprentice, you see, and Len wanted to give me a chance to see how this sort of affair worked."

Len caught her eye. He didn't do anything so blatant as nod or wink, but the tiny blink he gave conveyed his appreciation for her embellishment nicely.

"But if it does prove to be connected to a larger investigation in London, we will be sure to give you full credit for your aid in our report," he supplemented.

Gwen looked more cheerful at that. Clearly, she had great ambitions. Maia had no issues with that—she had been ambitious herself, when she started out. She supposed she still was, only her ambitions had changed.

She still wanted to be the best magician she could possibly be; she no longer cared so much about winning a high position. She wanted to do her work well, but she wanted it to be *her* work, no matter how humble it might look to Aunt Amelia or anyone else.

She paused mentally, though her feet continued to move down the road. When had that happened? When had finding the work for which she was best suited become more important to her than, well, being important? She couldn't remember.

Now was not the time to dwell on it. "Could you give us more details of the situation while we walk?" Maia asked. She had dressed sensibly for the outing in tweed suit, the skirt somewhat longer and fuller than fashion dictated, with sturdy walking shoes completing the ensemble. She hadn't minded before, not even on the train when some of the matrons and maidens had obviously sniffed at her, but she did wish now she had chosen something with more style.

Then they came to a muddy patch of road, and seeing the smears marring the bright polish of Gwen's shoes changed her mind on that point, at least. She'd rather look like a frump and not have her outfit ruined than be silly and stylish.

Best of all would be dressing stylishly and sensibly all at the same time, but fashion did not seem inclined in that direction. Perhaps Helen could make some changes that way once her career took off.

Gwen, while still casting curious glances at them, began her tale willingly enough, reciting memorized facts in a lilting voice.

"The hedgewitch, Miss Jane Ransom, has lived just outside Basingstoke for the last fifty years. Never qualifying as a magician, she was nonetheless a respectable sort, helping people who came to her for charms and potions, casting small spells, the usual. Even the non-magical folk around here knew of her, called her a 'witch' without ever really believing it, and generally accepted her. She wasn't hated or feared, as many hedgewitches are. She served as the local midwife, and the doctor had been known to call on her for aid in trickier cases."

"Not a likely candidate for murder, then," Len said.

Gwen shook her head. "Not exactly, no. The first we knew of it was when a local magician went to visit Miss Ransom and found her lying dead on the floor of her cottage, a bullet lodged in her heart. Sensibly, this young man contacted me— us—instead of the village constable, and set up a barrier to steer people away from the cottage. He also cast a cooling spell over the body to maintain it *in situ* until we could come look at the situation." Gwen's eyes shifted and a daft grin spread across her face. Maia speculated that this other magician might be the reason she was so eager for a good job.

"Any sign of the murder weapon?" Maia asked.

Gwen brought her attention back to the matter at hand. "No, but I examined the bullet as best I could without removing it—spells only do so much for that sort of thing, as I'm sure you both know. It came from a pistol, not a rifle or shotgun, and there was no spell upon it I could see."

"So, not likely to be from an unhappy farmer at a love potion not giving him the results he wanted. Are there many former soldiers in the area?"

Again, Gwen shook her head. "Many left, but only a handful returned. Of that few, only one or two are still mobile. Martin—that is, the magician who found her—did ask some casual questions to see if anyone had noticed anyone odd visiting the cottage lately, but nobody seemed to. Of course, since she lives out of town a ways—"

"Someone could have visited her without anyone else noticing," Len finished. He heaved a dramatic sigh. "Oh, for the gossip of a village!"

"I cast a relation spell on the bullet, to see where it came from," Gwen said.

Exactly what Len had been planning on doing with the bullet they thought had struck him.

"But it didn't point to anything in the area. So either the pistol's been destroyed, which seems unlikely, or it's outside the radius of my spell?"

"Is London inside or outside that radius?" Maia asked.

Gwen looked askance at her.

Len wiped a hand briefly across his mouth, perhaps to hide a smile. "Ah, few magicians would be capable of singly casting a spell that covers more than a few miles."

"Oh." She blinked. Aunt Amelia had never covered radii in her lessons—perhaps it was another one of those things that was so obvious to everyone who had grown up in the magic world that nobody thought to teach it. "So not London, then," she said, trying to cover her embarrassment.

"No, Miss Whitney," said Gwen.

"Maia, please, Miss Zhang."

"Then you must call me Gwen." She smiled almost shyly at Maia, who was relieved to find her *faux pas* over spell coverage hadn't turned the girl off her entirely. "NIMA gave me the job, both because I know Martin and as an aptitude test before graduation, and I immediately contacted MI in London."

"NIMA?" Maia didn't want to be thought an idiot again, but neither did she want to miss critical information. Better to look a fool than be one.

"Non-Integrated Magical Affairs," Len supplemented. "A fancy term for the branch of Domestic Protection dedicated to keeping track of hedgewitches and cleaning up their frequently untidy deaths."

Maia winced and nodded.

"That was good thinking, to contact MI," Len told Gwen.

She smiled. "It wasn't a typical hedgewitch death, and the circumstances looked fishy to me," she explained. "The agent I spoke to said as it was a non-magical death, I should let the constable handle it. I was going to have Martin dismantle his spells when I was contacted by someone else in MI saying that you two were on your way."

"Out of curiosity," Len said. "What was the name of the agent who dismissed you?"

Gwen paused and fished in her handbag. Len and Maia stopped walking as well, waiting. The birds sang madly in the hedges lining the road, and the scent of crab apple and damson blossoms drifted from the gnarled trees in the fields beside. Maia picked up the unmistakable heavy sweetness of lilac as well, too much when brought indoors but just right on a heady April day outside. It seemed far too pleasant a day to be looking into murder. If only they were in Leicestershire now, she would have begged the cook at Stanbury to pack them a picnic lunch, and she and Len could have gone out exploring, she could have shown him all the places she had run around when she was a girl …

"Here it is!" said Gwen, flourishing a piece of paper. It was a small handbag for such a seemingly large capacity; Maia wondered if there was a spell on it and if so, could she get a copy of it to use on her pockets.

"Amy Marsh," Gwen read aloud. Len groaned. "What?" asked Gwen, a crease appearing between her eyebrows. "What is it?"

Maia wondered that herself.

"Nothing," said Len. Maia glared, and Gwen raised her eyebrows.

"She's one of the agents assigned to the, er, other case, working under Barry," he said. "A good agent, but too much inclined to dismiss anyone and anything she doesn't find worth her attention."

"Rather like Barry himself," Maia observed.

"Except without his experience to justify it. His dismissal of people and notions is based on their relation to his cases.

Agent's Marsh's reasons are more … personal. She won't be happy when she finds out I've taken on a case she tossed aside as worthless." He paused. "On the other hand, she might be smugly pleased that I've fallen so low. Either way, she'll be even more unbearable than usual."

Gwen opened her mouth to ask another question, but was diverted by their approach to the yellow-painted, vine-covered cottage. Maia stretched out with her extra sense in a seeking spell, easy enough to require no words, just a momentary concentration, to see if there was anything to pick up about the site before they entered.

Beside her, Len nearly tripped, biting back a curse. Maia winced, guessing he had attempted to do the same, only to be brought up short when he couldn't. Habit died hard.

"Well," he said, a grimness to his voice she was unaccustomed to hearing. "Let's see what we can find."

Maia was unprepared for the overwhelming pity that struck her as soon as Gwen opened the gate for them to enter Jane Ransom's home. Such a tidy, well-kept place, with climbing roses growing up the yellow walls, a small garden full of old-fashioned flowers all blossoming bravely. The paint on the house was kept fresh, the windows sparkling clean. This was not the traditional witch of fairy tales, nor even the drooling, half-witted, sly old woman she had been unconsciously expecting.

Gwen unlocked the front door, and they stepped through into a cool, well-lit hall. Maia's pity increased, bringing with it another unexpected emotion—fury. The elderly woman sprawled on the floor very nearly at their feet was small and rounded, with grey hair neatly braided and coiled atop her head, wearing a print dress and once-clean apron. In life, her cheeks had obviously been rosy and her eyes sparkling. Some arrogant swine had taken all that away and reduced her to a sad heap crumpled on the floor of her own house.

It wasn't right. Nobody should be able to do this to another human being and get away with it. Somewhere out there this person thought he or she had the right to take life away from other people, and nobody could stop him or her.

She could.

And she would. Somehow, someday, whether this was the same person who had stolen Len's magic or not, Maia would bring justice to Jane Ransom's killer.

Gwen shifted her feet and edged away from her. Len cleared his throat.

"Uh, Maia?" he whispered. "You are … glowing."

Maia looked down. Sure enough, her hands were radiant with silver light. She hadn't even felt the magic gathering. Gwen wouldn't have been able to see it; her instincts must have warned her away. She wondered that Len could still see it, with his magic gone, but reasoned that a lifetime of having and practicing magic had left him still sensitive to their peculiar bond.

Maia closed her eyes and concentrated.

Strong emotions made her magic more likely to burst the bonds of her self-control. Aunt Amelia had told her that often enough. Maia had always kept herself tightly in check as a child and young lady, but it seemed that the older she grew, the harder it became. She was *tired* of always dampening herself down, both magically and emotionally. She wanted to be free to experience the full expanse of who she was, not keep herself in a tidy, safe box.

But more importantly right now, she didn't want to set the

cottage on fire or injure either of her two companions. She wrestled her magic as fiercely as though it were a physical opponent. It was like trying to shove a feather mattress into a too-small bag—as soon as one part was secured, another bulged free. She gritted her teeth and *pushed*, forcing it down by sheer willpower. Even then, there was still a hint of light around her hands, still a thread or two of magic unwilling to settle down (rather like loose feathers floating around even after the mattress was contained), so she channeled it into a spell and sent that spell through the window.

"*Custodiatur hortus.*"

Jane Ransom's garden was now guaranteed to survive the rest of this season, even without its mistress tending it. It was the least Maia could do for the old woman.

She opened her eyes.

"My apologies," she said to Gwen, who still looked thoroughly alarmed at these two strange magicians she had brought onto her case. "You can see why I'm still an apprentice." She trusted her voice had the proper wry edge to it, rather than bitter.

Gwen nodded, her shoulders relaxing. "One of my tutors had that sort of thing happen once or twice," she said. "The Dean said it's usually a sign of power."

Maia did not preen herself. Sign of power or not, uncontrolled magic could still kill her and everyone around her. Until she learned how to manage it properly, she had no hope of ever moving past her apprentice stage.

"Yes indeed, Maia is here to cast the spells as well as learn," Len interposed. "As you can see, she is well suited for the task." He smiled warmly at her, though his eyes held a new worry as he knelt down by the body. "My role is more along the investigative lines. I'm sure you've already covered this, Gwen, but Maia, could you double check to make certain she was indeed hit by a bullet alone?"

Not, Maia understood instantly, by a spell covered with or attached to a bullet. She concentrated.

"*Inveniatur ars magica.*"

A brief check was all it took. The only magic left in the building was that belonging to the wards set up by Gwen's sweetheart and the traces of Maia's garden spell. Maia closed her hands into fists. "Nothing, Len."

He nodded absently. "Mm-hm, about what I expected." He physically inspected the body, oblivious to Gwen's fastidious distaste. "Hm," he said.

He stood up and wiped his hands on a clean handkerchief, which he then folded neatly and returned to his pocket. First he strolled to the window and examined that, and then the door. "Hm."

While they watched, Gwen with growing interest and Maia with pointedly raised eyebrows, Len next followed the hallway into the main part of the house. They heard a sudden explosive, "Ha!"

"Is this how he usually conducts investigations?" Gwen whispered.

Before Maia could answer, Len's voice boomed out. "Maia, I need a spell in here!"

Maia pinched the bridge of her nose. "If it is," she said, more to herself than to Gwen, "then Becket needs a raise." Leaving a confused Gwen to trail behind her, she answered the call.

* * *

Len had his thumbs hooked in his waistcoat pockets, beaming avuncularly. "I have it," he announced. "Just need the magic to confirm my theory."

"Which is …?" Maia asked, holding on to her patience with what she considered commendable restraint.

"Observe, Watson," he said, and Gwen choked. Len tossed her a quelling glance.

A smile forced its way through Maia's reserve. "Stop being so theatrical and get on with it."

He tried to look hurt, but couldn't maintain it. "Don't spoil my fun," he said with mock reproach. "This is my big moment. I want plenty of 'oohs' and 'ahs' and 'Oh, Len, you *are* clever,' when I finish."

"We'll see," Maia said dryly. "Now, your conclusion?"

He pointed to the drying board beside the sink. "First, the observations. You will notice, two cups, washed and turned upside down to dry next to the teapot. I also observed in the hall that neither the door nor the windows had been physically forced open, and your spell told me they had not been touched with magic. Next, if you will examine this cake sitting under its glass dome, you will see that there's a large gap in it. Now, it is certainly possible that Miss Ransom cut herself an oversized slice, but combined with the other clues, what does this tell us?"

Maia beat Gwen to the response. "That Miss Ransom let her murderer in and had tea and cake with him or her. It wasn't a burglar or anything of that sort, it was either someone she knew or the sort of person she trusted, such as a client. Gwen has already checked and nobody local visited her recently, so that leaves a client."

Len patted her on the head. "Well done, my child."

Maia batted his hand away, but couldn't be too annoyed. The half-dead look in Len's eyes was gone for now, eclipsed by the thrill of the hunt, and she would endure any amount of teasing to ensure things stayed that way.

"Oh, Len, you are clever," said Gwen, surprising them both.

After a moment of silence, first Len, then Maia burst into laughter. Gwen settled back against the wall, looking pleased with herself.

"She has taken our measure, Maia," Len said. "Welcome down the rabbit hole, Gwen. We're all mad here."

"So," Maia said, bringing herself back to the task at hand. All this merriment and light-heartedness couldn't detract from the dead body in the hall. "What do you need a spell for, if you've got it all figured out?"

"Ah," said Gwen, catching on. "A shadows spell?"

Len nodded.

"Good!" Maia beamed. She'd been itching to do that spell ever since Len told her about it in the bookshop.

"I'll show you how to set the parameters so that it begins with her final visitor and ends with Miss Ransom's last moments. It …" he hesitated. "It won't be lovely."

Maia lifted her chin. "I've seen unlovely before," she said. "If it helps us catch her killer, I can endure it."

He gave her one short, sharp nod. "Gwen?" he asked.

She swallowed. "If this is part of the job …" she said, trying to hide the quaver in her voice.

"I'm afraid it often is," Len said.

"Then we'd best get it over with."

Len explained the spell to Maia. It wasn't tremendously complicated, though it did require precision and concentration, as he had warned. Maia could see the question in Gwen's eyes as to why Len wouldn't do such a simple spell himself, but she held her tongue, endearing her to Maia even more.

Unfortunately, Len saw the curious look as well, and his shell of bonhomie cracked a little. "Yes. Well. There you have it."

"Thank you," Maia said. She closed her eyes and sank down into herself, finding that waiting well of magic, ready to be called up at a moment's notice—a well now empty for Len (no, mustn't think of that, though something about how and why he could still see her magic did keep niggling at her, but there was no time to ponder it now, if she lost her focus this could be disastrous)—

She set the spell in her mind, and then spoke the incantation. *"Rursus apparatur umbrae ex praeterite."*

At first, it seemed nothing was going to happen. Then, shadows began to gather at the corners of the room. A shiver traveled down Maia's spine as they coalesced into two indistinct forms. There was something eerie about certain kinds of magic.

She understood now why Len had said this wouldn't show the murderer's identity. The shadows were just that—insubstantial, with no features or identifying marks about them, cloudy representations only of the two people who had been here last.

One shadow moved easily around the kitchen while Maia, Len, and Gwen silently pressed themselves back against the walls to watch without interfering. It went through motions Maia identified as preparing tea and fetching plates for cake. This, then, was the Jane Ransom shadow. The other stood in the doorway watching her, before drifting over to the table to sit and drink tea with the woman he was about to murder.

Once again, anger burned in Maia's stomach, threatening the stability of the spell. The shadows wavered, and Len hissed.

"Easy," he muttered.

Maia blinked away a droplet of sweat crawling down from her temple to her right eye. "Sorry," she said between her teeth, and tightened her grip on the spell.

"Not so tense," he said softly. "Breathe with it, not against it. Let it flow. It'll fight you more if you wrestle with it."

She only half understood his words, but tried to follow them as best she could. She breathed in and out slowly, calming down, and the magic steadied within her from a flickering, uncontrolled fire to a steady, easy glow.

"That's it," Len said. She nodded her thanks and turned her attention back to the scene.

The shadows drank their invisible tea and ate their invisible cake, and then the murderer-shadow leaned back while the Miss Ransom-shadow leaned forward, gesticulating with her hands as she explained something. Then she jumped up and moved to a shelf, taking down something that wasn't there in reality, and handing it to the murderer. He stood up, took it, pulled out a pistol, and shot her in the heart.

Maia and Gwen both gasped, though they'd known it was coming. Even Len, far more experienced, looked sick.

The murderer-shadow tucked the gun away and looped his arms under the Miss Ransom-shadow's arms. The watchers silently followed as he dragged her out to the hall and arranged her body there, atop the actual Miss Ransom's body. Nausea churned ever more violently in Maia's stomach at the gruesomeness of it, but remembering Len's injunction, she held her magic in a steady but light grip.

They came back to the kitchen, where the murderer walked

back to the shelf and took down something else from the gap between glass bottles, tucking it into his breast pocket. He neatly cleaned up after himself, including scrubbing the floor clean of any bloodstains, walked back past the dead body in the hall, and let himself out the front door, locking it behind him.

"*Finiatur*," Maia whispered, and the Miss Ransom-shadow vanished as the spell dissipated.

"That was—educational," Gwen said in a strangled voice.

"But *why*?" Maia demanded. "Why go to all that work? Why move the body?"

"To make it look like a stranger—a burglar—did it," Gwen said.

"To disguise the real purpose behind the killing," Len added.

"The whatever-it-was Miss Ransom gave him, and the other thing he took after killing her?"

Len nodded.

"I don't suppose there's a spell that will tell us what that is?"

"No," he said. "But some good old-fashioned questioning might. Gwen," he said, turning to the girl. "This Martin of yours, he visited Miss Ransom on a regular basis?"

Gwen bristled. "If you think for one moment that Martin could have killed—"

"Not at all," Len hurried to say. "I am only hoping to gain some more information about the victim."

"Oh," said Gwen, looking down at her feet. "Well then, yes. Martin is a proper magician," she added. "But he liked Miss Ransom for herself, and was interested in the different way she worked magic."

"Then he might know what was kept on that shelf?"

Gwen brightened. "Oh! That's a very good thought. Yes, he

probably would. I'll bring him here to ask, shall I?"

"Please do," Len said. The other magician hurried out the door, leaving Maia and Len alone with the dead body. Maia couldn't stop herself: she leaned forward and gently placed her clean handkerchief over Miss Ransom's face. It was the smallest of acts, but all she could do at the moment.

"Are you all—" Len stopped and started over. "Are you going to be all right?"

He placed a hand on the small of her back and guided her into the kitchen, where she dropped down into one of the plain wooden chairs.

"It's so cruel," she said, rubbing a hand over her face as though to wipe away the horror of it. "And so senseless. What could a hedgewitch have that a parasite would want or need? And why kill for it, when she was so obviously willing to give it to him?"

"To prevent her from being able to identify him," Len suggested. "Or to ensure that she didn't put two and two together when the leech spells started happening, realize who he was and why he'd wanted ... whatever he wanted."

"You think it was the parasite, then?"

Len raised his hands, open-palmed to the air. "My instinct tells me yes, that these two cases are connected. But I admit, I have nothing solid to build that on."

"Nothing but a lifetime of experience," Maia agreed sarcastically.

"Whatever that is worth now," he said. He sat down across from her and folded his hands together on the scarred tabletop. He looked ... old.

"Len," Maia began hesitantly.

He held up a hand. "Don't," he said. "Don't talk about it,

Maia. Please."

The "please" finished her. That Lennox Davies, of all men, should speak so humbly … she swallowed the lump in her throat and nodded.

"Dash it all," Len burst out after a few minutes of silence. "It doesn't seem real. I tried doing that damn—sorry—shadows spell myself three times before I remembered I couldn't. I mastered that spell as an apprentice, and now I can't … it's impossible. It's *impossible* that my magic is gone. It *can't* be true."

He stared down at his hands quietly before adding, so quietly she almost missed it, "But it is."

Maia stretched out her hand and rested it over his. "Maybe it's not permanent. Nobody has seen a leech spell in centuries. There has to be a remedy we aren't aware of. If you talk to a healer, maybe—" The thought she'd suppressed earlier returned. "After all, you can still see my magic. Maybe that means yours isn't gone for good, that there's some way it can come back. How else—"

He cut her off again. "I can't think like that. I can't hope. If I hope, and you're wrong, the disappointment will be worse than believing it impossible from the beginning. The healer said my ability to sense magic would fade only gradually." His brows lowered and nearly met over his eyes. "Us being able to see each other's magic, it was a fluke from the beginning. I can't believe that it means anything anymore."

Maia swallowed the unintentional hurt his words caused. She reached over with her other hand, and held both of his fast within her own. "Then I will believe for the both of us."

Tentatively, Len turned his hands over to clasp hers in return. His grip was firm, his hands strong and comforting, belying the way his pulse beat wildly against her fingertips. "Maia—"

The sound of the back door opening interrupted.

Maia jumped, and Len pulled back, and they were sitting demurely in their own seats with their hands to themselves when Gwen and her Martin bustled in.

Martin, when Maia was breathing and able to think again, was not what she had expected. Somehow she had pictured him as tall, lanky, practical, and plain. Instead, the magician was short, round, bustling, cheerful, and had a face like a Pre-Raphaelite cherub.

"Oh!" he said, upon meeting them both. "Gwen says you approve of the spells I set. I'm so glad. I was so worried I was doing the wrong thing, but I knew I couldn't leave her there for the constable to find if magic might be involved. Isn't it awful? I wanted to cry when I opened the door and saw her like that. But say, isn't it lucky that I'm the one who found her? Imagine if it had been a non-magician, we never would have even known about it. It just gets my goat, thinking about someone doing in our Miss Ransom like that. Anything I can do to help you folks catch the villain, Martin Redford's your man."

Len, better at presenting a mask to the world than Maia, made an appropriate response, and then asked the question about what Miss Ransom kept on her kitchen shelves. Maia took a few deep breaths to steady her whirling brain enough to take in the answer.

"Oh yes, that's where Miss Ransom keeps—kept—all her potions," Martin answered, waving at the glass bottles. "That row? Those were her glamours. That was her specialty, you know."

"How does that work?" Maia asked, frowning. "I thought

glamours were spells, not potions."

Martin beamed, apparently delighted at being asked to clarify. "Yes they are, for magicians, but hedgewitches don't do as much with spells, not formal ones with incantations and the like. Miss Ransom was a dab hand at potions. They were nothing on their own. A non-magical person could have blended the exact tincture of herbs and liquid and come up with nothing, but somehow she channeled her magic right into them. I think that's how she lasted so long without her magic consuming her, actually. Glamours were her best, they were at least as good as those a magician could cast, if not better."

"So the murderer took a glamour potion and killed her to cover it up. Two, actually. Why?" Gwen said.

"It's like Len said to me while you were out—he must have been doing something which required a glamour, and was afraid she would hear of it and remember him," Maia said. Something like disguising himself and his curse to land on Len in the middle of a crowd, for example. "Though if he's going to be wicked enough to murder her, I don't know why he wouldn't be wicked enough to scrub her memory."

Len, who had risen to his feet when Gwen entered, suddenly sat down again. "I do. Why would a magician need a glamour potion from a hedgewitch anyway? They aren't that hard. He would only need a potion if he weren't a very strong magician to begin with."

"You don't think he had the ability to do a memory scrub," Maia said, thinking it over.

"It's a difficult spell. Performed incorrectly, it will leave the person's mind mush. Or worse, backfire on the person casting it and turn *their* mind to mush." Len tapped his fingers on his knees. "There's a reason it's a forbidden spell."

Maia raised a hand to her throat. "An inadequate magician who takes a glamour in order to disguise himself so that he can leech magic from another magician without being seen and stopped?"

Len met her eyes. "I would say that's a reasonable conclusion, even without my instinct. I'll examine—I mean I'll have Becket examine the sleeve of the shirt I was wearing when the curse landed, see if it carries any trace of a potion left on it."

"And then match it against one of her remaining glamours," Maia finished.

"A leech spell?" Martin squeaked. Maia had almost forgotten the two junior magicians, now clinging to each other in horror. "You aren't serious—a parasite is on the loose?"

Len rose again to his feet. "I must request absolute secrecy from you both," he said. "These are grave matters. You have both been extremely helpful, and I shall give you the highest commendation in my report when this is all over. I assure you, there is nothing to fear. With the information we have gathered here today, we shall find the magician and stop him before he hurts anyone else. And now we must leave if we want to catch the afternoon train. Come, Maia."

He bowed and left before anyone, including Maia, knew what to think. She hurried after him, with Gwen's wail of, "But what shall I do with the body?" echoing in her ears.

"Cancel the spells and let the constable find it, we've gotten all we can from the scene," Len called back without breaking stride.

"Len," Maia whispered. "The next train doesn't leave for another two hours."

"I know," he said back. "But if I didn't get of there I was going to start breaking things."

She glanced at his face, swallowed her questions, and meekly followed along wherever he should choose to lead.

6

Speculations

As they had time on their hands when they reached the station, Maia went to work questioning the stationmaster and porters, anyone who might have noticed a stranger coming into town and asking the way to Miss Ransom's house. Len wandered around in a sullen haze while she toiled, eventually finding himself outside the wrought iron gates to the War Memorial Park. He stared at them for a few moments before deciding to go in.

He meandered down the path aimlessly before it ended at a small pond. Despite the chill of the April air, there were three small children paddling in it, much to the consternation of the woman who looked like their nanny.

"Now, Master Thomas, Mistress Nellie, Mistress Mary, you all come out of there, you're going to catch your death of cold, you are, and then what'll I tell your parents?" the small, plump woman remonstrated while wringing her hands.

The children, predictably, ignored her.

Automatically, Len began to calculate if there was a spell he could use to get them out. Nothing on the children themselves—human beings, especially children, were too wriggly and delicate for most benign spells. Could he conjure up a wind to whip them out? Not unless he wanted the nanny to have hysterics right there in front of him. Besides, that sort of spell was best left to weather magicians, as would one which would drop the temperature of the water to the point the children *wanted* to get out. Or he could—

"Goodness," said Maia, who had come up beside him unobtrusively. She spoke more loudly than her wont. "I hope the giant fish that lives in that pond isn't awake! It's bound to be hungry, and I believe children are its favorite snack. Why, it's so large, it could snap up two of those poor things in one bite!"

The eldest girl looked skeptical, but the smaller girl and boy both shrieked and sprang out of the water, fleeing toward Nanny with loud sobs. Heaving a great sigh, the elder child followed them up the bank. Rather than thanking Maia, Nanny shot her a most unfriendly look before gathering up her crying charges with coos and clucks and herding them away.

"Ha," said Maia, not discomposed in the slightest. "It got them out, didn't it?"

Len found his black mood lightened to a murky grey. "You, my friend, are unscrupulous."

Maia chuckled low in her throat. "One has to be, in dealing with children." She looped her arm through his and began walking, forcing him to keep up or be dragged.

"I was trying to think of a spell to use," he confessed in a low voice. "It's such a habit with me—with all magicians. I forgot I couldn't do it anymore."

"And yet," she said. "You were the one to tell me, back at the bookshop, to not rely on magic all the time, remember? I don't think you're as reliant on it as you believe you are."

He tilted his head to look down at what he could see of her face in profile. She turned to face him, wide mouth curved in a peaceful smile, cheeks glowing with exercise. "What do you mean?"

"Look at the way you deduced what had happened at Miss Ransom's cottage," she said. "Look at how your instinct told you there was a connection between the cases, and was proved right. Look at how you've handled yourself ever since losing the magic."

He glowered at her. "Don't patronize me, Maia!"

She rolled her eyes, pulled her arm from his, and threw her hands into the air. "Can't you tell the difference between honesty and condescension, or did the leech spell addle your wits as well?"

"Oh, I see," he spat. "I've always been a terrible magician, so what does it matter if I've lost my magic? It's not as if it happened to someone who would *matter*?"

The color drained from her cheeks as a fire sparked in her eyes. "Someone like me, is that what you are implying?"

Traces of silver around her gloved hands indicated she was dangerously close to losing control of her magic. He didn't care. "If the shoe fits. Come now, you think you'd be so rational and calm about this if you were the one to lose your magic?"

"Calm? You think I'm calm? If only you knew how I've—" She broke off and bit her lip, then stalked on ahead.

Len's rage still coursed through his veins, but now it was mingled with a thread of curiosity. He quickened his pace to catch up to her. "What? Knew what?"

She did not deign to look at him. "Never mind."

He could apologize and ask again—he should apologize, even if he didn't ask—but he couldn't. Not yet. All the hopelessness and fury and fear that he had been trying to suppress for three days had him in their grip, and he couldn't shake them.

"I could have accepted death in the line of duty—or injury—or any kind of ordinary curse—but this! How can you tell me to accept this, to hope that eventually I might find some way of being useful again, that it might not be as bad as it seems now! Platitudes, from you of all people!"

The more he ranted, the more his fury mounted.

"I never offered you a platitude," Maia snapped, still walking ahead of him and refusing to look over her shoulder. "If you would stop feeling sorry for yourself and think about what I actually said, you'd realize that."

"Sorry for myself? *Sorry for myself*?" Len drew a deep breath preparatory to launching into further invective when he came to a sudden halt.

Maia walked a pace or two more before she also stumbled to a stop. Before them stood the monument dedicated to the fallen soldiers, winged Victory perched atop a stone plinth, olive branch in one outstretched hand and wreath in the other. Plaques featuring the names of the war dead decorated the sides of the plinth.

"I probably nursed some of them, you know," Maia said at last, walking forward and trailing her fingers along the edge of a plaque. "We lost so many ... and even the ones we saved we couldn't heal completely. Missing limbs, blind, deaf, shell-shocked, lungs ruined from mustard gas ... many wept and begged us to let them die, rather than survive as they were." She turned to face him, fists clenched and eyes flashing. "I know you grieve for what you have lost. I will—and do—grieve with you. But if you are asking me to stand by and watch you give up—that I cannot and will not do. If you don't want my help,

I will not force it on you. If you resent me because I still have magic and you do not, I understand. I will not burden you with a friendship that now only brings you pain. But mark me, Len, I will *never* give up on you."

Without giving him a chance to answer, she turned in a swirl of green skirt and walked out of the park, walking down the street toward the station.

Len stayed by the statue until it was time to leave. He boarded the train alone, though out of the corner of his eye he saw Maia entering a different carriage. He sat alone, hoping she would come find him, but she did not.

He didn't see her again until they disembarked at Waterloo.

* * *

Len had anticipated they would all meet back at his flat to discuss the new developments. He had left Becket with instructions to search for the mysterious missing Whegg, and Maia had said something about Helen going to pump Matthew for information on how the official hunt was going, and it seemed logical to him that they all gather together to share information and make plans.

Maia didn't agree. "If you had asked me before we left, I could have told you that I need to spend some time back at Aunt Amelia's," she said, standing just outside Waterloo Station.

Motorcars whizzed by on the road, a cloud of pedestrians swirled and chattered around them, some laughing and chatting, some solemn and alone, some immersed in business. London at home.

"The servants are spying on me for her, you know—can you call it spying when you have been told that's what they're doing? At any rate, if I am never there or not keeping up with my studies, they will report that to her, and then not only will she return breathing fire from France, but she will drag my apprenticeship out even longer." Grim lines had settled into her face, making her appear older than her twenty-five years.

"But—" Len didn't know how to say it. *But how can we reconcile if you're not there?* was what he wanted to say, but he didn't think blurting that out right there in the middle of the teeming crowd was appropriate. He cast his mind about frantically. "But when can we meet, then?"

Maia tilted her chin to look him squarely in the eye. She was a tall woman, but he was even taller. "Are you sure you still want to?"

Harassed, Len pushed his hands back through his hair, knocking his hat off and barely catching it before it hit the ground. "Yes," he said. "Yes, Maia, I—look, we can't talk here. Can't we at least have tea before you leave? I told Becket to expect us."

She relented, her mouth curling in a half smile. "I suppose it would be rude to let Becket prepare tea in vain."

"Yes indeed, quite rude," he agreed eagerly.

She considered things briefly. "Let me go back and change out of my traveling clothes, and contact Helen, ask her to join us. Then I can honestly tell the staff that I shall be having tea with her, and will return after." She gave a little sigh. "To spend the rest of the evening there."

Always a stickler for honesty whenever possible, even to the servants. It was one of the many things Len admired about Maia.

"Half an hour, then?" he asked.

She raised an amused eyebrow at him. "Better make it three-quarters of an hour."

Ah, the mysterious way ladies always seemed to need heaps of time to change their clothing. He never could understand it—no man could, he supposed. At least it was better than it had been before the war, when it seemed the women of their class never did anything *but* change dresses.

They parted ways, though Len was tempted to walk her back to the Rawlings house and stand outside to wait for her departure. He resisted temptation and returned to his flat to make sure everything was perfect for tea.

He wasn't sorry for his feelings of anger and anguish. Those were normal, and as Maia herself had pointed out, part of the grieving process. He'd seen it in others—not magically, but injured soldiers trying to find their new place in a world which no longer wanted them. He'd always pitied such men. Now he was one himself. It would take time to come to grips with it, and the process would be both painful and messy. He knew that.

But he'd had no right to take out that pain and anger on Maia. First when she had spoken to him at the cottage, offering her support and faith, and he had dismissed it and her at the same time. How could she know how he had always secretly believed that their ability to see each other's magic was not, in fact, a fluke, but a sign that their souls connected on a deeper level? That they were destined for each other? Romantic rubbish, his common sense told him, but he'd never been able to shake it.

He hadn't been worthy of her even before he had lost his magic, and now, her hope in his ability to still see her silver aura was too much for him. Miss Fisher had said it was a phantom effect and would soon fade. She was a healer, she must know.

He couldn't afford to hope for anything more, but he shouldn't have spoken so to Maia. He should have explained to her instead of cutting her off. He most certainly should not have vented his anger on her at the park. Her final words of support, even flung in his face as they had been, had cut him to the bone. He didn't deserve that, didn't deserve her, and yet she refused to cast him off. She was as true-hearted a friend as ever a man could ask.

So then, not for his feelings but for his actions, he owed her an apology, and the sooner the better. He didn't think he could endure bearing a load of guilt on top of everything else he carried.

* * *

To Len's frustration, Helen arrived a few scant moments before Maia, depriving him of the chance to talk to her alone. He liked Helen, and would have liked her more had not their meeting happened in the midst of the worst crisis of his life, but just then he almost loathed her.

Reminding himself that his goal was to make amends with one woman, not offend another, he smiled and ushered them both into the sitting room, where Becket had set the tea tray. Scones with clotted cream and jam, toasted muffins with butter, and the dragon teapot with steam curling from its mouth went a disgracefully long way toward reviving Len's spirits.

"What an extraordinary tea set," Helen exclaimed, gliding over to pick up one of the ivory and charcoal cups. She handled it with utmost delicacy, turning it over to see the maker.

"A gift from a Japanese magician, an acquaintance I made last year on a mission," Len said. He smiled fondly down at the dragon winding its way around and across the teapot, with its open mouth serving as the spout. That had been a hair-raising time, and he and Hikaru had saved each other's lives and earned each other's respect before the end of it. He'd wished Maia had been there at the time, and even more so now. Hikaru's method of practicing magic would have helped Maia's struggles with her own power.

"Lovely," Helen sighed. She set the cup back in its saucer, a dreamy look crossing her face.

"Wonder about how you can incorporate that into your project later," Maia ordered. "Focus on the task ahead of us now."

Helen looked startled for a moment, then laughed. "Guilty, I confess. Very well." She dropped gracefully into Len's own particular green-covered armchair, while Maia perched primly on a more upright one. Len lowered himself into the matching upright chair, and Becket glided forward to pour the tea.

"I'll begin," Helen said. "I hinted, insinuated, and outright asked my brother about progress on the case, and he refused to tell me anything. So," dimples flashing, "I used a glamour to disguise myself as a maid and hung about outside the door when he and that odious Mr. Barry were meeting."

"I am impressed," said Len. She had the soul of a natural conspirator.

"Barry went on and on about assigning Agent Marsh to this lead, and Agent Driver to that one, and how he himself has been run ragged trying to organize and follow through with everything. Matthew has no underlings but managed to make himself sound impressive in his own efforts. To sum up their boring, self-satisfied conversation, they have made no progress in hunting down the parasite," Helen said. "What a waste of a good glamour," she added with a sigh.

"Nothing?" Maia said incredulously.

"I'm not surprised," Len said. He sipped his tea. "Your brother could be the best investigator in the world, Helen, but he is junior to Barry in this and as such, has to follow his lead. And Barry, while a competent investigator—" he had to admit that much, even though he couldn't stand the man— "is not up to this sort of thing. Any kind of subtle, tricky magic is outside his ken. Agent Marsh would be a better head to the team, but he is senior to her. She's the one with the tortuous mind. And torturous," he added despite himself, then hoped he hadn't offended the ladies.

Thankfully, Helen was laughing outright, and even Maia had a smile on her face. He hastily took another sip, and burned his mouth.

"What about Agent Driver?" Maia asked.

Len dabbed his mouth with a spotless white linen napkin. "He's a good enough fellow, but no gumption. I don't know that he's ever had an original idea in his life."

"Then you would say he has no *drive*?" Helen asked, eyes wide with mock innocence.

They all groaned at the pun on Driver's name.

"He told me you'd saved his life," Maia said.

Len blushed. "Oh, that. That wasn't anything—any agent would have done the same—and it isn't relevant to the case, anyhow." He stopped his stammering, tamping down his dislike of being lionized.

Driver should never have been assigned to that case alone, but he had insisted he could handle it, and against his better judgment, Harrison had agreed. Driver grew more and more secretive as the days passed, refusing to talk about his progress—or lack thereof—with anyone. Len would have left him to it had he not startled the man coming out of the Archives one day, a half-frantic look in his eyes and an air of desperation draped around him like a cloak.

Len hadn't bothered to ask if Driver wanted his help; instead he followed the other agent to his rendezvous the next morning and was in time to foil the trap that had been set for Driver. When asked, Len had claimed he happened to be nearby on a mission of his own and had happened to see it all in time to help. Harrison, of course, knew the truth, but he'd held his own counsel.

Len never did find out what Driver had been researching down in the Archives, but he assumed it was something— anything to help him against the rogue magician. Poor chap.

"Becket?" he said, once he recovered from his embarrassment. "Any progress on Whegg?"

His manservant came forward from the corner and shook his head. "It is most peculiar, sir. He was seen entering his shop Friday morning, and that's the last anyone can report of him. Even the beggars and children who usually see everything can't report setting eyes on him after that."

"Strange, you'd think they would have at least seen him leave," said Maia, absently crumbling a scone over her plate.

"Unless he didn't leave," said Len.

"Or he left under a disguise," said Helen.

"Such as a glamour?" Becket suggested.

Maia sighed. "I am getting most tired of glamours in this case," she said. "It seems we encounter them at every turn."

Helen raised her eyebrows as she helped herself to a muffin.

"Oh? Do tell your part now before we speculate further on the possibly evil Mr. Whegg. Poor man, he always seemed so humble and kind. Sorry! Didn't mean to distract. Go on."

Len nodded at Maia, who gave him a wry smile but complied with his unspoken request, telling their story in quick, concise terms. She left out what had happened *after* they had left the cottage. After she finished, there was a long pause.

"So," Helen said at last. "What does all of this *mean*?"

Len set his cup and saucer down on the side table and rested his hands on his knees. "That is a most excellent question," he said. "I have no idea."

Maia pulled her chair closer to the tea table, carefully moving aside the tray to clear a space. "Becket, would you be good enough to bring me paper and a pen, please?"

Becket slipped away without a word, returning moments later with the requested items.

"Thank you," said Maia. She began to write as she spoke.

"If we assume the same person is behind all of these attacks, here is how it stands. First, he steals a glamour potion from and then kills Jane Ransom. Then he uses a life-leeching spell on the still disgracefully unidentified man who stumbled into Aunt Amelia's house. Next, he casts a magic-leeching spell on Len, disguising it as a bullet. Since then ... nothing." She looked up. "Have I missed anything?"

"In between the murder of Miss Ransom and the dead man stumbling into your aunt's house, Mr. Whegg went missing," Helen said.

Len pulled his chair closer as well and took the pen from Maia's hand. "I also think it important to note that he—our killer—killed Jane Ransom with a gun, not a spell."

"Indeed," said Maia. "Naturally, when I say 'he,' I mean 'he or she,' as there's no evidence this is a man rather than a woman, only it's such a bother saying that every time." She looked around at the other three. "What can we deduce from all this?"

"He's a power-mad murderer?" Helen suggested.

Len glanced down at the timeline written in Maia's neat hand, with his additions scrawled atop her script.

1. Steals glamour potion from Jane Ransom in Basingstoke and ~~kills~~ *shoots her.*

2. Mr. Whegg goes missing.

~~2~~ 3. Uses life-leeching spell on unidentified man in St. James' Square.

~~3~~ 4. Uses magic-leeching spell disguised as bullet on Len in Piccadilly.

~~4~~ 5. Does nothing.

"The first thing we can conclude is that he must be about ready to do something else," he said. "All of this took place within a few days of each other, the life-leeching spell and the magic-leeching spell within hours. It's now been three days since I ..." he swallowed and forced himself forward. "Since I lost my magic. It's more than time for the next attack."

Becket had resumed his place in the corner. "Beg pardon, sir, but if he doesn't attack, that could be significant as well."

Helen looked from one to the other, brow wrinkled. "What do you mean?"

"You mean ... maybe he's already gotten what he wants?" Len said slowly.

Becket nodded. "Yes, sir. Exactly."

Maia had appropriated the pen again, and now tapped it on the table top. "I don't understand."

The tap-tap-tap started to get on Len's nerves. He captured the pen back from her, earning a scowl which he bore with equanimity. At least she wasn't ignoring him. "There's not much information out there about British parasites in the last three hundred years or so, but from the little information we do have, it's deuced odd for one to behave this way. Glamours, trickery, deceit … something about it doesn't ring true. A parasite is driven by pure greed—greed for magic, greed for life. They don't bother with all this slinking around. They take and take and take, and are usually all too easy to find. Agent Barry would be the perfect man for the case if this were a typical parasite. The difficulty lies in destroying one, not in discovering it."

"So now you think it isn't a parasite?" Helen asked. She rubbed her forehead. "I don't know whether to be thrilled or terrified by that. If it isn't, then what is going on?"

Len smiled wearily at her. "Again, you ask an excellent question for which I have no answer."

Thoughts of Joanna and Harrison knocked around in his head again, but he resolutely pushed them back. They weren't murderers. They didn't believe in vengeance, or personal vendettas. They had too much common sense to blame Len and Amelia Rawlings entirely for Alec's death, and to wait this many years for revenge.

Jo was his cousin, for pity's sake. They had known each other since Len was a baby and she a superior twelve-year-old. Harrison was his mentor, who had brought him into Intelligence and guided him throughout. He was ashamed of himself for even entertaining these doubts.

Yet no matter how many times he argued against their guilt, he couldn't banish the possibility for good.

He shook his head. "It's been a long day, and Maia, at least, needs to get back to the Rawlings house to keep the servants happy. I suggest we all sleep on the problem. Perhaps enlightenment will come in the morning."

Becket went ahead to fetch the ladies' wraps, Helen on his heels. Maia was on the verge of following them when Len allowed himself to lightly touch her arm.

What he wanted to do was fall to his knees and beg her forgiveness. Or even better, snatch her to himself and confess all that was in his heart. Instead, he forced himself to stay a respectable distance from her, allowing her to control the level of their interaction. It was the least he owed her.

"Maia, about earlier, in Basingstoke …" He swallowed. "Sorry is inadequate, but it is all I have to offer. It was wrong of me to take out my temper on you. And … and I want you to know how much—" His British reserve tightened his throat against the words he was trying to speak, but he forced them out. "How much your steadfastness means to me. I …" His throat closed entirely.

Thankfully, Maia didn't seem to need anything more. She studied his face and allowed a small smile to touch her lips. "That's all right, then," she said. "No need to talk about it. I know I can come across as patronizing without intending it. My sisters have told me so frequently. The fault was not all yours. So long as you know that everything I said, I meant."

"I know," Len said. "Your honesty is one thing in this world on which a chap can completely rely."

She seemed taken aback by that.

"Maia, are you coming?" Helen called from the foyer.

"Yes," Maia said, finally releasing Len from her gaze. "I'll be right there."

She moved to the doorway. "Oh, Len—I think I should go back to Whegg's shop. There's a chance there's a clue there we missed before, in our excitement over discovering the missing book."

He found himself able to smile and answer lightly. "Admit it, you want to try the shadows spell again."

She laughed. "Of course!"

"In that case, I'd better come along to make sure you don't set any fires," he teased.

She rolled her eyes. Then, with one foot across the threshold, she paused. "The advice you gave me, back at the cottage—who taught you that? And how exactly is it supposed to work?"

"I've picked up many different styles of practicing magic in my time traveling around to various lands," he said. "If you think it would help, I'd be happy to pass on all that I know, though I should warn you that I'm not a proper teacher."

She laughed again at that. "How fitting, as I am most certainly not a proper apprentice! So Aunt Amelia tells me, and I believe her. Tomorrow, then, after I've spent some time at the house appeasing the servants and putting up a good show, we will meet at Whegg's shop and do the shadow spell, and you can teach me your dangerous foreign ways." That last was said in a dead imitation of her aunt's voice and manner, and Len could hardly stop laughing long enough to bid her farewell.

It seemed they were friends again. He had lost his magic, but he hadn't managed to push her away.

There were no words to express his thankfulness for that.

7

Maia Uses Her Head

"Your aunt has contacted the household, miss, and wishes to speak with you this evening," Lorde informed Maia as soon as she entered through the door.

Maia pulled off her wrap, hat, and gloves and handed them to the footman with a smile and a "Thank you, Ben," at which he blushed to the edges of his outsize ears. Only then did she turn to the butler. "Excellent," she said brightly. "I look forward to hearing all about France."

He stayed stiffly still, eyes focused somewhere above Maia's head. "She had hoped to speak with you along with the rest of the household, miss, and was much surprised to hear you have been here so little the last few days."

What business was it of Lorde's how Maia spent her days? Even if Aunt Amelia had told him to keep an eye on her, that didn't give him the right to criticize Maia's actions to her face.

She allowed her displeasure to wash across her features and adopted her most imperious tone, the one which had always worked so well on recalcitrant patients in the wards (the

124

Yankees especially were impressed by it). "I am sure my aunt will inform me herself of any matters she wishes to discuss or any surprise she might feel, as I shall inform her of any information she should require from me. For now, I am going to my workroom. Have Elsie bring me a tray later; I shall be far too busy to eat in the dining room. Thank you, Mr. Lorde," she said as he opened his mouth to reply. "That will be all."

She brushed past him while his mouth was still open, whisked up the stairs and into her workroom, and closed the door gently behind her, resisting the childish urge to slam it. Of all the nonsense to have to endure right now!

In general, well-off magicians like Aunt Amelia employed staff of a magical persuasion without enough power or ambition to become full-fledged magicians themselves. Theoretically, Maia thought this an excellent practice. In reality, servants tended to resent more powerful magicians and took out that resentment on apprentices and those without the standing to command them.

She suspected Lorde would have been insufferable with or without magic. He was that type of man.

Over the next couple of hours, Maia worked her way steadily through the pile of practice spells and potions Aunt Amelia had left for her. She was pleasantly surprised to find how much easier it was to work through all of them without Aunt Amelia hovering nearby, snapping instructions and tossing out power-dampening spells every time she thought Maia might lose control. She found herself almost enjoying them, even the simple spells that usually irritated her no end due to their basic nature.

Now that she was able to look at them slowly and steadily, she saw they were similar to any other kind of exercise—scales for music or copywork for handwriting or tongue-twisters in elocution, any repetitive practice for any other accomplishment. They weren't designed to be ends in themselves.

She was two-thirds of the way through when there was a knock at the door, followed immediately by the housemaid Elsie bearing a tray covered in dishes.

"Your dinner, miss. And a silver bowl with water for when Miss Rawlings wants to contact you, so you can talk to her in privacy instead of coming downstairs."

Aunt Amelia, in keeping with many magicians, kept a scrying bowl next to her telephone so that she could easily contact anyone, magical or not, from the same spot.

Maia couldn't keep back a smile. Giving her privacy hadn't been Lorde's idea, of that she was certain! "Thank you, Elsie." She breathed in the savory aroma rising from the tray. "And pass my thanks on to Mrs. Oates, as well."

"It's our pleasure to do what we can for you, miss," Elsie said, with an ever-so-faint emphasis on the *you*.

Maia had to pause and assess the maid. Elsie appeared about twenty years old or so, a sharp-featured young woman who gave the impression her tongue could be just as sharp were she permitted to whet it properly. "What level of magician are you, Elsie, if you don't mind my asking?"

"Journeyman, miss," Elsie answered readily enough. "And never likely to go beyond. I don't mind, I never wanted to be a magician anyway. I've enough magic to be able to work for Miss Rawlings, which is better than service in a non-magical house, I can tell you."

"And what about the future?" Maia asked, genuinely curious.

Elsie smiled cheerfully. "Goodness, I don't know. Marry, perhaps, to a nice independent magician who can keep me and our six babies in a comfortable house in the suburbs!" She laughed. "Isn't that what every girl dreams of?"

Maia laughed as well. "Maybe not every one, but it seems perfectly reasonable to me." The water in the bowl trembled, though neither had touched it. Maia glanced down. "Ah, I believe that is my aunt. Thank you again for the meal, Elsie."

The maid bobbed her head in a abbreviated fashion. "Ring if you want anything else, miss." She exited the room, and moments later Aunt Amelia's face appeared in the bowl of water.

"There you are, Maia! What do you mean by all this gadding about, eh? I thought I could trust you to not lose your head with a taste of freedom, but according to Lorde, you're flitting off here and there, ignoring your studies and putting my household in an uproar!"

"Good evening to you too, Aunt," Maia said. She held the stack of finished work before her, where her aunt could see it clearly on her end. "As you can see, I have completed nearly all the work you left for me, and I have already found and shored up a few weak spots in my shield spell around the house. You were quite right to call it only adequate, though I was not pleased to hear it at the time."

Aunt Amelia blinked once or twice. "Oh," she said.

"As for going out, yes, I have been out a good bit the last couple of days. I am helping Helen Radcliffe with a project for the Magicians' Ball," Maia finished smoothly.

That was true enough, though by no means the whole truth. "I have not noticed any problems in the running of the house. Mr. Lorde gave me to understand he was able to take care of things perfectly well without any input from me, so I have left it to him." She let her eyes turn wistfully toward the tray of rapidly cooling dishes on her worktable.

"Well," said Aunt Amelia. "I see. Yes. Hmph. Lorde is a pompous old fool, anyway. I will be checking your work when I return, mind, so take care it isn't sloppy or rushed. Any problems with your magic while I've been gone? Blown up anything?"

"*No*," Maia said through gritted teeth. She remembered Len's advice to her that morning—goodness, was that only this morning? It felt like a month ago at least—when her magic struggled to escape her control, and how that had helped. "In fact," she continued. "I think I'm starting to improve my control."

"Indeed?" Aunt Amelia's skepticism was plain even through the water. "We shall see, when I return."

"And how are things on your end? When will you be coming back?"

"I had hoped to return in time for the Ball on Friday, but, er, matters of, er, great importance will keep me here." Was Aunt Amelia blushing? And stammering? Goodness, what was going on over there? Aunt Amelia cleared her throat and tried again. "The initial problem has been solved, naturally—I took care of that with my usual skill. But some, er, side affairs have come up ..." She trailed off again.

Maia had never seen her aunt behave like this. She was torn between delight and confusion. Telling herself that whatever was happening was none of her concern, no matter how oddly Aunt Amelia acted, she settled on delight. Aunt Amelia's unwavering competence and complacency did get so tiresome after a time. "I see."

"I presume you can accompany the Radcliffes to the Ball, as I won't be there?" Aunt Amelia said.

"I am sure—" Maia began, when a pure thrill ran through her.

If Aunt Amelia wasn't going to be at the Magicians' Ball, that meant Maia could spend as much time with Len as she wished, even dance with him without her aunt sniffing and scolding her publicly. In fact, once he heard of Aunt Amelia's absence, he might even ask her to attend with him. There she would be, in her spectacular gown from Helen, and there would Len be—

A sharp pin burst her silly schoolgirl dreams. Len was no longer a magician. He would be welcome at the Ball, she was sure, but she didn't know if he would want to attend now. Even if he did, they had a case to solve and a parasite to catch before they could think about such frivolities.

"I am sure I may," she said firmly to her aunt, and tried to put the matter out of her mind.

* * *

Maia had finished renewing (and improving) the shield spell the next morning and was thinking about breakfast when Helen burst through the front door without knocking or waiting for the outraged Lorde to announce her.

"Maia!" she cried, a shocking sight with no gloves or hat, hair disheveled and clothing mussed. "He came after *Matthew*!" She dropped her face into her hands and burst into tears.

Maia's breath caught. She'd never been particularly imaginative, but she didn't think anyone, even Len, could have ever pictured Helen so unguardedly upset. Her nurse's training kicked in.

"Mr. Lorde," she snapped, her tone drawing the butler's

attention despite himself. "Kindly send someone with a cup of hot tea and plenty of sugar into the Rose Parlor."

"I—this—your aunt—" he sputtered, only to wither when Maia turned the full force of her glare upon him. "I shall send Elsie," he finished.

Maia put her arm around Helen. "Helen, darling, have you eaten anything yet this morning?"

Helen raised her head. "How could I, when my brother—"

"And some toast," Maia added to her request. "Thank you."

She guided Helen into the Rose Parlor and sat her down on the chaise longue. Elsie followed a few moments later, bearing a loaded tray which she set down on an inlaid side table. "Mrs. Oates sent along some rashers and a bowl of porridge," she said. "If you need anything else, let me know." She bobbed her head and left.

Helen let out a hollow laugh. "Rashers," she said. "Who can think about rashers at a time like this?"

"They mean it as a kindness," Maia said. "You need to keep up your strength, after all. Whatever has happened to Matthew, you'll be no good to him if you starve yourself into a stupor." She poured a cup of tea for Helen, adding a couple heaping teaspoons of sugar, and pressed it on her along with a piece of buttered toast. "Now, drink and eat and then tell me about it, but slowly."

Helen sipped the tea and nibbled a corner of the toast. Once her breathing settled, she began.

"Matthew didn't return home last night. That's not terribly surprising, he often stays at his club or who-knows-where when work demands it. So none of us worried." She paused and shuddered.

"Take your time," Maia said.

Helen nodded. She smiled weakly. "I'm starting to feel like a fool. After all, he wasn't … but I'm getting ahead of myself." She sat up straighter and drank more of her tea. "Ugh," she said in an aside. "Maia, I loathe sugar in my tea."

"I know, but it's good for shock."

Helen made a face, but drained the cup, shuddering. She set it back down on the table and continued her tale, hands steadying and voice becoming more firm.

"He burst into the house a few hours past midnight, waking us all up, terrifying the staff and frightening Mama nearly out of her wits. Shouting and raving about the parasite, demanding we shield the house, insisting none of us go outside … it took ages to calm him down. I know, I know, he shouldn't have told us anything, but he was so shaken by the event that he couldn't help himself. It seems he was supposed to meet Miss Marsh at Intelligence headquarters last night to discuss some development the agents had made in the case. Instead, the parasite confronted him outside the building and threw a leech spell at him."

Though she had been expecting it, Maia felt sick at this confirmation. She raised a hand to her cheek and wished she had thought to ask Elsie for two cups of tea instead of one. "How dreadful. What did Matthew do?"

"He was prepared for it, thankfully. They all have been, since poor Len's attack."

Irrelevant as it was, Maia couldn't help flinching at that "poor." Len was *not* to be pitied! He was strong and courageous and the best man she knew, and he would endure this tragedy and emerge from it with his dignity and self-worth intact. She wouldn't stand for anyone diminishing him with their pity.

"At the first hint of magic, he threw up a shield spell, and the leech spell slid off and dissipated. The parasite vanished, and Matthew, so unnerved he couldn't think straight, bolted for home. He finally calmed down enough to return to Intelligence this morning, and naturally I slipped away as soon as he was gone to tell you." She rubbed her face. "It was dreadful enough when it was Len, whom I barely know, but … Maia, that beast came after my *brother*. What if it had—what are we going to do?"

Maia was cold from her fingertips to her toes. "We are going to stop him before he tries to hurt anyone else." She stood up and pulled Helen to her feet. "Come. Get yourself tidied while I finish dressing, and then we'll go take your news to Len and Becket. Between the four of us, we'll be able to make some sense of this latest development and use it to our advantage."

This time, the parasite had made a mistake, and Maia fully intended to use that mistake to end his magic-leeching career here and now. He hadn't stolen Matthew's magic, only put him on the alert. With any luck, he would have left behind some clues they could use to track him down. Even if not, the fact that he had tried to steal Matthew's magic meant either he had already gone through Len's, or the pursuit was making him nervous enough to act precipitously.

Perhaps he had heard about their visit to Basingstoke and it had made him nervous. Or perhaps that odious Mr. Barry and his team actually had made progress in tracking him down. Or maybe Matthew had stumbled across a vital clue without realizing it. Whatever the cause of the attack, Maia would take full advantage of it.

* * *

Len had not yet shaved, the dark scruff lining his jaw making him look startlingly older, but other than that gave no indication that his guests had come at anything less than an ideal time. His clothing was immaculate as always, worn with careless grace and unconcern. Maia smiled as he rumpled his hair with his hand, breaking the image of a dandy-about-town after a night of parties and drinks.

"We must go share our information with MI," he said at last after Helen had told her tale and Maia her speculations as to the cause of the attack.

"But—" said Helen.

"We can't—" said Maia.

Sympathy and frustration radiated from his eyes as he looked at them. "I know," he said. "Barry is going to be furious at me for interfering with his case, even unofficially. Your brother will no doubt be outraged at you, Helen, for putting yourself in potential harm's way to chase down the parasite, and with me for allowing it."

Helen, now almost fully recovered from her fright, sniffed at that "allowing."

"The information will surely leak back to your aunt, Maia, and then she will return in righteous indignation against all of us as well."

Maia shuddered at the thought.

"But it must be done. If the parasite has attacked someone else, the investigators need all the information we have gathered. It would not be right to hold it back from them. Someone else could get hurt."

Maia knew he was right, but she couldn't help protesting further. "We are the ones who followed the unlikely leads, who have gathered together these threads, while Barry, his team, and Matthew have ignored the possibilities within them! Why should we hand it over to them? They most likely won't even use it, they'll dismiss us and all our suppositions. We haven't even come to any solid conclusions yet, what makes you think they will make more sense of it?" Besides, they didn't know yet if these threads did add up to a pattern or if they merely made a snarl.

The threat of Aunt Amelia finding out troubled her less than the idea that somebody else was going to make a mess of their investigation before she had a chance to figure it all out for herself. Her aunt would return breathing fire, no doubt, but eventually she would snort and let it go, holding a tighter rein on Maia's activities but nothing more. It might delay Maia's progression from apprentice to journeyman by another year, but that was the least of her worries at this point.

"Perhaps we haven't been able to make sense of it because we don't have their information, and they haven't been able to because they don't have ours," Len said. "Collaboration, rather than competition, is generally the thing."

"Dear me," said Helen, striving a little too obviously for lightness. "How unsportsmanlike."

"Murder, espionage, curses, and traitors … one thing you learn quickly in the Intelligence business is that this is no game," Len said, his voice quiet and even. "The goal is to prevent people from being hurt, not to win."

There seemed nothing more to say to this.

"Sir, allow me to go in your stead," said Becket, hovering nearby as usual.

"What? Send you to face the lions while I cower here in safety? Never!" declared Len. "Though I do thank you for offering, my friend. No, we shall all go." He clapped on his hat and pushed his arms through his coat sleeves, looking at the two ladies, who hadn't even bothered to remove their wraps when they came inside, so eager were they to tell their tale. "At least there's one good thing to come from all this," he said, ushering them back outside, Becket following loyally.

"What's that?" Helen asked.

"Nobody can say I made up the leech spell, now that your brother has been attacked as well."

"What?" Maia demanded. "Who has been saying that?"

He looked at her furious face and hurried to speak. "Er—just rumors, gossip, you know—nothing to get worried about. How, er, how is your magical control doing?"

She concentrated on taking deep breaths. "It's just fine," she snapped. "Though if one more person asks me that I might accidentally lose my grip on it and explode something."

Len gave her a nervous and unconvinced smile. "Ha ha," he said. "Remind me later that we need to have a conversation about separating emotions from magic, and ways to control said magic that your aunt is not likely to teach you."

Maia returned to the main point. "How anyone could think that you would make up a story about a parasite is beyond—" She stopped. Len, Becket, and Helen walked on a few paces, noticed she was not with them, and came back.

"Maia?" said Helen. "What is it?"

"Is it commonly known where MI headquarters are?"

"No," said Len. "Why?"

"How did the parasite know where to find Matthew?"

They all looked at each other.

"Perhaps the parasite intercepted Miss Marsh's message," Becket suggested. "Miss Radcliffe, did your brother mention whether it was a magical or ordinary message, or any details about it?"

"I can tell you that," said Len. "Ordinary. Marsh's not a good enough magician to send magical notes willy-nilly. She has to save up her magic for the big spells."

"Actually, no," said Helen. "Matthew said the parasite must have been following him, because Miss Marsh's message had come through magical means and Matthew destroyed it after reading, so no one else could have read it."

"Hm," said Len. A look of surprise had crossed his face at that. "Amy—that is, Agent Marsh—must be improving." Maia thought she detected some displeasure in his voice, though she wasn't sure why. She herself felt slightly disappointed at Matthew's eminently logical and prosaic explanation.

"That makes sense. Although …"

"Go on," said Len. "What are you thinking?"

"Only—why strike at him so close to a building which must be teeming with spells? Unless the parasite was waiting for Miss Marsh as well, but then why strike at Matthew before she arrived? And if he wasn't waiting for Miss Marsh, why not throw the leech spell at Matthew in the street, or at his club, or someplace where he wouldn't be so on his guard?" She saw Len's wince and felt bad for mentioning it, but it was a legitimate concern.

"What exactly are you suggesting?" Len asked, voice deep with suspicion.

"We have already started to suspect that perhaps this isn't a true parasite," she said. "What if it's someone from within Intelligence? What if they saw the note on Miss Marsh's end, or saw Matthew waiting, and decided to put an end to his investigation?"

Len turned away sharply, before spinning back to face her.

"No! None of us would betray …" His voice trailed off. Perhaps he was thinking of the number of agents, magical and not, who switched allegiances and sides so frequently nobody knew exactly who to trust. Even Maia had heard the stories of such. Or he might have been thinking of magicians with too much power and not enough boundaries, who went bad.

"MI does attract magicians with lesser abilities," Helen said, reluctance to consider the idea plain in her voice, as well. "That might explain why he needed the potion, or why he wanted to leech magic from others at all."

"Or if he's a turncoat agent, he could be trying to weaken our own defenses, attacking both Intelligence agents and someone from Domestic Protection," Becket suggested.

"I can think of dozens of unethical ways to gain more magical powers—or I could, when I had them—that are far less risky and noticeable," argued Len. "If this is an agent gone bad, why do something so spectacular? Why this pretense?"

"To spread fear," Maia promptly countered. She didn't like the idea herself, but she wasn't sure why Len looked so sick at the notion. "If they are working against England, think how paranoia and terror over a parasite would help … whoever our enemies may be."

"Fascists," Len said. "Russia. Any number of countries. Germany, seeking revenge. Our own Socialists, trying to start a revolution. You're right, of course. Any amount of chaos and fear contributes to an enemy's cause." He swallowed. "Or it could be personal. Intelligence agents have personal lives too, you know."

Maia wondered what he was leaving unsaid. This was something more than the possibility of an agent-gone-bad. Something deeply private was troubling him.

"Did the note come to Mr. Radcliffe at work or at home, miss?" Becket asked Helen.

"Certainly not home," she said. "Mama refuses to let him bring his work home, which is another reason why he spends so much time at his club."

"It could be someone from Domestic Protection, then. Even if he destroyed the note, the parasite could have seen him receive and destroy it, followed him to see what the note was about, and then lost his nerve when he noticed, as Miss Whitney mentioned, the spells surrounding the building, and decided to do away with Mr. Radcliffe then and there. It's not as likely as an Intelligence agent, but it is a possibility."

"Why go after Len, then?" Helen asked.

"Len was outside a magicians' club," Maia said. "It is possible the parasite was lurking in that location, and Len was the first magician to come in his range."

"What about Whegg, though?" Len said, eyes distant, as though he was arguing with himself. "Didn't we think he was the likeliest candidate for the parasite?"

"And we mustn't forget Miss Whitney's dead man," Becket put in, scratching his head. "Seems to me his identity must be the key to this whole thing, or it wouldn't be hidden so well. How does he fit in to all this?"

"Perhaps the so-called parasite kidnapped Mr. Whegg, in case he needed more information than what the book could give him," Helen suggested, eyes bright. "And the unknown man was a witness to the kidnapping, so the parasite had to kill him."

"Or Mr. Whegg might be in league with the agent—or whoever the parasite is," Maia said. She felt like stamping her foot. Too many possibilities! Events kept happening too quickly for any real reasoning to take place. All their facts kept giving them more options, without paring any of them down.

"Then how do we know who to trust?" Helen said.

"We don't." Len rubbed a hand across his jaw, grimacing at the bristles. "We can't take what we know to MI. I was wrong. If there's even the slightest chance that someone there is corrupted, the only possible way to stop them is by working outside the official lines." His eyes brightened momentarily. "Maybe that's why …" he murmured, then caught himself.

Maia respected his choice to not speak his private thoughts in front of Helen, but she vowed that the minute they were alone she would force him to tell her whatever it was he feared or suspected about his colleagues.

"But what about Matthew?" Helen pleaded. "We know *he's* not guilty. And the parasite attacked him! Surely we can, and should, tell him what we've learned. I don't want the parasite trying again, and maybe breaking his shield. Even if he will be angry with me," she added with a sigh.

Len didn't say anything. Maia guessed at his thought: one, that ignorance might have saved Matthew up until now; and two, that no one had actually witnessed the attack on Matthew, and faking such a thing would be an excellent way of diverting suspicion from oneself. It was done in many of the detective novels, at least.

Maia didn't think that Matthew was the parasite. Even aside from the fact that he was Helen's brother, he seemed a decent, upstanding citizen. But she understood that Len didn't want to take any chances.

"I'll meet up with Mr. Radcliffe," Becket offered. "I'll talk to him, find out what I can, give him enough information for him to be on his guard. I won't tell him everything, but I will caution him that the parasite is likely someone who found him either through MI or Deep, and tell him to keep a close eye on his colleagues."

Maia knew they could trust Becket. If, heaven forbid, Matthew was the parasite, Becket was discreet enough to keep him from being suspicious of *their* suspicions. And if he was merely an innocent bystander, Becket would give him what he needed to protect himself without putting him in more danger from an increasingly erratic and deadly enemy.

"Excellent," said Len. "I'll talk to Har—er, my superior again, and see what developments there might be on his end. He's going to want to hear my report from Basingstoke, anyway. It'll give me a good chance to snoop around and see if anyone's behaving suspiciously. I might drop a hint to Driver, as well, if he's there."

With the debt Mr. Driver owed to Len, he was the last person Maia would suspect of leeching Len's magic. That should be safe.

"And what will Helen and I do?" Maia asked. "Sit home and knit?"

His grin was full of warmth and unexpectedly endearing. "I'm sure you'll find something."

Helen cleared her throat. "As a matter of fact, I'm at the point where I need you again for the glamour over your gown, Maia."

Len rubbed his hands together. "Perfect!"

Maia could see no way out of it. "Very well," she capitulated. "But I am going back to Mr. Whegg's to cast that shadows spell this afternoon, whether anyone accompanies me or not."

"You mustn't go alone!" said Helen, eyes wide. "It isn't safe."

"I don't particularly care about being safe, I care about

stopping this person," Maia said, eyes snapping.

"I shouldn't be more than a couple of hours," Len interposed. "I will meet you at the shop at noon, Maia. We need all the information we can get. In the meantime, all of us should be thinking of ways to identify the dead man. There *must* be a spell to tell us who he is!"

They promised to put their minds to it, and Maia also promised herself that when she and Len met at Whegg's, she would make him tell her his suspicions. If they were truly unofficial colleagues, he had to trust her enough to tell her the truth.

"I suppose so long as you and Len are together …" Helen said.

"Don't worry," Maia said, summoning up a smile for her concerned friend. "I promise to stay in one piece at least long enough for you to display your project to England's magical elite."

Helen relaxed enough to grin back. "Good. You may be as reckless as you like afterward, but do please stay sensible before then!"

On those words, they parted ways, Len to snoop around Intelligence, Becket to discreetly pump Matthew, Helen to work on her masterpiece, and Maia to be a dressmaker's dummy again.

One day, she reminded herself, she would no longer be an apprentice, and could utilize her talents with the best of them. But first, to catch a parasite.

8

Shadow Spell Again

Precisely at noon, Len and Maia met in front of Whegg's shop. Before then, Len had shaved, met with Harrison, eaten breakfast, and fretted, not necessarily in that order. He wasn't sure how to act with Maia, since their exchange in Basingstoke and subsequent reconciliation. Did he try to explain to her the emptiness inside him, how he felt hollowed out and cast aside with his magic gone? Did he try to convey some of the rage simmering barely below the surface at the person who had done this to him? Did he cast aside English reticence to tell her all that so that she understood some of what was behind his lashing out? Did he thank her again for her faithful friendship? He knew he could never, ever tell her how deeply he had desired their relationship to move beyond friendship into something deeper, not when he had nothing to offer her now.

Maia took the decision out of his hands. "Shall I check to make sure nobody has come by since we were last here and laid wards against us?"

"Excellent," he affirmed, wriggling his shoulders a little to shake himself out of his mood. Dash it, this leech spell had affected more than his magic alone! He was not generally the introspective nor dithering type. The mater had always called him impulsive—Len preferred to think of it as decisive. Once one wanted to do a thing, why waste time fretting over whether or not it was the right thing? Make the move and accept the consequences, eh. Take one's hedges as one came to them, to borrow his brother-in-law's hunting cant.

Maia tilted her head, and Len took comfort in seeing the familiar silver mist around her hands as she spoke and gestured. "Nothing," she said after a moment, and stepped back to let Len use his lockpicks. An empty gesture, since he knew perfectly well she could have undone those locks with nothing more than a hairpin, but one he appreciated.

He wrestled briefly with the lock, made clumsy by his dashed eagerness to impress (as though he were a fresh-faced schoolboy again, get a hold of yourself, Davies), then pushed the door open. The hinges creaked, something old Whegg never allowed when he was there. Creaking doors, he claimed, disturbed the books.

Maia followed him inside, ducking down to peer beneath his upraised arm. "No, it certainly doesn't look like anything has changed since we were here. Good. Now we can talk."

Len switched on the electric light. "I thought you wanted to cast the shadow spell and work on your magic?" he said, suddenly panicked. What if *Maia* wanted to talk about Basingstoke? He didn't think he was ready for it after all.

"Whom do you suspect at Intelligence of being behind the parasite?" she asked, folding her arms across her chest and focusing her piercing glare on him.

"Oh," he said, torn between relief and a new kind of panic.

"That."

"Yes, that. I didn't press you in front of Helen, but I need to know."

He couldn't argue with her logic. "Thank you for your discretion," he said. She inclined her head. "It's not a suspicion, not really. It can't be true, it's mad to think it … but I can't get the 'what if' out of my head. That's the reason I didn't want to talk about it. I don't want anyone thinking ill of a person I respect. And," he surprised himself by adding with raw honesty, "it's painful to think about, much less talk."

"I understand that," she said. "The question is, do you trust me enough to maintain a proper judgment about this person and respect your pain or not?"

Put like that … he'd already slammed the door on her friendship once. He wasn't going to make things worse by showing a distrust of her character.

When it came down to it, he *did* trust her. Implicitly. And part of this story she already knew.

"Do you remember, when we first met, my telling you what was behind your aunt's and my dislike of each other?"

Maia moved over to the nearest pile of books and seated herself. "It was because she agreed to let your cousin go on a mission with you into Germany, to stop that magician assisting the Kaiser. You didn't believe your cousin was ready for such a dangerous task, but my aunt thought otherwise, and he … was killed. You blamed my aunt, who refused to accept responsibility for it but obviously felt some guilt anyway, as she has disliked you ever since."

"What? You think that's why—never mind." Now was not the time for Maia's conclusions about her aunt's behavior or inner thoughts. He was impressed she recalled it so perfectly.

On the other hand, it perhaps wasn't that surprising, given her sharp mind and the emotional circumstances under which he'd shared that tale. "Yes. Alec—my cousin—had an older sister, Joanna, who is married to my mentor and superior at Intelligence, the one who brought me in when I was still a young magician."

"Harrison Eastwood," Maia said slowly, putting the pieces together.

"Yes," he confirmed, once again impressed with her acuity. "And there's a part of me that keeps thinking, what if this isn't a parasite, but is an ugly revenge scheme cooked up against your aunt and me for letting Alec die? What if it's Harrison, or Jo, or Harrison and Jo together? What if the cursed man was supposed to infect your aunt, only the curse was too virulent and he died too soon?"

"Then why Matthew?" said Maia, forehead wrinkled in thought as she worked through the implications of this. Len was relieved that she neither dismissed his fears as ridiculous nor jumped to the conclusion that this must be the solution.

Len shifted half a pile of books and sat down on the ones remaining. "Either because Matthew had found a clue, or to reinforce the idea that it is a parasite, not a personal vendetta."

"And why send you to Basingstoke? Surely it would be in their interests to keep Miss Ransom's death separated from their efforts?"

Len looked down at his hands. "That's what I told myself," he said unhappily. "We concluded that the parasite took the glamour potions because he or she didn't have enough power to cast a glamour and throw a leech spell at the same time. Both Harrison and Jo are more than adequate magicians; and if they are working together they certainly wouldn't need a potion."

"Exactly," Maia said.

"But what if Harrison sent me after Miss Ransom as a red herring? So that I would come to that exact conclusion, and therefore dismiss him from suspicion?"

Maia put a gloved hand to her head. "If this sort of twisted reasoning is typical of Intelligence agents, I think I'm glad I'm not qualified for the role."

"You have no idea," Len said, smiling faintly.

"It's a plausible theory," she said after a moment. "But by no means certain, and to my mind leaves several questions unanswered. For one, would they really wait this long before enacting revenge? And if Miss Ransom is a red herring, who *did* kill her, and why? Not to mention your opinion of them as people. Clearly you think this sort of action foreign to them. We should not dismiss that lightly. People do act out of character, but only under great provocation. Has anything happened recently that might have triggered this need for vengeance? A particular anniversary, or activity, or remembrance, or anything at all?"

Len cast his mind back. "Not that I can tell," he said. "But who knows what goes on behind closed doors."

"Indeed." Maia was silent for a moment. "We shall keep this as a distant possibility, but for now, if you say you think it *practically* impossible, I will trust your judgment and continue to search for other suspects."

Len felt like he could take a proper breath for the first time in days.

"Excellent," he said, suiting action to impulse and taking a deep breath. Once he stopped choking on all the dust, he finished speaking, Maia sitting patiently with hands folded in her lap all the while. "Do you want to cast the shadow spell now, or work on those non-traditional methods of magical control first?"

"Which would you recommend?" she asked gravely.

Len was touched. "Let's save the shadows spell for the end," he decided. "That way you can test your new methods on it. That way, too, if it shows us anything interesting, we can immediately go to work on that, instead of having to set it aside for school." He smiled whimsically at that, and Maia smiled in return.

"You may begin, *Magister*."

He appreciated the word play, and the idea it conveyed. Even if he was no longer a magician, he could still teach. "I assume Miss Rawlings is teaching you the same way I, and most British magicians, were taught. There is only one proper way to perform magic. Emotions must be controlled, spells must be in Latin, you must never loosen your grip on your magic lest it destroy you." He seemed to remember telling Maia some of those truisms himself back when they first met.

"You mean that is *not* the case?" Maia asked, eyebrows going up.

"It is and it isn't," Len said.

"Lennox, you can be the most maddening man. For heaven's sake, say what you mean and say it straight out!"

He grinned. "I've seen enough other ways of practicing magic in the last ten years to think our traditional methods are too rigid, and that perhaps we should approach magic differently. Is that blunt enough for you?"

"Goodness," said Maia. She blinked a few times. "Aunt Amelia would consider this heresy."

"She and most magicians of her generation," Len agreed.

"Times are changing! It's a big world. During the war, I saw many different types of magic and magic-users from different countries. So did Miss Rawlings, for that matter, only she was too narrow-minded to think anything of it. 'Those sorts' of magical practices might be good enough for foreigners, but not for the British."

Maia's mouth curved upward. "That does sound like her."

"Ever since the war, I've studied foreign magic on my own, whenever I've had the opportunity. Some types I don't think we could ever successfully adapt to our way of thinking—one would have to have been raised in the Japanese tradition in order to work one's magic in their style, for example—but I think there are some general principles one can apply." It was something he'd planned on passing along to his apprentice, if he was qualified enough to take on one when he was retired from field work. He was well and truly retired now, but it didn't seem likely he would ever gain an apprentice. He winced and pushed the thought away. No matter. He could help Maia, at least. Perhaps, in time, he could assist in training others as well, even if he could never have a proper apprentice.

"Such as?" she asked, leaning forward in her interest.

He considered his words carefully. Now was not the time to wax enthusiastic about the alternative forms of magical theory and practice he had learned. Maia was a practical person, and in need of immediate aid. He would keep it simple and to the point. "The first thing I have to tell you is that there's no precise formula for any of this. You will have to work much of it out for yourself."

She grimaced.

"Sorry," he said, though he couldn't help grinning. "I don't think you necessarily need to keep a tighter grip on your magic, or fight with it so much. If you had—let me see—ah, yes, if you had better-than-average hearing, you wouldn't wear a muffler around your head, would you? Even though the noise might be disturbing and distracting, even painful at times, you would train yourself to filter it out, do mental exercises to sort the jumble of noise into meaningful sounds, that sort of thing. Wouldn't you?"

"Not having better-than-average hearing nor being a doctor, I couldn't tell you for certain, but that certainly seems logical," said Maia.

"Well, I don't know about any of that for certain myself," Len admitted. "I'm guessing. But it's a useful analogy for my purposes."

"In that case, by all means, carry on."

"The point is, you wouldn't try to subdue your hearing or work against it. You would learn to work with it. You would neither squelch it down nor allow it to overwhelm you to the point of madness. That, I think, is the folly in how we British approach magic. 'Oh no, it's too powerful, we must quench it lest it destroy us!' Instead, we should train ourselves to work with it. Breathing exercises are good, as are visualizations and mental sorting. Anything to help us control without crushing it." He pulled a sheaf of papers from his pocket.

"Back at the cottage," Maia said slowly, eyes unfocused, "Trying to keep from losing my grip on my magic gave me the image of pushing a feather mattress into a too-small cover."

"Ah, that would be the wrong sort of visualization right there," Len said. He put the papers back in his pocket. Maia was quick. She grasped the idea right away, without needing any of his other notes on the matter.

She looked at him briefly and smiled. "But when you helped

me, it *did* become easier … as though the mattress were slithering into the bag. Which is nonsense, because mattresses don't slither," she ended briskly.

"No, but you're on the right track!" Len enthused, nearly toppling off the books before he regained his balance. "Close your eyes," he ordered.

Maia gave him one sharp blue-green glance and obediently lowered her lids.

"Now, feel your magic at your core." He instinctively attempted to follow his own instructions, and shuddered anew over the emptiness. "Imagine it a snake, coiled and asleep," he hastily continued, hoping she wouldn't hear the change in his voice.

"Yes."

"Now, awaken it."

She opened her eyes. "What spell?"

"No, no!" Len said, and momentarily he was transported back to Russia, being lectured by a tiny *babushka* when he did the same thing under her tutelage. If he tried, he could almost smell her *pryanik*, that delicious Russian spiced gingerbread. "*Nyet, nyet,*" he murmured under his breath. Generously, he spared Maia the names the babushka had called him, of which "idiot" was the kindest. "Eyes closed, magic awake."

"But for what spell?" she asked again. He almost thought he could hear panic in her voice, though he dismissed that at once. Maia did not panic. "Magic is simply another sense, it doesn't exist in itself, we use it to interact with the natural world around us in ways that most people cannot." The speed with which she recited this confirmed his earlier impression: she truly was on the verge of panic.

"Think of it like your vision," he said, trying another route.

"You don't only open your eyes to see one particular thing. You open them to see the world, and after they are open, you pick things on which to focus. So, awaken your magic as though you were opening your eyes. Only these are your inner eyes, not outer."

"Len," Maia said, her voice small and serious. "If I set fire to this bookshop or lose control of my magic, you can't stop it."

Her words stabbed him in the gut. He shunted the pain aside. This time, it wasn't about him. It was about Maia defeating her fears.

He rose to his feet and crossed the room to stand behind her. "If you can't trust yourself, trust me," he said. "I am telling you that you are not going to lose control." Ever so gently, he rested his hands on her shoulders. "You are going to wake up the sleeping snake and lull it back to sleep, and you will not fail."

He felt her shoulders tense under his hands, but she drew a deep breath and began. After a few moments, the familiar silver aura came to life around her, a gentle mist surrounding her entire body and enveloping his hands. He stared at it wistfully, wishing it were possible to absorb some of that into his skin.

That, he reminded himself, was the sort of thinking that led to leech spells.

"It's awake," she whispered. "And—it's hungry. What do I do, quickly?"

"Breathe in and out," Len said, his voice steady and deep, hands firm but calm on her shoulders. "Your magic is part of you, just another sense. It does not control you, but you don't have to battle it. As simple as closing your eyes, settle the magic back down. It's a snake, being lulled to sleep by its charmer;

a bird, not fluttering madly to escape its cage but sitting on a branch and singing; a steadily cantering horse being brought down to a walk and then stop."

The aura dimmed and winked out.

Maia placed her hands on her cheeks. "Oh my."

Len reluctantly let go of her and stepped back around to see her face. Two red spots glowed between her fingers on her face, and her opened eyes were dazed. "Did it work?" he asked.

"I have never … not since starting my apprenticeship … never …" Maia stopped and tried again. "That is the first time I have ever experienced my magic like that. I've never been able to feel it active within me without using it for a spell lest it spill over. It's as if …" she stopped and laughed. "I'm picking up bad habits from you, thinking of metaphors and analogies for it. It's as if it was a turbulent river before, always wanting to spill over the banks, but now it's a calm stream. It is still there, still flowing and active, but not needing to be actively contained."

Len recalled the words of the one who had taught him this method of self-control. "A river in overflow is no longer a river, but a flood," he said. "So it is with your magic. Only when it remains within its bounds is it properly magic; otherwise it is an empty and destructive force."

Whereas his was now a dry bed. Once again, Len moved past the thought. This was a tremendous moment in Maia's development, and he was dashed proud of her, and of himself for helping, and he wasn't going to let any sorrow over his own loss interfere with that. "This is only the start," he said, speaking with his own words again. "Keep practicing, and before long you'll have such good control even your Aunt Amelia won't be able to shake it."

"Won't that be a triumph!" she said, but beneath the light

mockery in her tone he could hear the wonder still existing. "Thank you, Lennox."

"It was my pleasure," he said. "And now, I suppose we should get on with the shadows spell."

"I hope this helps," Maia said, rising to her own feet and composing herself to stillness. "I am tired of chasing after clues and never reaching any conclusions."

She wasn't the only one.

* * *

It was remarkable how much more smoothly the shadows spell flowed from Maia on only her second time around. Whether it was from the control experiment or simply because she had already done it once Len wasn't sure, but he was impressed.

"Did you remember to set the parameters?" he asked in a hushed voice once she'd set it.

She opened her eyes and glared at him.

"Ah. Of course."

From all corners of the shop, shadows rolled, stretched, trembled, and finally coalesced into two human forms. Len, watching narrowly, narrated the events as he saw them unfold. It was a trick to help him make sense of what could often be confusing with this type of spell.

"Customer has entered. Whegg behind the counter. Greets customer but does not come out personally to shake his hand—either a stranger or not someone he knew well, then."

"Was that his custom, to come out to personally welcome those he knew?"

"Oh yes, frequent visitors to the shop got quite the royal treatment," Len said. As he watched, the customer-shadow, browsing the shelves, meandered in the direction of the back room, the one they and Becket had found torn to pieces, while Whegg stayed behind the counter. Maia and Len trailed after the customer-shadow.

"And now he looks through the books back here," Len said, resuming his narrative. "Sees one—can we safely assume it is *the* book? I think so—drops everything else, picks it up, opens it, reads." The caressing way the shadow's hands slid over the non-existent book's pages made him shudder.

Maia tugged him out of the way as the Whegg-shadow rushed through the doorway.

"He sees the book, tries to take it from the customer," Len murmured, eyes glued on the tug-of-war. Even in shadow form, Whegg's perturbation was plain to see. "The customer refuses. All around them, books topple to the floor. At last, the customer punches Whegg in the stomach, backhands him across the face, and clutches the book to himself."

"Shame," Maia said, lips tense and white. "To treat an old man so."

"Unless Whegg is the parasite and wants the book for his own vile purposes, and this customer was only trying to keep it safe," Len said, without any real conviction in his voice. More and more, this scene showed Whegg as another victim, not the perpetrator.

Still holding the book to his chest, the customer-shadow threw out his free hand, fingers moving in a complex pattern Len, sickeningly, recognized. The Whegg-shadow staggered and fell back a few paces, now clutching at his own chest.

"A curse!" Maia breathed.

This was followed by the customer-shadow rushing upon Whegg, pulling something out of his pocket.

"He uncorks it," Len said. "Then, while Whegg is kneeling on the floor, defenseless, pours it over his head. Whegg shudders, staggers to his feet, and …" they all trailed behind … "goes out the door into the street."

"From whence he is never seen again," said Maia. "But why—" She swallowed the rest of her question as the customer-shadow did not fade away as the Whegg-shadow had.

"He turns back, destroys the rest of the books in the back room, does a cursory search behind the counter, puts up the closed sign, and leaves," Len said. The shadow finally dissipated, leaving the magician and former magician staring at each other.

"Nobody saw Whegg leave," Maia said. "How could people miss that?"

"Even more perplexing," Len said. "Why toss a potion over a man you've already cursed? Is it a glamour? Is that why nobody saw Whegg leave? But why? And even with a glamour, he should have been found by somebody, with a curse like that."

"What sort of a curse was it?" Maia asked. "You looked as though you recognized it."

"I did," Len said, a heavy weight settling on him with each word. "It's a basic curse taught to every Intelligence and Domestic Protection agent as soon as they enter training. It's meant to be used in self-defense alone, but of course, there's no safeguard to prevent one from using it as an attack."

"Aside from one's own principles," Maia said.

"Which this person does not have," Len finished.

"One more piece of evidence pointing toward MI or Deep," Maia said. She shook her head. "Appalling."

"At least we can now categorically state that Whegg is not

the parasite."

"Unfortunately, we still can't find him. That curse—it kills?"

"It can," Len said. "Depending on the strength with which it was cast, and the intent. You can cast it to kill instantly or to merely impair a person. It affects the heart, either stopping it entirely or else slowing it to the point where the body can't function. If imprecisely cast, it will slow a person and then eventually kill him."

"So Whegg could be dead, dying, or gravely injured." Maia flung her hands into the air. "Couldn't we get at least one piece of evidence in this case that doesn't muddle matters even more?"

"Would that we could," Len said.

"So what do we do now?"

"Before we go any further, I must ask this, and please don't be angry." Maia looked apprehensive, but nodded. Len drew a deep breath. "Do you think Matthew Radcliffe could be the parasite?"

"No," she said promptly, looking neither angry nor surprised by the query. He was so relieved. "I thought you might suspect him, and I agree, it seems logical enough due to that unexpected and unwitnessed attack on him, but I don't see Matthew as power-mad or selfish. If anything, he seems eager to prove himself on his own merits, not those of his siblings or parents, and he genuinely seems to care about other people's wellbeing. No, I don't see him as the parasite."

"Good," said Len. "I would hate to have to tell Helen her brother was a murderer and a leech. And that also means we don't need to conduct our investigation behind her back for fear of her accidentally spilling the truth to her brother." He rubbed his hands over his face. It had been a long day, and it showed no signs of ending soon. "I will talk to Harrison again."

"Even with your suspicions?" she asked.

He nodded. "The best way to make him think I'm not suspicious is to keep him updated regularly. I'll tell him about the connection with Whegg we've now proven, and see what he does with it. If he is innocent, he might have some good ideas about where to look next. If he's guilty, I ought to be able to pick up some clues by his reaction."

"Len—if it isn't Harrison or your cousin, or Matthew, who do you think it is?"

"There are any number of MI agents in London right now," Len said. "Even more Deep. Most of them I know only a little or not at all. I spend so much time in the field, with Becket as my backup, reporting only to Harrison, that I don't know my colleagues as well as I would like. It could be any of them."

"Are there—forgive me—are there any with a particular grudge against you?"

"Heaps," he said promptly. "You already know Barry and I loathe each other—well no, that's not true. I loathe him; he despises me. He couldn't have done this, though."

"Why not?"

"At the time I was getting cursed, he was overseeing the investigation of the dead body at your aunt's house, remember? Not even a parasite can be in two places at once. Agent Marsh isn't particularly fond of me, either."

"She was also at Aunt Amelia's, though," Maia pointed out.

Len shook his head. "I checked, casually, this morning. Barry sent her and Driver off with the body while he stayed behind to interrogate people and oversee the curse removal team. It's just possible that she could have left the Deep officers to carry the body back to their morgue and dashed off to curse me before returning to meet Barry and the rest of the team at HQ. Not tremendously likely, but possible. Those are the first two that come to mind. Plenty of people in MI think I only rose to my position because of my familial connection with Harrison. They'd all be happy to see me undone. As for Deep, well, I can think of one or two officers who feel I stole a case from under their noses. Not to mention the general dislike in Deep for MI agents. It could have been an attack against any MI agent, not me specifically."

"Marvelous," Maia said. "And while you're filling in Harrison and possibly exposing yourself to the parasite yet again, I suppose I'm meant to go home and practice my magic again?"

He sympathized with her frustration. Idleness never sat well on him either. "The best thing you can do for us right now is think," he said. "Your brain is top-rate—no, I'm not flattering you, it's the plain truth. Where I batter my way through a brick wall, you step back and examine it for cracks and figure out its weak points so you can dismantle it with one push." Good lord, was she blushing? Hah, well, if so, good. Maia didn't get anywhere near enough praise, in his opinion. It would do her good to hear the truth about herself for a change.

They exited the book shop, locking it behind them, and started down the street. Not half a block away they crossed paths with none other than Jasper Driver.

"Driver, old boy!" Len said, surprised to see him.

"Oh—Davies," the man stammered, falling back a pace. "Miss Whitney. I—yes, that's right, Miss Whitney, y-you said the two of you were a-acquainted."

"What brings you to this part of London, Mr. Driver?" Maia asked, slipping her hand into the crook of Len's elbow so casually it almost failed to fluster Len.

"Er …"

"It's all right, old chap, you can speak freely before Miss Whitney," Len assured him.

"Agent Barry sent me; he heard about Mr. Whegg's disappearance and wants me to check to see if he c-could be the … you know."

The parasite. Took Barry long enough to get there.

"As a matter of fact," Maia began. Len tightened his arm muscles beneath her hand. She took the hint and fell silent.

"Good luck," he interposed. "I hate to think of that old man falling so low, but on the other hand, best if we get this cleared up right away, eh? Don't want anyone else ending up like me."

As he'd hoped, such a blatant reference to his loss caused Driver to wince and hurry along, not asking them any more questions.

"Why did you stop me from telling him that Mr. Whegg is a victim, not the culprit?" Maia asked once they were out of earshot. "I thought you trusted him."

"I do—but I don't want anyone connected with this case to know how deeply we are involved. The more we stay on the outskirts of this, the better."

Maia stopped at the next street. "This is where we part. Be careful, Len."

"I will. Remember what I said: *think*. You've said it yourself, we are missing some key parts to make all the pieces fall into place. If anyone can figure out what those parts are, it's you."

9

The Pieces Start to Fit

Maia spent a good two hours after breakfast and household duties diligently working through more of the spells and charms left by her aunt. Then she took half an hour—locking the door to her workroom first to keep out nosy servants—to practice the breathing and control methods Len had shown her. At the end of that time, she was amazed at how calm she felt, and how smoothly her magic flowed through her. Generally after a practice time with Aunt Amelia, she was all on edge, and her magic kept fizzing erratically out of her pores. Either that, or she was so drained and exhausted she couldn't have lit a candle without a match.

She'd have to tell Len what an excellent teacher he was. Even if he couldn't be a magician, perhaps he could find a future for himself in training up other magicians. She doubted he'd want to hear that right now—teaching was quite a step down from a practicing magician and Intelligence field agent—but perhaps after they'd caught the parasite and he'd had a chance to come to terms with his loss, it would hold more appeal.

If, that was, his magic was irrevocably lost. She still refused to believe there was no possible way of regaining it. Surely there must be a spell to drain it out of the parasite and restore it to Len without resorting to black magic! Or a way for him to re-grow it, or … something. Simply because the healers said it was gone forever didn't make it so. After all, all the books and training she had received up until now had told her there was only one way to control her magic. It took Len's experience with other cultures and practices to show her otherwise.

Perhaps the thing for Len to do after this was all settled was to travel around the world and find out what other magicians knew about leech spells. That, she would suggest to him right away.

Having settled this in her mind, she turned her attention, as Len had suggested, to the case.

Glamour, she thought. This all centered around glamour. Not only the magical kind, but deception and trickery, things made to appear one way to draw the eye away from what had really happened. The witch who was known for her glamours murdered, two potions stolen. One most likely used to hide Mr. Whegg's identity (but why? What was the purpose? Why did he have to be disguised, why was it so important no one find him?); one used in the process of casting the leech spell on Len (was the glamour attached to the leech spell itself or to its user? Did the person disguise him or herself in order that Len might not recognize him or her, or simply as a basic precaution?). The murder of Miss Ransom made to look non-magical. The murder of the man who started it all, a curse so deadly it still couldn't be examined fully for fear of contaminating the investigators …

Maia stopped. She turned to her books, flipped through

them frantically. Somebody had said something about this recently, but she hadn't really listened, hadn't heard ... oh, where was it? She slammed the books closed and made for the door. One of the servants could tell her, she was sure. A voice in the back of her mind whispered it was disgraceful to inquire of servants for such matters, but she ignored it. Where truth was to be found, there could be no disgrace in the method of seeking it out.

"Elsie!" she said, finding the housemaid crossing the hallway alone, to her relief. Far better to ask the friendly young girl than pompous Mr. Lorde, though she would have done even that if necessary. "Elsie, are non-magical people able to see glamours?"

Elsie blinked. "No miss," she said. "If you want to deceive a non-magical person you have to use a different spell, like that there chameleon spell you do so well."

Elsie knew about her sneaking around under the chameleon spell? Maia filed that away under the *not relevant* section of her brain and determined to think about its implications later.

"Didn't you know that, miss? Everyone—"

"Everyone knows it," Maia said through gritted teeth. "Everyone except me, it seems." Blast her ordinary upbringing!

Her better sense stepped in at once, reminding her that Helen had most likely told her this more than once—that was why it had been tickling at the back of her mind—and she hadn't listened because she found glamours boring. In this case, she could blame neither her aunt's tutoring nor her upbringing. It was her own fault. Now that she did know it, she needed to see Helen at once.

"Thank you, Elsie," she said. "That was just what I needed to know. Kindly let Mrs. Oates and Mr. Lorde know I am going out, and I'm not sure when I'll be back. If my aunt contacts the house, tell her I am researching something crucial!"

She whisked down the stairs, flung a wrap across her shoulders, and left the house, only just holding herself back from a run. Eager as she was for the truth, a lady did not scamper through the streets of London like a ragamuffin. Alas.

By the time she reached the Radcliffe residence, she was nearly dancing out of her skin with impatience, but she composed herself enough to ring the bell and await someone answering the door, rather than barging in. She didn't want Mrs. Radcliffe thinking she'd lost her wits and was no longer a fit companion for Helen.

The pretty young housemaid opened the door on the second ring, cautiously cracking it at first and only opening it fully after seeing Maia's face. Of course, with the scare Matthew had had, they'd all be on edge. Maia had extra need for calm and caution here.

"Hello, Miss Whitney," the housemaid said, scanning the street up and down behind Maia.

"Hello, Anna," Maia said, summoning up a smile. "I am here to see Miss Radcliffe, is she in?"

"Yes, she's upstairs in her sitting room." The maid stepped back to let Maia enter, quickly closing and locking the door behind her.

"No need to announce me, I'll go ahead up," Maia said. She left the maid no time to argue, briskly heading out of the entry hall and up the stairs to Helen's pretty white-and-gold sitting room.

Unfortunately, that door was locked as well. Really, this was carrying things a bit far! Maia thumped her fist against the door, losing grip ever so slightly on her patience.

"Helen, it's Maia, open up!"

She heard the sound of a bolt being slid back as well as the murmur of a spell being ended, and then the door cracked open to show Helen's worried face.

"Is Mother with you?"

"Of course not, why would she be?"

Helen reached out a hand and dragged Maia inside, before she closed, locked and re-activated the spell on the door. Seeing inside the room, Maia understood her friend had a different cause for her paranoia than the housemaid had.

A simple silken gown, its lines pure and undecorated, stood on a dressmaker's dummy in the middle of the room. Surrounding it were reams of papers, beeswax candles, bunches of rosemary and cedar, and scraps of fabric with gossamer threads appearing and disappearing randomly across their faces.

"All of this for my gown?" Maia asked, overwhelmed.

Helen nodded and pushed her hair back from her face. Dressed in an old day frock and apron, free from jewelry or other fripperies, she looked the picture of a hard-working magician, not much like the frivolous young lady of society she so often appeared. Maia felt a pang. This was Helen's passion, that which meant more to her than anything else, even her generally neat and tidy appearance. It was both good and painful to see her friend so in her element. Would Maia ever have that same passion for an area of magic?

"I'm not ready for another fitting," she said. Each fitting worked as a way to anchor another layer of glamour to the frock—it had less to do with fitting the dress to Maia as fitting the glamour to the dress and to Maia.

"I know," Maia said, recalling her errand. "I need to ask you about glamours. How do they work, how long do they last, and how do you dispel a glamour somebody else has cast?"

Helen wrenched her attention away from the gown with difficulty. "I've told you all about glamours before and you never cared. Why do you need to know all that now?"

"Oh," said Maia, not answering the question. "I also need Matthew to get me in to see the body from Aunt Amelia's."

Helen stared at her for a long moment, then untied her apron and blew out the candles. "Not without me, you aren't."

* * *

Matthew was understandably displeased with his sister's request. Once he was done shouting at her for disregarding his express orders by involving herself in the case and risking the parasite coming after her, he started in on her "ghoulishness" in wanting to see the body.

"Besides, if you think I'm going to risk you near that curse …" he sputtered.

Helen cut him off, having borne all this with remarkable patience. "Have a little sense, Matthew. Don't you know me at all? I am the last thing from a ghoul, nor would I want anything to do with the, the *corpse* were it not for the fact that Maia thinks the curse is a glamour."

Matthew swung around to stare at Maia, who had been standing in the background during the brother-sister spat, gladly not interfering. She knew better than to get between squabbling siblings. Far too often, she had been one herself.

"And I think his identity has been obscured as well," she said.

Matthew's mouth worked for a few moments before he finally managed to get words out. "That's … not something that had occurred to us," he admitted. "I'll mention it to Barry and see if we can get a glamour expert in. Not, however, my younger sister!"

"Oh, Matthew, do be reasonable," Helen said. "Why go through all the formal channels when you can simply whisk Maia and me in, have me examine him—er, it—for a glamour, remove it if it's there, and whisk us out again?"

Matthew proved stubborn. He left to contact Barry, and Helen turned to Maia, her shoulders slumped.

"Sorry. I should have known better. Always by the book, my brother. I don't suppose we can sneak in ourselves and uncover the truth before MI and Deep get there?"

Maia knew it was irresponsible, but she rose to the challenge. She and Helen spent the next fifteen minutes discussing ways and means before acknowledging it simply couldn't be done. For one thing, they didn't know where the morgue was.

Maia sighed, resigned. "So long as they find the truth, I suppose it doesn't matter who does the finding."

"Of course it matters!" Helen said. "I want our proper share of credit!" She looked so fierce Maia couldn't help but laugh.

She sobered when Matthew re-entered the room. The expression on his face resembled his sister's, so much so Maia was taken aback.

"Agent Barry wasn't there. Agent Marsh, however, says there's no need to check the body for a glamour, that the curse experts would have done that right away, and that only someone from Deep would make such an elementary suggestion," he said.

Goodness, he must be upset to speak so frankly.

"Well, really!" said Helen. "No wonder Len doesn't like the agents working this case."

Maia heartily concurred. He did have a point, though. "If the curse people already checked…" she said.

Matthew shook his head. "That's just it, I don't think they did. They were told it was a curse, they checked and saw evidence of a curse, and nobody wanted to get close enough to the body to do a proper examination with all the residue it's still leaking. They've been mostly studying books and reports to find out what sort of a curse it was, but not the body itself. They didn't even take it back to MI, left it in our morgue instead."

"Then that is simply unacceptable sloppiness," Maia said, pursing her lips together.

Matthew put his hands in his pockets. "It is a nasty bit of magic," he said apologetically. "Even your aunt didn't want to do a proper examination."

That was true enough. Maia remembered the wave of revulsion that had swept over them all as soon as Aunt Amelia had attempted her diagnostic. She felt a pang of doubt. "Could a glamour really produce that strong of an effect?"

Helen nodded. "I couldn't, but a master glamourist could."

"Or a well-brewed potion?"

"If it was exceptionally well-brewed, yes." Two pairs of eyes met across the room with perfect understanding. "Looks like it's our plan after all," Helen said, turning to her brother. "Sneak us in and out again."

"Hel, I told you—" he began, then stopped. "Even if I wanted to, do you have any idea how much trouble I would be in if anyone saw you?"

"Maia has mastered a chameleon spell," Helen announced. "She could make it so that no one would even see us. Or I could glamour us to look like somebody else. Nobody even needs to know we were there. Until afterward, when we are proven right and the accolades are being handed out."

"You don't have to tell anyone at all," Maia said, attempting to quell Helen with a glance. It had generally worked on her sisters, but made no impression on the stronger-spined Helen. "Tell Barry that you decided to double-check, or that the glamour fell away on its own. Or don't tell him anything, solve the case yourself!"

Matthew straightened, the weariness starting to smooth away from his face, replaced by speculation. "Hm," he said. "Maybe I could make it work."

"You mean we," Helen said tartly.

He managed a faint smile. "Of course," he said hastily. "We, naturally."

For a moment, Maia wondered if this was the right choice. What if her judgment was flawed, influenced by her friendship with Helen, and Matthew really was the parasite? She and Helen would be putting themselves in terrible danger. He could kill both of them and blame it on the curse residue, and no one would know.

Len and Becket would figure it out. She had utter faith in them. All the same, that would be cold comfort if she were dead. She ought to have consulted with them first before rushing in like this. It was the sort of thing Len would do, not she! The only explanation was that she was so eager to solve this case and help Len regain his magic if possible that she had lost her head. That would never do.

Maia resolved to keep her wits about her and her magic ready at a moment's notice. She didn't really think Matthew could be a villain, but if she was wrong … she would be ready for whatever he might try.

He nodded. "Right. Better make it the chameleon spell. And

whatever you do, don't let Mother know, or she'll have my head!"

Pausing only long enough for Maia to cast the chameleon spell and Helen to set a glamour to make it appear as though the two girls were still having tea in her sitting room, the three left the house and went straight for Domestic Protection.

A boxy brick building with dusty windows on a remote side street, Domestic Protection had none of the imposing grandeur of New Scotland Yard, which was just as well, since the goal was to not draw attention from the general public. Magicians knew where it was located and what was inside, and that was all that mattered.

Matthew murmured the spell which allowed him to get through the side entrance reserved for those who worked there—people coming to make a complaint had to go to the front desk and wait their turn. The chameleon spell was harder to maintain in a large group of moving people; Maia was relieved to not be put to the test.

Trailed by the unnoticed ladies, Matthew made his way through the corridors, past offices filled with desks and filing cabinets, before stopping before an iron door marked "Morgue." Maia heard an audible gulp beside her. Matthew must have heard it as well.

"Last chance to turn back, Hel," he whispered out of the side of his mouth.

"Don't be ridiculous," Helen's voice hissed back at him.

Matthew shook his head, whether at his sister or himself Maia was not sure, and pushed the door open.

"Hullo, Radcliffe," said the man sitting at the desk blocking the way into the rest of the room. "No new information on your corpse, I'm afraid. Nobody can get near him at all still."

"I think I may have a lead," Matthew answered. He tugged his collar. "I'd prefer to check it myself, though, in case I'm wrong. Don't want to contaminate anyone else."

The man looked at him closely. Matthew pulled out his handkerchief and blotted his forehead. Maia hoped he would get them through soon. This was the longest she'd held the chameleon spell, and she was getting tired.

"Agent Barry know?"

Matthew tucked his handkerchief away and drew himself up to his full height. "Do we really need to check with MI for permission to conduct an investigation on a body in our own morgue? After all, if Agent Barry had wanted it, he could have had it taken to MI, but he left it with us. I think that means we can do with it as we please."

The man laughed. "I can't argue with that. I hope your hunch pays off! I'd love to see someone get the best of those toffee-nosed Intelligence chaps. Intelligence, ha! I'll show them intelligence." He pressed a button beneath his desk. "You lot clear out, Officer Radcliffe's coming in to do some work on his corpse."

As the desk officer sat back with his hands folded over his stomach, six men paraded out of the space behind him, stripping off gloves and other protective gear and dropping them in a bin beside the desk. They all nodded at Matthew and filed through the door.

"All yours," the desk officer said as the door closed behind the last one. "You know where the gear is. Don't forget to get some for your company as well." He winked.

Helen incautiously exclaimed "oh!" and Maia dropped the spell, seeing there was no point in keeping it up any longer. She wasn't sure whether to be furious or merely dismayed.

Matthew, to her surprise, laughed, his overly cautious manner replaced by smug humor.

"I should have told you ladies, Officer Park here specializes in seeing through disguises, but I rather wanted to see your reaction."

Helen stamped her foot at her brother. "How like a man!"

Not usually one for generalizations, here Maia couldn't help but agree with her friend.

"Not to fret, I won't tell anyone you're here," Officer Park said. "I didn't see nor hear nothing." He picked up a newspaper, rustled it ostentatiously, and buried himself beneath its folds.

"You made Maia waste her energy on an unnecessary spell for a laugh?" Helen demanded of her brother.

"The spell was necessary to keep others from knowing you were here, but I knew I could trust Officer Park. Don't be such a fussbudget, Helen. Come on," Matthew said, and led them, still fuming, past the desk and into the cavernous space beyond.

The temperature dropped several degrees as soon as they were behind the desk, and all outside sound vanished—magically controlled, Maia guessed, since there was no physical barrier to mark the difference. A row of tables, some bearing a sheet-covered body, some not, went down the middle of the space. At the far end, partitioned off from the rest by glass walls laced with spells, rested their corpse. Even from this distance Maia could sense the evil pulsing off him. Her shiver had nothing to do with the temperature. What if she was wrong? She could be endangering Matthew and Helen on nothing more than a whim … perhaps they should turn around and leave right now, before anyone got hurt. Glancing at her companions, she could see the same thought echoed on their faces.

"I've changed my mind," Matthew said abruptly. "It's too dangerous. I can't risk you ladies here. Come on, we'd better get home before Mother realizes you've left."

"Maybe we should," Helen agreed uncertainly, and that was enough to snap the fog of fear and repulsion clouding Maia's mind. Helen, meekly agreeing with her brother's protection? Something was off here, and it was not residue of a wicked curse. Nor was it Matthew's doing. She could see on his face how little he wanted to be here.

"You may both flee if you wish," she said curtly, pressing her gloved hands against her stomach to hold down the nausea that bubbled up as soon as she made up her mind to go forward. "I have no intention of quitting now."

Confusion, shame, and determination passed plainly across her companions' faces. "Matthew, is there such a thing as a spell to misdirect and repulse?" Maia asked.

Comprehension lit up his face. "Of course! You think that—" He broke off, pointed across the room toward the box, and was about to speak the counter-spell when Helen grabbed his arm.

"You idiot, not with the protective spells set up around it!" She pulled gloves and smocks from the closet nearest her and bundled them into the others' arms. "Honestly, you two would bring the building down around our ears without me around. No wonder Lennox needs Becket, if this is any indication of agents and officers."

Properly protected, they walked across the room, fighting the miasma of distaste the entire way, until they were at the glass walls. Matthew glanced at the girls. "Ready?"

Maia nodded. Helen gulped and followed suit.

Matthew laid his hand on the glass walls and spoke the spell to drop the wards. In almost the same breath, he brought up his other arm and spoke a counter-spell to break the repulse charm.

Before the girls had more than a moment to brace themselves against the full weight of the loathing coming off the body, it vanished. Maia gasped, and Helen slumped against her brother before she caught herself and straightened.

"Well thought, Maia," Matthew said. "I can't believe it didn't occur to any of us."

"You thought it a curse, and it was, only not the kind you believed," Maia said. "Our perceptions matter more than we realize."

"We didn't think of it because what we did see matched our set ideas," he nodded, then turned to his sister. "Go ahead, Hel. Dazzle us." He grinned down at her.

She sniffed. "First, we check to see if there is a glamour attached to the poor man." She closed her eyes and mumbled in Latin. "Yes!" she said triumphantly. "A glamour potion. Now to dispel it." She drew in a deep breath and waved her hand.

Before Maia's eyes, the body rippled and shimmered, causing her stomach to churn for an entirely different reason. Human bodies ought not to *do* that, particularly dead ones. Then the last of the glamour vanished, and there lay a small, white-haired, neatly dressed old man.

"Whegg from the bookstore," Matthew said, sounding stunned. "We'd heard he was missing, but nothing that would connect him to this."

"How was he killed?" Maia said. She was fairly certain she already knew, but she needed Matthew's confirmation.

"An ordinary defense curse," Matthew said after a moment. "Sloppily cast. That's why he lasted long enough to get from his shop to your aunt's."

Maia stared at the body, no longer a thing to cringe away from, merely a kind, book-loving old magician cut down before his time to serve the desire of a wicked man. "A pity he couldn't have held on a bit longer to tell us the name of his murderer," she said.

* * *

"Are you going to tell Agent Barry of our triumph?" Helen asked her brother as they walked back toward the Radcliffe house.

He shook his head, not necessarily in a negative, but more in a contemplative manner. "I know I ought to. MI has the lead on this case. But aside from the fact that I ought never to have allowed you two ladies in there and he can justifiably rip me to shreds for that—"

Helen made a face. "I cannot believe I'm suggesting this, but don't tell him it was us, then. Let him think you did it. You can give us credit after it's all over and the parasite caught," she added hastily.

Matthew smiled at her. "A truly generous suggestion, little sister."

"You said aside from that?" Maia prompted.

Matthew rubbed his face. "I know I'm a lowly Deep officer, and he's a proper MI agent with years of experience behind him. I ought not to criticize. But I can't say I'm pleased at all with how he's handling the case. He hinted at first that perhaps your aunt was involved, Maia! Just because the man came to her house to die."

Maia found herself less affronted by the thought that Aunt Amelia could murder a person than the idea that she would do such an untidy job of it.

"And then he wondered about your servants. He didn't believe the attack on Agent Davies was genuine until I was also attacked—" He shivered.

Maia hadn't considered any of the servants. She rather liked the idea of Lorde as the parasite, only there wasn't enough evidence to support such a fanciful theory. "The butler did it?" she said under her breath. Sherlock Holmes might approve, but Hercule Poirot, never!

"His team is no better. Marsh said their people had already checked for glamours when they hadn't, Driver sits around and waits to be told what to do. They have no leads, no suspects, and if I hand over the information about Whegg to them who knows what they'll do with that?" Matthew caught his breath and seemed to remember his audience. "Sorry," he said. "I shouldn't be saying all this to you."

"Trust me, it isn't anywhere near as dreadful as everything Len says about Barry and Marsh," Helen said.

"Still," Matthew said, sighing deeply. "It wouldn't be right to hold evidence back, either. My visit to the morgue has been recorded, and somebody is going to notice that the effects of the curse are gone. If Barry finds out that I did this and didn't tell him the results, he could get me kicked out of Deep. No, I think I must pass the information along, much as I hate to."

Maia would pass it along as well, to a far more competent agent than that Barry person or any of his so-called team. She checked her wristwatch, wondering if he'd be back from meeting with Harrison yet. "Helen, Matthew, I think I will leave you here," she said, stopping at the street corner.

"Are you sure you don't want to come back with us to tea?" Helen asked.

"Please do," said Matthew. "I owe you a great deal."

She smiled at them both. "I thank you, but no. I'm afraid there is still a considerable amount of work left to be done before this case is solved, and as you so accurately pointed out, Matthew, Agent Barry and his team aren't going to do any of it." She nodded and left them, hearing their conversation follow.

"A considerable amount—Helen, have you two been investigating on the sly?"

"What do you think, that the idea about the glamour was a sudden inspiration from the clear blue?" Helen's sarcasm was withering even from a distance.

"But—but—it's not proper!"

"I didn't hear you complaining about propriety when we identified your body for you!"

As they moved further down their chosen path, their voices grew fainter and fainter. Maia made her way through the bustling streets of London toward Len's flat. Surrounded by people, shoes clicking on pavement, she felt a longing for the green fields and wide spaces of Stanbury, the smells and sounds of the country, the small village where every shop owner and delivery boy knew her by name. London was exciting, vibrant, and alive, the heart of wizardry in England, but oh, she did miss having room to breathe. Perhaps when this case was wrapped up she ought to go home for a visit. If nothing else, a few days in her mother's company would make Aunt Amelia seem almost palatable in comparison!

She ran lightly up the steps to the front door and rang the

bell. She had only the briefest moment to wait before Becket greeted her.

"Miss Whitney! What a pleasure to see you. What can we do for you?"

"Is Len in, Becket?"

The short, slight manservant shook his head. "I'm sorry, miss, he's still out."

"Oh." Maia's enthusiasm dampened. "Do you know when he'll be back?"

"Knowing Mr. Davies … no, miss. You are welcome to come in and wait, if you like."

Maia was tempted. Even if Len was gone for the next two hours, waiting in his quiet, comfortable sitting room, reading one of his books while being waited on by Becket was far more tempting than returning to Aunt Amelia's. She released the vision with a sigh.

"Better not. If you could tell him when he returns that we have determined the dead body who started all this is Mr. Whegg, killed by that curse we saw used in the shadows spell at the shop, and he was disguised by a glamour and the curse made to seem worse by some sort of charm, I would be most grateful."

Becket's training proved itself during this recital. He did not turn the proverbial hair. "Very good, miss," was all he said. "I will tell him."

"Thank you, Becket," she said. She gave him a conspiratorial smile. "Don't worry. We'll catch the person who did this to Len. We're getting close, I can tell."

"Yes, miss," said Becket. "I certainly hope so."

10

A Suspicious Invitation

Len had never minded walking into MI London before. Similar to Deep, it was an unobtrusive box of a building, though built of stone instead of brick, and it did boast a few gargoyles on the roof. Broken and battered, the ordinary eye would pass over them without taking any particular notice. In fact, they housed highly effective and nasty guard charms to be released upon any non-cleared person crossing the perimeter.

Though they let Len pass without trouble, he couldn't help but feel a fraud as he entered. The feeling increased as he faced the five doors opening off the main corridor inside the big front door. Without the proper spell, the doors would either refuse to open or else would lead to the basement, which had an entire webwork of spells laid over it so a person could, theoretically, wander around endlessly in an enchanted labyrinth down there until he died of hunger, thirst, exhaustion, or sheer frustration. The lowest level agents were supposed to go down once a week and check for unwanted visitors, but stories abounded of skeletons in the corners, intruders who'd been missed or, more frequently in the stories, whom nobody had bothered to rescue.

Without his magic, Len could go no further this way. Luckily, once in a while they needed to work with non-magicians, and so there was an alternative.

There were three doors on the left side of the corridor, two on the right. Len went to the blank space facing the third left-hand door. Feeling something like a fool—all agents had to learn this method of entry, but he'd never had to use it before—he tapped the wall in a specific pattern.

"One two three, one one, two three four, one one," he said under his breath as he tapped. Non-magical persons were told this released the catch to a secret passageway. It in fact released a doorspell crafted especially for non-magicians.

Sure enough, a large rectangle showed as he finished tapping, and a door creaked open.

"I hate this," he muttered.

He passed through the doorway, stood still so the watcher spell could identify him (non-magician guests were told this pause was necessary so their escort could disable traps), and then climbed the twisting staircase to the top floor of the building. There, he paused before another blank door for one final identification and nerved himself to open it.

Entering the main room through this door would announce his loss of magic to everyone, mark him indelibly before his peers. Even though they all knew it already, he still wasn't entirely sure he could do it. To face all their pitying expressions, the shock in their eyes that Lennox Davies, one of Intelligence's best, was now magic-less.

He rolled his eyes. "You aren't that important, Davies," he told himself. Most agents sitting in that room at the moment would be convinced he or she was Intelligence's best and that any agent who was fool enough to get caught by a leech spell deserved what he got. "Don't be such an ass."

He pushed open the door and entered.

The main room was a long rectangle, filled with desks and tables, people sitting at the former scowling at paperwork, or grouped around the latter examining a spell. The air smelled a little singed and a little stale; the sun filtering through the grimy windows competed with the *lux* lights clustered above everyone's heads; the murmur of well-bred English voices arguing (constantly) over various points sounded like the hum of angry bees chasing an intemperate gardener away from the roses. It felt like home.

It didn't feel anything like home.

"Good morning, Len," said Joanna Eastwood. His cousin sat at a desk near to the door, one of the few people who had looked over when it opened; the only one who hadn't flinched and immediately averted their gaze. Joanna looked demure as always in her dowdy brown dress and softly waved bob. Newcomers nearly always mistook her for a secretary, something in which she took wicked delight.

The truth of the matter was that she had one of the sharpest minds and wits of anyone Len had ever known, not even excluding Maia. Her mother and Len's were sisters; that alone explained much about Joanna.

"Good morning, Jo," he said, leaving his post near the door to perch on the edge of her desk. "Heard there was another parasite attack last night."

Her eyebrows lifted, making her look like a surprised kitten. "Now how did you hear that? Have you set spies among us?"

He grinned at her. "I have my ways, you know. Besides, the

parasite is personal."

"That's why you shouldn't be involved in the matter at all," she said, but her gentle voice lacked conviction.

"That's why I have to be involved," he contradicted. "Come on, Jo. I know you know all about it."

She sighed. "Haven't you already discussed it with Harrison?"

Of course Harrison's wife knew that Len was meeting him on the sly—had already met him this morning, in fact. "You know Harrison," he said. "Far more interested in getting information out of me than sharing any."

"So you think his wife should share it instead?"

Len tapped his fingers on the desk.

Jo sighed. "Why does everyone gossip around me? Would that I could tell you I know nothing about it!"

"They forget you're there."

"They forget I have ears and a brain," she rejoined, which was true enough. It was one of the aspects that made her such a marvelous agent: nobody ever suspected the short, plump, middle-aged woman with the purring voice and sweet face of being capable of thinking about anything more complicated than her children's accomplishments or a tricky knitting pattern. Len, with vivid memories of his youth, was not fooled.

"Very well," she capitulated. "But if anyone asks, you didn't hear it from me."

"Cross my heart and hope to die," he chanted, drawing a finger across his chest in an "x" pattern.

She snorted absently. "You already know that the so-called parasite attacked Matthew Radcliffe around midnight last night, when Radcliffe was supposed to be meeting with Marsh. Radcliffe, the young idiot, sprinted home instead of entering here, where we might have been able to mobilize a few of us to search—ah. That's how you heard about it. Radcliffe's younger sister is friends with your paramour Maia Whitney. He told her, who told her, who told you."

"Maia Whitney is not my paramour," Len said, hoping he wasn't blushing. He didn't bother denying the rest of it.

Joanna smirked. "Of course not. By the time Radcliffe reported to Barry and Barry told the rest of us, the parasite was long gone, leaving no evidence behind."

"I already know all this, Jo," Len said, trying to hide his impatience. "There has to be more to it."

Jo leaned forward and lowered her voice. Out of habit, Len glanced around, but nobody was watching them. He gave her his full attention.

"According to Marsh, she never sent that message to Radcliffe."

"Someone else did?"

"Or Radcliffe made it up."

Len pulled back. "But why—ah. You think he faked the attack on himself."

Jo shrugged. "He seems like a nice enough boy, if terribly wet behind the ears, but you and I both know that means very little in our business."

Len could see how it would make sense. Radcliffe setting it up to make it look like he was attacked to throw off suspicion. A young and ambitious Deep officer, desperate for extra power to help him rise through the ranks.

Balanced against that were Len's instincts and Maia's certainty that Matthew Radcliffe was not the parasite. Those were two substantial weights.

Not much point in saying that to Jo. Still, he could plant a suspicion or two. "If it's not Radcliffe, then who would have sent that message? It would have to be someone from here."

She tapped a pen thoughtfully against her chin. "Yes, that occurred to me. That could be why we found no trace of evidence afterward. Easy enough to attack Radcliffe and then slink back inside."

"After all, Radcliffe didn't even know me before this case began. Why would he use his first leech spell on me? If it was another agent …"

Jo nodded. "A reasonable point. But who?"

He watched her. Her brown eyes were clear as brook water. She seemed the very picture of innocence.

That meant nothing. Jo was one of the best liars he knew, she could hit you across the face and then lie so convincingly she made you believe you did it to yourself (that was not a random example. Granted, he had been an obnoxious adolescent at the time and had deserved what he got).

Even so, watching her now, he couldn't help but believe her trustworthy. Maia's question at the bookshop returned.

If not Harrison or Jo, then who? It was true he had enemies, but most of them were either imprisoned or far away. Even the people who disliked him here wouldn't go so far as to use a leech spell. Barry had an alibi and considered Len beneath him anyway. Radcliffe wasn't the type. Marsh … it was too arrogant to think she hated him this much simply because he'd rejected her romantic advances. One of the other agents on Barry's team? He couldn't believe it of Driver, not after he'd saved the man's life. A random agent? A Deep officer?

The possibilities were vast, and no matter what he did, he couldn't seem to narrow them down.

"Davies!"

Len jumped off the desk and nearly snapped to attention before catching himself. Joanna grinned wryly at him, patted her hair, and went back to her paperwork.

"Sir!" Len said, as his former chief approached.

Harrison Eastwood glared at him. "My office," he snapped. "Now."

"Yes sir," he said. He glanced at Joanna. "I'll be visiting Pippa and Cam soon, if you want to send them anything."

"I've a baby blanket almost all finished, I'll get it to you by the end of the week," she promised.

Len's arrival might not have garnered much attention, but Harrison's bark did. Agents all around the room stood and turned as Len trailed after Harrison toward the office. He could hear the whispers, feel the stares burning into him. He swallowed and fixed his eyes on Harrison's tweed-covered back.

Not many people had proper offices in the building. Harrison and a few other senior agents, retired from the field and directing affairs and other agents, merited their own space, the walls being put up by either spells or shaky carpentering. Harrison being the type of man he was, his office was also laced with anti-eavesdropping spells. Once the office door closed behind them, Len allowed his shoulders to relax.

"What are you doing here, Len?" Harrison asked. "I thought we'd agreed it was best if you didn't come here until all this was sorted. What was so important you couldn't send me a message to meet elsewhere?"

Len watched him closely while telling him about the results of the shadows spell at the bookshop. Harrison didn't flinch at the news.

"But no sign of Whegg himself?"

"No sir," Len admitted.

Harrison sighed and sat down behind his desk. "Have a seat, Len," he said, waving toward the other chair. Len would have preferred to remain standing, but he couldn't refuse with Harrison staring pointedly at him.

"Now. You could have told me that in a message. What really brought you here. Just to pump Jo for scuttlebutt?"

Len had no intention of telling Harrison his true motives—to examine his cousin for signs of guilt.

Thankfully, he had other perfectly legitimate reasons for being here.

"You must see as clearly as I do that the evidence is pointing to MI, sir. I wanted to look through our files, see if any of our agents had had contact with Jane Ransom in the last year, that they would know about her skills with glamour potions."

Harrison raised an eyebrow. "You think an agent is behind this?"

Len's blood ran cold at that tone. "I don't want to," he said hastily. "But the evidence does seem to indicate—"

"The other solution hasn't occurred to you?"

Len's heart began to beat faster. Was this it? Was Harrison going to confess? Would he admit his guilt and then attempt to finish the job by killing Len? Would he—

"Matthew Radcliffe."

Len blinked a few times. "Oh," he said flatly. "That."

"Yes," Harrison said. "That."

Was it Len's imagination, or was Harrison watching him more closely than usual? He struggled to appear casual. "I suppose Radcliffe is a possibility," he said, examining his fingernails. "I would like to eliminate any chance of it being one of our own first, though."

"Fair enough," Harrison said, coming to his feet with that litheness which was always so surprising in such a big man. "I'll shout at you first, and then if anyone sees you in the Archives, they'll think you went in there to weep." His grin was downright wicked.

Len wasn't sure whether to laugh or be furious at that.

Harrison sobered. "We'll catch the bastard, Davies. Cold comfort, I know, but at least we'll prevent him from doing this to anyone else."

Unexpectedly, an image of Jane Ransom's crumpled body rose before Len's eyes. Perhaps even more important than stopping the parasite before he stole anyone else's magic was stopping him from hurting and killing any more innocent victims, men and women like Miss Ransom and Whegg.

"Right," he said, closing his eyes briefly and releasing much of his tension in a single breath. "Of course we will, sir."

"And when it's all over, before you go off to Scotland, come to dinner with Joanna and me. Bring that Whitney girl. I'd rather like to meet the niece of Amelia Rawlings who can catch your eye."

He moved to the door before Len could react to that, throwing it open and standing beside it with arms akimbo.

"I told you before, Davies, you're done! I feel for you, we all do, but there's nothing to do about it. You're no good to us now, a liability instead of an asset. Maybe you were one of the best once, but it's time to let others take up the reins. Go home. Visit your sister. Find something else to do with your life. Leave the parasite to us."

Len stepped through the doorway into the main room, ducking his head to avoid hitting it on the lintel. He turned back to Harrison, now framed in the doorway, and bowed deeply and ironically.

"Yes, *sir*," he said, letting all his true frustration hiss between his teeth on that "sir."

"And don't come back here trying to worm secrets out of the other agents or my wife!" Harrison shouted as Len spun on his heel and stalked away.

Most of the other agents refused to meet his gaze, but Edwin Barry stepped into Len's path, forcing him to stop and face him.

"Hard luck, old boy," he said, smiling thinly. "But don't worry. We'll sort it for you."

Len was hard pressed not to grab the weasel by the throat and fling him out the nearest window. Only the knowledge that it would undoubtedly please Barry all the more to know he'd gotten under Len's skin held him back.

"I appreciate that," he said instead, with grave courtesy.

Barry's smile didn't reach his eyes as he continued, ignoring Len's tone and words alike. "I realize it must be embarrassing for you, having been fooled by a glamour at the same time the parasite stole your magic, but not to fret. I'll catch him in the end. I'll make him regret ever tangling with MI. A pity that won't return your magic to you, but at least now you don't have to wrestle with your conscience anymore over the more— challenging cases, or look for an excuse to take easier ones. Perhaps it's all for the best, eh?"

"I look forward to the successful end of the case," Len said, and walked away before he could lose his temper fully.

He left by the same door he'd entered, only this time he turned left instead of walking straight down the staircase. It looked as though he was walking into a solid wall, and just before contact he flinched back, unable to believe he wasn't about to break his nose.

"Curse it," he said. He wasn't going to be defeated by a shoddy little spell like this!

He clenched his fists pugnaciously and walked forward with chin tucked and eyes glaring. Sure enough, he passed through the mirage of the wall and found himself in a long, winding, windowless corridor. He hoped he could remember where the door to Archives was without his magic to guide him.

Halfway down, he blinked in surprise. The door to Archives was outlined as it always was to magical eyes, a shimmering green rectangle. No non-magician could see it. He had assumed he would have to operate by memory, but he could see as easily as he ever had.

"Huh," he said. He'd expected his ability to see magic would have worn off by now, Maia's aura excepted. He knew it wasn't logical, but he felt that he'd be able to see her aura forever, long after his own magic was nothing but a dim memory.

That he could see other spells but not use them felt rather like salt in the wound, but for the moment, he was grateful. He hadn't been looking forward to pushing every likely-seeming spot on the wall until he blindly stumbled into the proper one.

The door swung open with a simple touch, and Len stepped into the cool comfort of Archives.

The small room had windows on all three sides—Len had never been able to figure out where it was actually located within the building, magical logistics made his head hurt— and was always flooded with light, whether it was cloudy, nighttime, or high noon. He had never been able to spot any obvious lighting, either. The room was one of the oldest within the building; nobody knew the name of the magician who had designed and built it, but it housed over one hundred years of Magical Intelligence history, and rumor had it that if the entire building burned to ashes, this room would turn up in the next building built on the spot. Rows upon rows of boxes filled the space, stretching beyond where Len's eye could see.

With so much information in there, finding anything ought to have been an onerous task. Thankfully, its architect had been as canny in that area as in all the rest. Beside the door was a tiny card cabinet. Len placed his hand on the drawer.

"Ransom, Jane," he said. The spell was triggered by his voice; no magic required of him at all. "Profession, hedgewitch. Location, Basingstoke." He opened the drawer.

One card awaited him. He picked it up and examined it. *Row 12, Section 30, Box 14*, it read.

One of the main reasons paperwork was so important to the agency was this room. Anything filed properly in here was easily accessible to any agent at any time, even years after. An improper filing, however, meant the information got lost somewhere in the bowels of this magical room, never to be found again.

Len walked down the room which, tiny though it appeared, expanded as far as he kept walking. He came to the neatly labeled Row 12 soon enough, stepped down said row to Section 30, and counted until he reached Box 14.

It wasn't there.

Len stepped back a pace and looked again.

"One, two, three, four …" he began counting. Sure enough, the empty space was right where Box 14 ought to have been.

A cold chill trickled down his spine. He brushed a hand over his upper lip and wished he didn't have such an aversion to firearms. A pistol would have been a dashed bit of comfort right about now. He'd used guns in the past—in his line of work, there were times he'd had no other choice. He always preferred spells, though, an option he didn't have right now. Nor could he set up a warning system to let him know if someone entered the room after him. He was far enough away from the door; he'd never see if someone came in.

Who could have known he was coming for Box 14? Harrison, but he hadn't had time to get ahead of Len to remove it. Joanna could have done it while Harrison distracted Len, but how would she have known? Len hadn't told her or anyone else about his desire to look up information about Miss Ransom until he'd mentioned it to Harrison.

Maybe the person hadn't removed it for him specifically. Maybe he or she had done it as a precaution when he or she went after Miss Ransom in the first place. Or maybe he'd spotted Len coming in and decided to take care of it to be safe.

Maybe this wasn't a trap for Len.

His instincts still told him he was in danger.

There—he heard a creak. The door? Was that a footfall? Len slid around the sections into the next row, and waited. If anyone was coming after him, he wasn't going to stand there as a perfect target.

That was *definitely* a footstep. Len wished for a properly shadowy library and pressed against the opposite stack of boxes. A spell, any spell, he wished desperately, unable to keep from probing the empty well of his magic. Nothing, not the smallest drop left. He could have screamed with rage would it not have given away his position.

A flash of light indicated the newcomer had sent a curse rocketing down Row 12. Len instinctively ducked, though he was one row over. Even with his head covered, he saw the light stop as suddenly as though it had hit a wall, and reverse back on itself.

There was a yelp—whether male or female he couldn't tell—and then Len was running, sick of hiding, sick of feeling like half of himself with his magic gone, sick of this entire situation. He didn't need a gun or a spell, if he got a grip on the scoundrel he'd flatten him with one blow.

He burst out of the rows to find a scorched spot on the door and no intruder in sight. Len slowed to a stop, feeling foolish. What had happened?

Ah. Of course. A slow smile broke over his face as he put it together. Of course the room's architect would protect against curses and spells. Likely the curse has brushed too close to the boxes and hit a shield, which ricocheted the curse back on the original caster. From the look of the door, the chap had escaped just in time.

Sure that he was too late, Len crossed to the door in one bound and jerked it open, looking down the hall both ways, ready to pull his head back instantly should another curse come for him.

Nothing. No curse, no magician, nothing. The corridor was as empty as it had been before.

Or was it? Len left Archives slowly and carefully, every nerve tuned for a trap.

No one jumped out at him, no spell tripped him up. He made it to the small object at the end of the corridor and cautiously picked it up.

A small box, neatly labeled *14*.

Len carried it back to Archives. Sure enough, it fit perfectly into the slot in Row 12, Section 30. He shook his head.

"What game is being played here?"

Ready to duck, hoping that the strange magic in the room

would protect him if the parasite had jinxed the box itself, Len removed the lid.

No jinx. Only a file containing the name of the agent who had first discovered Miss Ransom's talent with glamours.

Agent Amy Marsh.

* * *

Len exited the building a short time later, his thoughts whirling. *Amy?* Could it really be Amy—clever, beautiful, ambitious Amy—behind the murder and leech spell? *Why?* She had more magical talent than most in MI; she had chosen this role due to a love for adventure and England rather than because she had no other options. In fact, if he recalled correctly, she had had to fight to prove she wouldn't be corrupted by the role before they would accept her. Oh, he had toyed with the idea of her as the villain, but never seriously. It didn't make sense.

No, Amy wouldn't turn parasite for more power. Then why? The personal angle he and Maia had decided could be behind it? But that made no sense, either. True, she had boldly cornered him six months ago and told him they would make an excellent team on and off the field, emphasizing the "off." When he had hastily declined (less than politely, if truth be told, but he'd panicked), she had seemed to accept it with equanimity.

Or had she? Len thought back. What had she said?

"Your choice, Lennox Davies," she'd said, no rancor evident in her voice. "I warn you, though, you'll regret it."

He'd thought it a sign of her supreme confidence, that she was certain one day he'd look back and wish he'd hitched his wagon to her rising star. What if it had been a threat?

Just how dense was he?

No good to jump to conclusions. He needed proof, hard proof. Where had Amy been during the times Miss Ransom, and Whegg had been attacked? He already knew there was a chance she could have cast the curse on him. If she had an alibi for the other two, well and good. If not …

It would be better than Harrison and Jo, but not by much. He liked Amy, doggone it! Not in a romantic way, no woman could ever tempt him since meeting Maia, but as a colleague and person. He appreciated her confidence, her boldness, and her sense of humor. He didn't want to think of her as a parasite and murderer, the person who had entered Miss Ransom's house under false pretenses and then shot the poor woman through the heart. It was easier even to think of Amy leeching away his magic in revenge for his refusal than to picture her doing *that*.

"Davies!"

He flinched. Speak of the devil … He swung around and tried to look pleased.

"Hullo, Marsh."

She was a tall woman, even taller than Maia. Thinner than Maia, too, older as well. Amy Marsh was closer to thirty than twenty. Her dark hair was cut in a severe bob, her blue eyes piercing, her cheekbones sharp enough to slice cheese. She was beautiful, but far too efficient and cold-blooded for Len's romantic tastes.

"I wanted you to know that it isn't just Barry handling your case. Driver and I are doing everything in our power to work beyond him and catch the parasite. It isn't easy, what with the tight leash he keeps us on, but we have no intention of letting him botch this." Two red spots burned on her cheeks. "Driver has even started pursuing leads of his own accord, if you can believe it."

Was she lying? Sincere? Len couldn't trust his instincts anymore, didn't know what to think or who to believe. "Thank you, Marsh," he said, that seeming the safest all around answer.

"And what are … what are your plans now?" she asked, leaning forward slightly. Len stopped himself from backing up a pace. Was this what Maia meant when she told him not to loom? He resolved never to do it again. "Are you going to Scotland, as Eastwood said?"

"Yes," he said recklessly. He was going at some point, anyway, even if not immediately. "I need some time to think about my future."

"Of course," she said, straightening.

"Why?" he couldn't resist asking.

The red spots on her cheeks returned. "I only thought—I thought if you were going to be in London, you might want to go to the Magicians' Ball with me tomorrow."

The Ball. Tomorrow? He silently cursed. He'd forgotten all about that.

He'd missed the Ball before. Too many years he'd been on assignment when it took place. He didn't always attend even when he was in London at the proper time. Balls and dances were not among his favorite activities.

This year was different. Maia was going to be there. Even when he'd thought Miss Rawlings would be there as well, he'd hoped for at least one dance, a few words of conversation. He'd even allowed himself to imagine taking her outside for a stroll at one point, and there, under the moon, with the strains of music wafting to their ears from the open windows, telling her … it didn't matter now.

"I hardly think I'm eligible," he said curtly to Marsh. "After all, it's a Magicians' Ball. I am no longer a magician."

"Anyone who tries to tell you that you don't belong in our community will have me to deal with," she responded, her tone just as curt as his.

If she was the parasite, she was playing a deep game. If she wasn't, he was touched. Either way, he had no intention of accepting her offer.

"Thank you," he said. "But I do not plan to attend."

"Lennox Davies, hiding? Afraid?"

He tilted his chin, looking at her silently. She smiled.

"That's what they'll say, you know. Barry and his kind. That you can't bear to face other magicians, now your magic is gone. Are you going to let them get the best of you?"

He knew she was trying to needle him. Her words did bite, but they didn't sink in. Still, he laughed. Whatever her game was, she was playing it well, and he was genuinely curious. What was she after? Only one way to find out.

"Well, Marsh, when you put it that way … I accept."

"Good," she said, nodding once, a short, sharp jerk downward of her chin. "I expect you to pick me up at seven o'clock. Try to not be late."

With that she walked off, drawing the eye of every man on the street with her elegant posture and striking good looks. Len wasn't sure if he'd grabbed hold of a tiger's tail or not, but he had no intention of letting go until he was certain.

For now, home, tea, Becket, and figuring out what to do with today's information.

11

Stars in Their Courses

Before going to bed that evening, Maia received a note from Len *via* Becket's spell-working, as before.

Becket told me about your deductions and the proving of them concerning Whegg. Well done! That's one part of the puzzle unraveled, at least.

She told herself it was ridiculous to feel a thrill at another's praise, but to no avail. She took pen in hand to respond, whispering the words of the spell as she did.

Thank you. How was your meeting with Mr. Eastwood?

She was glued to the paper as word after word appeared, detailing his conversations with Joanna and Harrison, his adventure in the Archives room, the box left for him to find, and his interaction afterward with Agent Marsh. She was surprised to feel a frown on her face when he told her of his intention to attend the ball with this Marsh.

Are you sure that's wise? If she is the one behind all this?

Perhaps not wise, but sometimes the only way to get answers is to take a risk.

What she wanted to write was, "Please Len, it's hard enough

seeing you without magic, I could not bear to lose you entirely." What she did write was,

So long as you've enough sensible precautions in place behind the risk.

Was she imagining the cheerful tone behind the response of, *Of course I have! I've told you.*

She couldn't be too angry about that, though the amount of trust he placed in her was sometimes staggering. *What do you expect I can do if Agent Marsh tries to kill you? I am only an apprentice.*

Bosh, was his heartily rude response. *Do you still have your war souvenir?*

Shooting Agent Marsh would be one way to stop her, though Maia hesitated to do that. Only once had she shot a person in cold blood—not to kill, but to injure. That was bad enough. She didn't want to go through anything like that ever again.

On the other hand, should she witness the parasite attempt to kill Len, she might be angry enough to not even care.

I'll have to ask Helen to include a special pocket in my gown for it, she wrote dryly.

This time there was a brief pause before he replied.

My apologies, it finally came. *I was laughing too hard to write. In all seriousness, my friend, I have complete faith in your ability to perform whatever spells of protection or attack are necessary tomorrow evening. If we are lucky, nothing will be required.*

Do you really want to trust in luck? she asked.

Have faith, then. In you, in me, in Becket in any higher powers you might believe in, in the strength of goodness to prevail over evil. In justice.

"Trust in God and keep your powder dry," she quoted under her breath. Turning to more practical matters, she asked, *If*

Agent Marsh is the so-called parasite—which term I suppose I will keep using even if we prove her to be doing this for personal reasons, as "the villain" seems far too melodramatic—then why would she leave the box for you to find? And you didn't say exactly what you think her motivations are, only that they would *be personal, not professional, so to speak.*

She tapped the pen against the side of the desk and waited for his response.

My theory is that she needed to get back into the main room before anyone noticed she was gone, and didn't want to draw attention. Boxes aren't supposed to leave Archives; we are supposed to look at the files there and take notes. Once they leave Archives, they aren't protected anymore. So she left it there because she had no choice. And remember, she didn't even see me. She might have thought that since her curse missed, I had already left, or had not arrived yet.

And her motivation?

Again, there was a discernible pause before he responded. Maia didn't think it was due to laughter this time, though.

*I rejected her half a year ago. She suggested we partner in the Agency, and—*here some words had been scratched out before they had time to come through—*she also made it clear she was interested in a closer relationship personally. I was interested in neither.*

"I see," Maia said under her breath. *One rejection alone might be too dramatic for motive—no matter what the novelists say, few women will go to such extreme lengths out of wounded vanity—but the combination of the two could, I suppose, make her want to enact some sort of vengeance. I suppose I can see starting out thinking of a leech spell, evil directed solely at you, something to make you suffer but not kill you, and then little by little it got out of hand, and she got in over her head until the evil swallowed her up.*

As it has a tendency to do, was his grim reply. Neither wrote anything for a few moments. Then Maia wrote,

By the way, you never told me exactly how it was you saved Agent Driver's life.

Driver? Not that interesting a tale. He was hunting down a rogue magician, I happened to be nearby on a different mission, saw that the rogue had some friends and had gotten Driver in a trap, and neutralized them long enough to haul Driver out of there.

Maia suspected that was a far more exciting story than he made it sound, but she let it slide. *At least there's* one *agent working this case you can trust.*

True enough, Len wrote. Then he asked, *Will I see you tomorrow before the Ball?*

No, Maia reluctantly responded. *I have to renew the shield spell one final time—Aunt Amelia is supposed to return tomorrow—and then spend the rest of the day with Helen so she can set the glamour on my gown.*

I see, he wrote back. *Stay safe. I'll see you at the Ball. Good night.*

Good night, she wrote, and when nothing more appeared on her paper, pushed back her chair and rose to prepare for bed.

She didn't like any of this. It was all wrong. It felt wrong. Something was going to happen, something dreadful, and she didn't know how to stop it. She didn't even know what *it* was! She paced her small room in a fury, while at the same time unconsciously practicing the breathing and relaxation techniques Len had taught her for keeping her emotions and her magic separate. It worked: she did not blow anything to pieces.

She glanced over at her desk in her pacing and saw more words appearing. She dashed back only to find the note was not from Len.

Maia! Did you know those beasts at MI suspect Matthew of being the parasite? How dare they? Did you know? How could you keep this from me? Maia, you must tell them he is innocent. You do believe he is, don't you? You can't possibly think he's guilty! If you do, I'll never speak to you again! Matthew could never hurt anyone!

Since Helen's flow of indignation didn't seem like it was going to end any time soon, Maia decided to cut the eloquence short.

Helen! Of course I know Matthew is not the parasite. And so does Len, as he told his chief this very afternoon. Now calm down and tell me what's happened. Please.

Calm down? How can I calm down, when those idiots have accused my brother of such a vile—yes, well, thank you for saying that you and Len defended him. But he shouldn't need defending at all! One has only to look at Matthew to know what a gentle, innocent soul he is!

Maia bit down her impatience. *Helen. I cannot help unless I know what's happening.*

Oh, very well. After Matthew informed that odious Barry of our discovery—that the dead man at your aunt's was really Mr. Whegg, and that he was covered with a glamour and a misdirection spell and Barry and that Marsh agent were wrong about everything, stupid people (not that Matthew called them stupid, you understand: that's my choice of words), Barry showed up at Deep and ranted, simply ranted at Matthew in front of all his colleagues! Told him he had overstepped his bounds and behaved in an unprofessional manner, and that he, Barry, had already developed suspicions and that now he, Matthew, had proven those suspicions to be true, and that he was going to report this to his, Barry's, superiors and that they would no doubt arrest him, Matthew, as the parasite before dawn. Maia, what are we going to do?

"This is dreadful," Maia murmured. She scratched her nose with the end of the pen as she thought. *Stay calm,* she wrote at last, knowing it was probably a useless request, but needing to make it anyway. *Len has a new suspect, one far more probable than your brother. And I don't think his chief will allow Matthew to be arrested on such a flimsy pretext. You know what a bully that Barry is, I'm sure he just wanted to feel powerful by threatening Matthew. Matthew did try to consult with him beforehand and he wouldn't listen, so the blame, if there is any, lies with him.*

Very well, came the grudging response. *But if my brother is blamed for this ...*

He won't be, Maia wrote, pressing firmly with the pencil. *I will not allow Matthew to be a scapegoat.*

Good, Helen answered. *I suppose I will see you tomorrow for preparing your gown. Good night.*

Good night. See you tomorrow.

Tomorrow seemed both very far and all too near. Right now, Maia needed her bed. Perhaps sleep would clear away the cobwebs and allow her to see this case clearly.

* * *

Despite everything, Maia felt a thrill as she slipped into her gown for the final laying of the glamour before the Magicians' Ball. Elsie, accompanying her to the Radcliffe house as lady's maid for the evening, had done wonders with her hair, and her silver jewelry was laid out on the dressing table. She was powdered and perfumed: all that was left was the gown.

Helen had covered the glories of her own crimson and gold gown with a voluminous apron, looking incongruous contrasted with her carefully coiffed hair, the golden silk headband appearing almost part of her black curls, so artfully was it arranged. She paged through her sheaf of notes one final time.

"Helen, you've practiced this half a dozen times and you already laid the foundations," Maia said. "What do you have to be so nervous about?"

Helen raised her head to glare at her. "See if you're so calm when it's your turn to present a master's project to the world, which if it succeeds will break your mother's heart and if it fails will break yours."

Put like that, Maia could only bite her lip and school herself to stand still and wait patiently.

Her own mother had no idea that magic even existed. Maia still wasn't sure how that worked, how there could be families with one child a magic-user and the other not, the non-magical one growing up utterly ignorant of magic entirely. Especially if one or both parents were magicians, as her grandparents had been!

For the first time, Maia felt a pang of sympathy for her mother, left out of this one special gift that bound the rest of the Rawlings family so tightly together. It was no wonder she turned to drama and developed an unhealthy possessiveness of her own family's lives. Even the most insensitive soul would feel it, always being on the outside.

Still, her mother's ignorance of Maia's magic meant that Maia had no expectations on her shoulders. Her grandparents were dead, her father's family non-magical (so far as she knew); Aunt Amelia was her only living relative who shared her gift for magic. Maia's relationship with her aunt *as* an aunt was distant enough that she didn't particularly care what her aunt wanted of her magical career.

Nor did she think Aunt Amelia had specific hopes and goals for Maia, simply desiring her niece not "waste" her talent on someone like Lennox Davies. She had no real idea of the kind of burden Helen was under. Her friend, Maia realized now, was far braver than Maia had imagined.

Finally, Helen stepped back. "There," she said. "All I need to do is speak the final incantation over it before you enter the dance, and it will come to life."

Maia looked down. The dress, a sleeveless blue silk with a hem that went just past Maia's knees, looked as simple and unadorned as ever to her eyes, though she had watched Helen lay a dozen base spells on it: spells to anchor and secure the glamour, spells to make it move when Maia moved, spells to preserve it through the night, and the groundwork for the glamour itself, to be released when Helen said that final incantation.

"It will be perfect," she said. "I had no idea how much work goes into a glamour. I always thought of them merely as masks."

Helen sniffed. "Some, perhaps. Mine is different. To attach a glamour to a person is one thing, you can drape it over them like a cloak or, as you say, a mask. But to attach it to a piece of clothing and make it seem as part of the gown itself, to have it almost woven into the fabric, is another matter entirely. And that is what I hope to do more of, if this works tonight. I don't care about glamours for disguise; I want them to enhance what is already there."

She continued to chatter as she stripped off the apron and peered into the mirror to make sure her curls were in place, but Maia barely heard a word. Disguises … enhance what is there … what is there … or not there.

"Helen!" she said, cutting into Helen's sentence and causing her to jump.

"Goodness, Maia, what on earth—?"

Maia interrupted again. "Matthew said MI's curse experts left Mr. Whegg's body at the morgue, correct? And he said Agent Marsh claimed they had already examined the body, but none of them realized it wasn't a genuine curse. Isn't that what he said?"

"Goodness, I don't know, you don't think I ever listen to my brother, do you?"

But Maia wasn't listening again. She grabbed a blank piece of paper off Helen's desk and started scribbling down dates and times.

"Mr. Whegg was cursed in the morning … he came to Aunt Amelia's and died … the investigation started … and then Len was cursed. *Then.*" She straightened up. "Ha! I can prove Matthew is innocent. And what's more," she whirled to face her bewildered friend. "I think I know who the guilty person is."

"Who?" Helen gasped.

Maia shook her head. "I need to talk to Len first. What time is it? I must get to his flat before he leaves for the Ball!"

Helen grabbed her arm. "Don't be absurd. There is no time! Likely he's already left to pick up Agent Marsh. If you try to hunt him down, we'll be late."

Maia shook her off. "Helen, I don't care if I'm late to the Ball. Don't you understand? This is life and death!"

"And that's my master project!" Helen cried, gesturing to Maia's dress.

That got through. Maia paused for a moment, breathing

heavily. "Very well," she conceded reluctantly. "I will talk to Len at the Ball."

They'd waited this long, another hour wouldn't matter.

"Ladies!" Mrs. Radcliffe called up the stairs to them. "Aren't you ready yet? Helen, your father and brothers are waiting. At this rate, we will miss our table!"

"Coming, Mother!" Helen called. Mr. Radcliffe had made reservations for all of them, Maia included, at the Ritz for dinner before the Ball. It was one of the few times Maia had ever dined there, and under any other circumstances she would have been thrilled. As it was, she had to strain every nerve to keep a smile on her face and answer ordinary, pleasant questions and conversation from the Radcliffe family. Helen kept eyeing Maia's dress and muttering under her breath. Matthew jumped every time someone spoke to him. All in all, it was not the most successful of dinners, and more than Maia breathed a sigh of relief when they left.

"I don't know what's got into everyone lately," Mrs. Radcliffe said as they drove to the Ball. "Matthew's abstraction I can understand, though I do wish he would leave his work *at* work and make an effort while at home, or with his family. But the rest of you—! It must be excitement over the Ball," she decided, settling back with an indulgent smile. "I remember how nerve-racking and thrilling it was for me the first few years. Why, I believe that's where your father and I met, in fact, and it was while dancing the waltz that we fell in love."

She sighed happily.

Maia had first met Len at a dance, though an ordinary, non-magical one, hosted by her friends Julia and Dan Foy at their country house. It was that dance that led her into the world of magic, murder, and mystery, though she and Len had not fallen in love at it. To the best of her recollection, they had merely tolerated each other at first. She had been irritated at the secrets he was so clearly hiding from her. He, she was fairly certain, had suspected her of being cut from the same cloth as Aunt Amelia—arrogant and careless of other people's live.

They were both wrong, and their friendship was all the stronger for the difficulties they'd overcome. But they certainly weren't in love.

At last, the auto pulled up before the long, low building with lights blazing out of every window and strains of music reaching their ears even above the noise of countless magicians arriving all around them. They disembarked, and with a bit of judicious maneuvering, Helen managed to lose her parents in the crowd of people entering.

"To the powder room?"

It was full of ladies at first, all laughing, chattering, and comparing gowns and gossip. Before long, the sound of music coming from the main ballroom changed from tuning to tunes, and the ladies cleared out, leaving Maia and Helen alone.

"Ready?" Maia asked her friend, who looked utterly wretched now the time had come.

Helen didn't wring her hands, nothing so weak-livered as that, but she did bite her lip. "I don't know."

"I have faith in you," Maia told her. "I have never seen someone put so much effort and attention to detail into a spell. You have been an inspiration to me this week. You may not think you are ready, but I know you are."

At that, Helen raised her chin and smiled. "Yes," she said. "I believe I am. Hold still. *Efficiantur incantationes has movere se.*"

Maia's dress sprang to life. Starting at the shoulder seams, silver threads unraveled and crawled down to the dropped waist and thence to the flounced hem, leaving glowing starbursts and constellations in their path. By the time they finished, Maia's entire dress appeared to have been dipped in stardust, the stars gleaming even under the harsh light of the powder room. The dress shimmered as Maia moved, swishing her skirts and staring in awe at the living light in which she was clothed. She had seen the practice versions and the design sketched on paper, but the end result was magnificent beyond anything she could have imagined.

"Oh ..." she breathed.

Helen stood back and smiled, a mix between tremulous and proud. "That's the reaction I wanted."

They had spent a considerable amount of time settling on the design. Silver to represent Maia's magic, which when set against the deep blue of the gown led naturally to a night sky design. Maia hadn't objected—it reminded her of the first spell she'd ever performed, a *lux* spell with Len's guidance as they practiced deep in the woods late at night. When Helen first heard of that event, she'd wanted to recreate a woodland scene, with vines and leaves as well as trees, birds, and deer. Maia didn't feel that such a rustic scene represented her well—while she appreciated nature, she wasn't particularly devoted to it. Helen agreed and settled on the stars and planets, deciding that was symbolic of the *lux* spell, and better suited to Maia's nature.

The glamour was crafted so carefully as to look woven into the fabric of the gown, the countless spells laid by Helen doing their part of seamlessly blending glamour and gown. It was the most breathtaking thing Maia had ever seen, much less worn.

"All right," Helen said, swallowing. "This is it. Are you ready?"

"Lead on," Maia said.

They left the powder room, walked through the abandoned hallways, and entered the crowded ballroom together.

Maia felt rather like Cinderella. A collective "ohhh," echoed through the room as people turned as one to see them coming. Panic seized Maia with all those eyes on her, and she understood why Cinderella had fled so precipitously, even without the fairy godmother's warning about midnight. She reminded herself that they were looking at Helen's work, not her, and walked slowly into the room to give everyone a chance to see. Helen trailed behind, practically radiating delight.

"My dear!" fluted a tall, elderly woman, bustling out of the stunned crowd to halt Maia's progress. "What a stunning piece of magic! Who created that dress?"

This was the moment. Maia let her voice ring over the entire hushed room. "Miss Helen Radcliffe did, ma'am."

The elderly lady brought her lorgnette up to study the design more carefully. "Remarkable," she said. "Truly remarkable. Miss Radcliffe, am I to understand this is your master project?"

Helen drew a deep breath. "Yes, ma'am."

"Excellent. Come with me, my dear. Miss … sorry, what was your name?"

"Maia Whitney, ma'am."

"Ah yes, Amelia's girl. Miss Whitney, we'll need you later, but for now, enjoy yourself while I question Miss Radcliffe about the design of these spells." She whisked a dazed Helen off, leaving Maia suddenly alone and at loose ends.

She wandered the floor a bit, losing herself in the crowd as the musicians began playing again and the dancing started up once more. She greeted people who were enthralled by her dress and allowed them to examine the work for themselves. Across the room, she saw Mrs. Radcliffe's face and hastily decided to walk in a different direction, wondering if she ought to find a different ride home as well. All the while, she searched for Len and his escort, that Marsh woman. Now that her part in Helen's reveal was done, it was time to focus on her other job: stopping the parasite and seeing justice done.

* * *

She didn't find Len, but she did see Becket standing near the windows, and so she made her way through the crowd to greet him.

"Good evening, Miss Whitney," he said, bowing. Dressed in evening clothes, he looked every inch a proper gentleman. Maia remembered for the first time that he was a magician in his own right, not merely Len's valet and assistant, and was distracted from her mission by wondering how many of those here were servants in everyday life. Despite the hidden prejudices still existing in this world, it was heartening to know that some differences were blotted out by magic, if not all. The servants would go back to serving tomorrow, but for tonight, they were all here on equal footing.

Outside the magical community, someone with Helen's skin coloring would not be afforded the respect she deserved. No one would glance at her artistry and work, or if they did it would be as an oddity, not out of recognition of her abilities and ambition. A girl like Gwen Zhang would be hard pressed to be awarded a degree from Cambridge were she not attending the magical school there. Becket would never be able to ask a gentleman's daughter to dance under ordinary circumstances.

It wasn't right. Yet more injustices Maia couldn't fix. She was sure there were countless more, knew that she herself had prejudices so deeply ingrained she didn't realize they existed. She couldn't change the world, but she could do her part to see to it that the voiceless had a voice, that there was justice to be found for all, even and especially the ones usually denied it.

At that moment, with blinding clarity, she knew what she wanted to do with her magic. Aunt Amelia would be furious, but Maia didn't care. This, *this* was her calling, the reason she'd been given her magic, and she would follow it to whatever end, no matter how many obstacles were put in her path.

She blinked, realizing she'd never answered Becket's courteous greeting, standing there like a half-wit while all these thoughts swirled through her head. "Good evening, Becket," she finally said. "You look quite dashing."

"Thank you," he said. "May I say how lovely your gown is? Miss Radcliffe's efforts have certainly paid off."

"Yes indeed, they have. Becket, I believe I have pieced together some more clues, and I have a theory as to the parasite's identity. Where is Len? I'd like to tell both of you at once."

Becket set his champagne flute down, face full of concern and curiosity. "I've not seen him since arriving. I helped him prepare for the evening, of course, and he went to pick up Ag—Miss Marsh. I finished my own preparations and came here, expecting to see them, but so far I have not."

"Oh dear," Maia said.

"I expect, if he is here, he will find us soon enough. Your frock has drawn the attention of all, and continues to do so."

"A beacon in the night," Maia murmured whimsically.

"Quite so."

They were silent for a few more moments. Then—

"Oh, this is ridiculous," Maia burst out. "I will just tell you my deductions and then you can give me your thoughts on the matter, and if Len hasn't arrived by then, we will figure out what to do ourselves."

Becket's face remained sober, but Maia thought she saw amusement flicker in his eyes. "Very good, miss."

"I think the parasite is—"

Before she could finish, quite in the dramatic fashion required by this entire case, beginning with a mysterious man dropping dead on Aunt Amelia's doorstep, a loud commotion broke out in the foyer, spilling into the ballroom itself. The musicians came to a stop as everyone turned to stare at the doors once again. This time there was no grand entrance by a young lady in a stunning frock. No, this time two men struggled into the room, one attempting to pull away from the other, who continued to twist his arms into painful positions behind his back while dragging him along. Maia recognized the first man as Matthew Radcliffe, and when his opponent turned his head, she saw him for Jasper Driver.

"I have captured the parasite!" Driver proclaimed.

A few women screamed. Mrs. Radcliffe found herself standing alone as her companions drew away from her. Maia's blood coursed through her veins with sudden fury. Magic sparked at her fingertips, matching the silver glow of her gown.

"Go to her, Becket," she hissed. "Don't let her stand alone."

"But Mr. Radcliffe—"

"I'll help Matthew. Go!"

Without another word, Becket slipped through the stunned

crowd to offer his arm and silent support to Mrs. Radcliffe, just as Mr. Radcliffe reached her from the other side. Maia forgot about looking for Len as she pushed toward the front of the rows of standing, silent magicians.

"Driver, what on earth …?" said a portly man, bursting through the ranks.

"Sorry to do this so publicly, sir, but he was beginning another leech spell," Driver panted, as Matthew redoubled his efforts to escape. "I had to stop him."

"I did no such thing," Matthew sputtered. "You've lost your mind, Driver."

"Sir, you can see the stolen magic leaking from him," Driver protested, sorrow and goodwill practically radiating from his round, reddened face. "Examine him yourself, right now!"

Not only the portly man, but all those nearby murmured the spell to reveal traces of recent magic.

"It is a leech spell!" cried one woman, fainting into her companion's arms.

"That evil magic is dripping everywhere!" said another older man, shuddering and drawing away. "We must leave at once!"

Matthew stopped struggling, his jaw dropping. "But I—I didn't—I'm not—I don't understand."

But Maia did. Not Matthew, not at all. A setup, another misdirection spell and glamour cast over him to make it appear he was the parasite, just as had been done to poor Mr. Whegg. And because she was perhaps the only person who could see the aura of Len's magic, she knew, by the bronze color shimmering about Matthew's person, that the same person who had cast the spell on him was the one who had leeched Len's magic away in the first place.

How badly had Driver resented Len stepping in that day

with the rogue magician, saving Driver's life and in the process making the other man appear weak and Len a hero? Very much, it seemed, for him to go to such steps to discredit Len and gain stature for himself. To not only steal Len's magic, but to create a false parasite so he could be a hero, solving the case and saving the day, no matter who else he hurt along the way.

But he hadn't counted on this case being connected with the death of Jane Ransom, an insignificant hedgewitch. He hadn't counted on Helen's ability to create and take apart glamours. He hadn't counted on Matthew's trust in his sister. He hadn't counted on them investigating the bookshop before he could eliminate the clues. He hadn't counted on Len's investigative abilities being only sharpened by the loss of his magic.

He hadn't counted on Maia.

She channeled her rage into her magic, funneling it into a precise point. She took what she'd learned of glamours from Helen and her ability to see Len's stolen magic, and without bothering to use an incantation she dispelled the glamour, freeing Matthew and knocking Driver back a step.

"Matthew Radcliffe is not the parasite," she said, her voice once again carrying across the entire stunned room. "You, Jasper Driver, are."

There was a brief moment while everyone renewed their seeing spells to take in what had just happened. That moment was all Driver needed. He pushed Matthew aside, backed up even further into a clear space, and pulled out a gun—the same one, most likely, that he had used to shoot Jane Ransom.

"Everyone stay back!" he cried in a shrill voice. "I have a shield spell to protect me from any of your spells, and I'll shoot anyone who tries to come near me."

Maia squinted, saw the shield spell, and coldly dispelled that as well. Driver spun to see the source of the magic disrupting his. His eyes landed on Maia, standing apart from everyone else, distinctive in her midnight gown with the silver stars blazing across it. His face darkened, and he raised the gun to point at her.

Which was when Lennox Davies crashed through the windows and landed on Driver, bringing him down to the floor and knocking the gun out of his hand.

12

All is Well …

en saw Driver's face, startled and suddenly afraid, and then saw nothing else.

When he came to himself again, Driver was unconscious and Len's hands were around his throat.

"You got him, son," came Harrison's voice in his ear. He felt Maia's hand rest on his back.

"Len," she said. "Len, it's over. It's done."

He stood up, shaking all over. "Are you safe?" he asked Maia, ignoring the blood on his face and hands from his impetuous crash through the windows, and the bruises beginning to form from what must been Driver's ineffective attempt at defense.

"Yes," she said, holding his eyes with her own. "Yes, quite safe. Thank you."

Len breathed again, and felt the last of the tension leave his body. Maia must have felt it too, for she broke eye contact and stepped back a pace. She looked down at the inert body lying at their feet.

"He doesn't have any of your magic left. He must have used the last of it in his shield spell. Wastrel!"

Len felt sick at the idea of that scoundrel using his magic—his!—to hurt other people. He trusted Maia: if she said it was gone, then it was. At least if he couldn't have it any longer, neither could Driver.

"Could someone please explain what is going on here?" demanded one of the more important Council members clustered around.

Matthew Radcliffe stood up and straightened his evening jacket, tugging at his bow tie. "I'd rather like to know that myself. Since this is my case, and since he accused me in front of everyone."

Len stepped away from the body. "First, Harrison, I think you'd better take care of … this." He nudged Driver with his toe. "Before he comes to and I have to hit him again."

"I … don't think there's much danger of that," Harrison said. Nevertheless, he looked around for minions.

Agent Marsh stepped forward, sleekly elegant in a black frock that paled beside Maia's glory.

"I'll take him, sir," she said. "Barry!" Agent Barry also appeared out of the crowd, his face white with fury, though whether at missing the fact that his subordinate had been the villain all along or at Marsh's preemptive order, Len wasn't sure. Either way, this was not going to look good for Barry on the official report.

The two grabbed Driver, one under each arm, and began hauling him away. Marsh paused long enough to make eye contact with Len. He nodded; after a moment, she dipped her chin fractionally in return. Then they were gone.

He would never understand women.

Harrison whispered to the older Council member, who then stood forward to make an announcement.

"Friends, I know that what you just saw here was shocking and probably a little frightening!"

"Probably?" whispered Maia.

"A little?" added Helen, who by now had joined them, Becket by her side.

"But rest assured, the matter is contained! You may have heard rumors of a parasite roaming the streets of London, but they were just that: rumors. Thanks to Matthew Radcliffe's willingness to take a false accusation in order to bring about justice, and the actions of our other fine magicians here, the culprit has been apprehended, and nobody has been hurt. Once the window has been repaired—someone get on that, please—we can continue our Ball, safe and secure in the knowledge that once again, the brave men and women committed to protecting us have done their duty nobly."

He stepped back. "Now," he said in an ordinary tone. "Someone explain to me all that nonsense I just babbled."

Len waved at Maia, who shook her head. "Oh no," she said. "First I want to hear how you appeared so perfectly on the scene."

"Very well," he said. "Should we move into one of the card rooms?"

They accordingly moved—Harrison, Matthew and Helen, the Council member, Maia, Becket, and Len. At the Council-man's wave, they seated themselves around the table, and Len began.

"Half a year ago, I thought I rescued Jasper Driver from a mission gone wrong. As I recently found out, he had planned the entire thing. He had arranged to meet with the rogue magician he was supposed to capture, as well as that magician's contacts—every person connected with that magician whose name we have in our Archives—and learn their methods of easy power. Far from rescuing him, I ruined his plan and humiliated him. I believe he began plotting my downfall then and there. It never occurred to me that harmless, inoffensive, plodding Agent Driver was seething with rage and thwarted ambition all along. My mistake." He looked down at his bleeding hands, tiny cuts he once upon a time would have been able to heal with a single Latin word, and continued.

"From what Miss Whitney, Mr. Becket, Miss Radcliffe, Mr. Radcliffe, and I have all been able to piece together—Agent Marsh assisted with that as well, earlier—he came across a book for leech spells at Mr. Whegg's shop and that set this entire plan into motion. He had learned of the existence of Jane Ransom last year, thanks to a casual word dropped by Agent Marsh about a hedgewitch who channeled her power into potions and therefore avoided losing control. Amy—Agent Marsh even remembers commenting that she specialized in glamour potions which were on par with or better than a trained magician's. So Driver set the stage. He visited Miss Ransom first and stole the two glamour potions, killing her to prevent her ever telling anyone of his visit, and setting up a spell to delay the discovery of her body. Then he went back to the bookshop, took the book and cursed Whegg, casting one of the glamour potions on him for another delay, this time in identification. He was just smart enough to know that a single leech spell against me would arouse suspicion and focus attention on my acquaintances, whereas if he made it look like a parasite had arisen, it would distract from me and give him a chance to play a hero's role. I'm not sure when he settled on Radcliffe as his scapegoat—"

"Before we removed the glamour from Mr. Whegg, I think,

but after we found Jane Ransom and he met us leaving the bookshop," Maia interrupted. "I believe he never intended that leech spell to work on Matthew; he wanted it to look like Matthew had falsified the attack. After we discovered Mr. Whegg's identity, he knew we were getting close. Also—and this took me until today to realize—Matthew was asking questions about the supposed curse on Mr. Whegg's body. Driver never brought the experts to the morgue. He left Aunt Amelia's house to go cast the leech spell at Len, and only got to the morgue in time to meet the other agents and report that the curse team had already examined the body. Nobody questioned it until Matthew found out the curse wasn't a curse at all. After that, it was only a matter of time before somebody realized that Intelligence-trained curse experts ought to have discovered that immediately and found out Driver had never fetched them at all. So he had to cast the blame on Matthew instead."

Matthew put his head in his hands. "Some investigator I proved to be," he said, his voice muffled. "I never even made that connection."

"What an odious, wretched, *abominable* man!" Helen cried, eyes flashing indignantly.

"Quite so," Harrison said.

Len took up the tale again. "When I came to HQ to ask for permission to look through the Archives for information on Jane Ransom, that was bad timing for Driver. He knew you had assigned me to that case—"

"I didn't make any secret of it," Harrison admitted. "When Barry refused to look into it, I told him in front of the other two that I was giving it to you. Thought it would spur him on to making a greater effort. I felt that Barry was leaving too much to the other agents on his team, considering himself above doing the work himself."

"Which he was, and which Driver took advantage of," Len said. "He slipped down to Archives and pulled Jane Ransom's box as soon as he saw me come to HQ. He didn't know for certain I was there for that, but in the manner of all guilty people, he assumed I was on to him. He hid himself with a chameleon spell, blast his eyes, waited for me to show up and then tried to curse me, only to have it rebound on him. When he escaped, he left the box behind hoping it would make me suspicious of Agent Marsh."

Maia drew in a deep breath. "That explains it!" she said.

Len nodded. "It worked, too, at least at first. But then I had Becket look into dates and times, and Marsh had an alibi for every single one of the events—Miss Ransom's murder, Whegg's attack, even the leech spell on me. She had met with some contacts to ask them to keep their ears open for a sociopathic magician, and they vouched for her. So I knew she had to have been set up."

He'd almost been convinced it *was* Harrison and Jo at that point. Who else could have framed Amy so neatly? It was only in talking to her over dinner that very evening, and hearing her reports of Driver's activities and mysterious absences, and hearing that Driver was the one who had started reluctantly murmuring suspicions to Barry of Matthew, that the truth had blazoned itself across Len's mind.

He had leapt from his chair, leaving Amy still seated, and bolted from the restaurant without a word of explanation. One thought consumed him: *Maia was in danger*.

He ran the entire way from the restaurant to the Ball, and was almost at the building when he saw a narrow beam of silver light, so potent it seared across his vision even through the walls, slice through the night. He'd recognized it at once as Maia's magic, and it turned his run into a sprint. He'd made it onto the ground and was heading for the door when he saw her cast a second, similarly powerful and controlled spell. Through a window, he saw her standing apart from everyone else in her blazing dress, surrounded by a nimbus of silver magic. He saw Driver turn the gun on her.

He'd abandoned all thought of the door and went straight for Driver's throat, careless of the window and people between. He hadn't spared one more thought for Amy Marsh until she appeared to drag Driver away.

Someday he'd have to apologize to her, as well as to Harrison and Jo, for his unfounded suspicions. But not tonight.

"And so I came here to confront Driver, only to find Maia had done it for me," he summed up.

"And how did you know Driver was a fraud and Radcliffe innocent, Miss Whitney?" the Councilman asked her.

Len found himself hoping she wouldn't mention her ability to see his magic even after Driver had taken it. That was … rather too personal to be shared with all these people.

He needn't have worried. Maia was too private for that.

"I knew Matthew was innocent, and something about the evidence pointing to Agent Marsh didn't seem right. Looking at who might hold a grudge against Len and want to get rid of Agent Marsh and Matthew at the same time, at first Agent Barry seemed the only logical choice. But he was at my aunt's for the entire morning, bullying the servants and throwing his weight around. He simply couldn't have gotten to the club to cast the spell at Len. Then I remembered that Agent Driver had left before anyone else to bring the curse experts to the morgue, and I remembered Matthew's comment of how odd it was they hadn't discovered the truth. After that, all the other suspects seemed so many red herrings. Agent Marsh was on the case with Driver, sharp-witted and ambitious. She was both a danger to him as regarded discovering the truth, and as a potential rival in the agency. As for Matthew, we've already covered that. I had hoped to see Len before making any public accusations, but when Driver made his accusation against Matthew, I was left with no choice. I knew I had to expose him publicly in order to clear Matthew's name."

"And a neat bit of spellwork it was," said Harrison. "I will be passing that along to your aunt."

Maia blinked. "Thank you."

Len was prouder of her for that than almost anything else in this entire case. She had finally mastered her magic, instead of letting it master her when her emotions were roused. He had no idea what Miss Rawlings would make of it, but if she'd been his apprentice, he would have elevated her to journeyman status for that. It was a tremendous step for anyone, to learn that kind of control under that kind of pressure, but even more so for Maia, who had *such* power.

"And I helped," Helen said. She leaned back in her chair, looking smug.

Harrison coughed into his hand. "Well, that does seem to straighten it all out. Councilman, any other questions?"

"I do not believe so at this time," said the Councilman. "An abominable man. You've all done a fine bit of work in clearing it up. Most commendable. My thanks, and the thanks of all England's magicians. Eastwood, I trust you will take care of this Driver properly?"

"Oh yes," said Harrison. Len knew that face, and that voice.

If he'd had any room in his heart for pitying Driver, he would have felt it then. As it was, he merely felt a deep sense of satisfaction.

"Then that takes care of it! Everything solved, nothing more to worry about." The Councilman placed his hands on the table and pushed himself to his feet.

"Except for Mr. Whegg, Miss Ransom, and Len's loss of magic," Maia said.

"What's that? Er … yes. Quite right. Terribly sorry about your magic, Davies. Maybe the healers will be able to help, what? Er … I'm sure something will turn up. And the main thing is, you caught the chap. Yes. Well done. Back to the party, everyone! Now we've really something to celebrate!"

He left the room, not noticing Maia seething in her chair. "He didn't even care about the deaths," she said in a low, fierce voice.

Len pushed a hand through his hair, wincing as bits of glass tinkled to the floor. "Yes, well … the one is a hedgewitch, the other a lonely, obscure bookseller. Why should a big, important Council member care about them?"

"But you care," Maia said, turning to him with a smile. "You care about the ordinary people. The ones nobody else notices."

Len didn't quite know how to respond to that. Becket, as usual, saved him.

"Sir … you're still bleeding."

Len looked at his hands. "Oh! Dashed if you aren't right, Becket. Excuse me, all. I'd best go get cleaned up."

"Len, you will stay for the rest of the Ball, won't you?" asked Helen. "Don't worry about the state of your clothes. I can glamour them to look normal, no trouble. After Maia's gown, it would be easy."

He gave his full attention to Helen's creation for the first time. It was stunning, but to his mind not half so stunning as the woman who wore it.

"Besides," Helen added. "If you stay, you can dance with me."

He smiled. "How can I resist such a generous offer as that?"

* * *

After Becket got him cleaned and patched up as best as possible, Len submitted to a hasty glamour by Helen, and joined the Ball. Not many of his fellow magicians outside the agency knew of his loss yet, and all had seen his spectacular capture of Driver, so he had to endure an uncomfortable amount of praise. Even if his magic loss hadn't ended his Intelligence career, he ruminated, this display would have. A secret agent who was no longer secret was not much use.

He was surprised to find the thought didn't hurt as much as he thought it would—certainly not as much as being magicless. From what Harrison had said, Len had been on his way out from active field work as it was. And he *had* been feeling restless for quite some time, he could see that now.

The problem was, he didn't have one dashed clue as to what to do with his life.

He didn't have to decide tonight. Tonight was for celebration.

He got in his dance with Helen, who was in fine form between her sartorial success and her brother's vindication. Nothing official could be decided tonight, but it appeared as though Maia's dress would gain Helen her status as master magician in the field of fashion glamour—the first ever to successfully blend the two. Len was pleased; if anyone deserved to be rewarded for her efforts and perseverance, it was Helen. She had become a good friend through all of this, and he was glad of it.

After Helen, Len was finally able to dance with Maia, even if it didn't match his romantic dreams. She spent their first dance scolding him for endangering himself by coming to her rescue like that, and their second talking excitedly about the new control over her magic he had helped her develop.

By their third dance, Len lost patience, and whisked her outside to walk on the verandah with him.

"Remember our first meeting, at a dance like this?" he asked, awash in memories the cool evening brought to him.

"Not that we ever danced," she said with a reminiscent smile. "I had gone outside because I was angry at the world, and you followed and spun me a tale to distract me from following you as you attempted to sneak after your suspect."

Len couldn't help but laugh. His memories were more romantic, but Maia's were probably more scrupulously accurate. There was still no place for romance in her view of their relationship.

Friendship, though: that always had a place, and was just as important in its own way.

"Not that my best attempts worked," he said. "You've always been able to see right through me."

She turned her head to look at him. "I suppose I have. And you can see me as I am, too."

"And yet somehow neither of us has left yet," he said lightly, teasing.

"That is not something I think either of us ever have to worry about," she said, smiling at him, her expression visible in the starry glow from her gown.

He didn't remember reaching for her hands, but somehow they were tucked securely within his own, and he was looking down at her face with a smile of his own. "No indeed."

He might not have his magic anymore, but he had Maia. That went a long way. She couldn't replace his magic, nothing could, but he wouldn't lose her because he was no longer a magician. She would stay by his side no matter what, just as he would should anything bad ever happen to her. No matter what, they still made a good team. And they always would.

"I do like this gown," he said, turning the conversation to lighter matters, mostly to distract himself from wanting to tuck that wayward tendril of hair back behind her ear. "It reminds me of your first spell."

"You can see the glamour?" she said.

"It hasn't faded yet," he responded. For once, the thought brought no pain. If the last bit of magic he saw was Helen's work on Maia's gown, it was a worthy ending.

"And you can still see my magic?"

"Always." That was a vow he ought not to make since he had no way of knowing if he could keep it, but he couldn't help himself.

"Hm."

"What's that supposed to mean?" he asked, mildly alarmed.

She released his hands and tucked one of hers in the crook of his arm. "I'm not sure yet. Something that's been teasing at the back of my mind. We can talk about it tomorrow, after I've had a chance to think some more. Come, let's return inside. They have the food buffets set up—all that work earlier has made me dreadfully hungry."

Len let it go—for now—and walked back inside with her.

He would have walked to the ends of the earth with her, had

she asked.

He was happy to still be able to do so.

* * *

Len didn't see Maia the next day after all, nor the next. He heard that Amelia Rawlings had returned, and decided that the formidable Miss Rawlings was so furious over her apprentice's participation in tracking down Driver that she had forbidden Maia from ever seeing him again. Resigned, he started packing for Scotland. It would be good to see Pippa and Cam again before the baby came, good to have a chance to be with people who knew nothing about his magic or loss thereof. So far as his sister and brother-in-law were concerned, Len was a gentleman of means who sometimes amused himself by discreetly helping the government settle potential unpleasantness. It was never spoken of openly, and as it did not affect the family, was mostly ignored.

The day before he was due to leave, Becket entered his study with a surprisingly open smile on his face.

"Miss Whitney is here to see you, sir."

Len sprang to his feet. "Maia! Splendid. I'll have a chance to say goodbye. You've put her in the sitting room, of course? Excellent. Be a good chap and make us some tea, will you? Do we have any of those lemon biscuits she likes?"

Becket vanished in the direction of the kitchen and Len entered the sitting room. Maia sat in the upright, uncomfortable chair (he really needed to get rid of that thing and replace it with another armchair), ankles crossed, lips compressed, eyes bright. In the midst of Len's delight at seeing her, it occurred to him that she didn't seem as happy to be here as he would have hoped.

Nervous now, he dropped into his own seat. "Dashed good to see you, old thing," he burbled. "Caught me before I left. How are you? Miss Rawlings not too angry, I hope?"

Maia shook her head and a small smile played across her lips. "Aunt Amelia apparently began a 'friendship,' so she calls it, with a French magician while she was over there, and returned home more amiable than I've ever seen her."

Len burst into laughter. So much for all Miss Rawlings' prejudices and pride! "So she was not upset by your actions helping MI?"

Maia rested her hands in her lap. "Quite the opposite, in fact. Aunt Amelia examined me after hearing from your Harrison Eastwood and the other Council member about my magic use. She determined that I had finally obtained sufficient control to attempt the testing marking the end of my apprenticeship."

Len leaned forward. "And?"

Maia looked down at her folded hands. "And … I passed. I'm a journeyman now."

"By all that's wonderful! Maia, that's tremendous!" He leapt to his feet. "We must celebrate. Dinner? Becket, have you heard? Maia is a journeyman!"

Becket hurried in with the tea tray. "Allow me to offer my congratulations, Miss Whitney," he said, beaming at her.

Maia waved at them, unusually flustered. "Thank you. That's not actually why I am here."

Len sat back down. "Oh."

Becket coughed discreetly and started to back out of the room.

"No, stay please, Becket," Maia said, stopping him. "I want you to hear this too." She squeezed her hands together one last time and finally met Len's eyes.

"Lennox, I think you can get your magic back."

The air rushed from Len's lungs in one explosive "whoosh." He stared at her, helpless, until she spoke again.

"I never believed it as hopeless as you did, you know that. Even though the healers said it was impossible, there hadn't been a leech spell in England in a thousand years, how could they know? And after what you told me about the different ways of using and controlling magic, well, I believed even more strongly that there had to be a way.

"It seemed strange to me that even though you had lost all your ability to perform magic, you could still sense it. You could still see glamours, and residues of other spells, and you always could see when I was using magic. You told me the healer said it was left over from the removal of your magic and would fade over time, but that didn't make sense to me. You and Aunt Amelia had both described magic to me as an extra sense. I started to wonder how it was even possible for that sense to be removed. One loses a sense by damaging something physical, generally: you lose your sight because of hurt caused to your eyes or your brain, for example. But if magic is not tied to anything physical, how could it be removed entirely?

"It seemed to me that instead, it was as though the leech spell had sucked you dry, as though draining a pond. But you showed me that magic is not a stagnant pond; it is a river. A river can be drained, I suppose, given enough force all at once, but it will always refill. I speculated that it might be so with magic, that yours might start to trickle back in time."

Len couldn't think. He couldn't speak. He could only stare.

"The only difficulty with my theory was that it was too

simple, I thought. Surely, if that were the case, others would have learned it by now. So I spoke of it to Aunt Amelia. Imagine my surprise when she didn't pooh-pooh it out of hand! She thought that if it were the case, magic would return so slowly to people, and their assumption would be so firmly fixed that it was gone, that by the time it came back they had lost the ability to use it. As muscle atrophies from disuse, so with the practice of magic. And I remembered, too, that your way of thinking about magic was not practiced by most in England, and so the comparison might not occur to others. I've researched everything I can think of—I didn't want to offer you false hope—but I am here now because I truly believe you can regain use of your magic. Perhaps it will never be as strong as it once was, but I think you can at least get it partially back."

She peered closely at him. "Len?"

He said nothing.

"Len?" She started to sound worried. "Becket?"

Becket came closer and gave his shoulder a shake. "Shall I administer smelling salts, sir?"

At that, Len shook himself out of his daze. "No! Dammit, Becket, I am not a fainting Victorian maiden—apologies Maia—wait a moment—Maia, *what*?"

She patiently repeated everything she had said. It took two more repetitions before it finally sank in.

His magic wasn't gone forever?

His magic wasn't gone forever.

His *magic* wasn't *gone* forever.

"Oh dear," said Maia. "I think we've lost him again."

13

… That Ends Well

After Len finally came to his senses, they went to his workroom to perform a few tests. Maia still wasn't sure how this would work, or if it would at all. She wondered if she was a fool for attempting it, but she knew she couldn't go through the rest of her life knowing there might have been a chance and she had missed it out of fear.

First, Maia cast a few spells for Len to see and identify, which he did with no difficulty. Then Becket did the same. Len had to work harder at identifying those, but in the end he could.

As last, Maia told Len to try the simplest spell he knew.

"I can't," he said, surprising all of them. "What if you're wrong? What if my ability to see magic *is* a fluke, a leftover? I can't do it."

Maia braced herself. No time for her vapors now; Len needed her to be strong for the both of them, until he could carry himself again. "You certainly won't be able to do it if you refuse to try. Lennox, are you going to waste all my research?"

She watched him steel himself. No, Len Davies would never let somebody else's effort be in vain. He cared too much for other people, valued them and their time too much.

He closed his eyes, perhaps afraid of what she might see, and said, "All right. I'll try."

Her heart squeezed as she watched him steady himself. "Talk us through what you are doing," she whispered.

The narration came as easily to his lips as it had in Whegg's shop that day. "That well of *extra* is still empty," he said. "I can't feel—wait. There is something. Not a full sense. Not enough to let me twitch those invisible threads in the fabric of nature. It's more like a, a, a ghost of a sense. There, at my core. There is *something*."

"Try a spell," Maia breathed, afraid to break his concentration. Oh, let it work!

"*Lux fiat*," he said, his voice flat.

Nothing. He could tell without even opening his eyes, she saw it by the slump in his shoulders.

"Don't give up," Maia said, keeping the tears back out of her voice by sheer stubbornness. "Try again. Please, Len."

She could tell by his stance that he didn't think there was any point. But he did try, for her. And tried, and tried.

"It's no good," he said at last. "I can almost sense the magic, almost gather it, but it slips through my fingers every time."

"Here," she said, making up her mind in a moment. She stepped right up to him and wrapped her hands around his larger ones. Aunt Amelia wouldn't approve, but Maia was no longer her apprentice.

She was her own woman, at long last, and hang disapproval anyway.

Before he knew what she was going to do, she closed her eyes and expanded a tendril of her own magic. No spell, no violence, just her voluntarily feeding him some of her own magic. Shared, not stolen.

"Maia—no—it isn't safe!" he said, trying to pull away.

"Just use it, Len," she said. "For now."

He knew her well enough to know when she wouldn't quit. He groaned a little, and she felt him retreat into his own core.

It was the oddest sensation, feeling her magic being used but not using it herself. It was almost too intimate an experience. Maia shut down that train of thought and concentrated.

It would have been the easiest thing for Len to use her magic to gather threads of light out of the air and form them into a ball. He refused to squander her gift that way—that wasn't Len.

Instead, he used her magic to reach out and coax his to the surface. —There! Maia could almost see it herself behind her closed eyelids. A faint bronze shimmer, floating up to meet and mingle with her own silvery glow.

"*Lux fiat,*" he said one last time.

A strangled noise from Becket tore both their eyes open.

Hanging in the air before Len's nose was the tiniest, faintest hint of coppery light, woven through with strands of silver.

Now came the trickiest part of all. While Len held the spell balanced within his will, Maia slowly and carefully withdrew her magic, reeling it back in to herself. When she was finished, his light remained, hovering proudly on its own.

Len stared at it in disbelief.

It was his. It was back.

It was the most magical thing Maia had ever seen.

Len closed his hand into a fist. "*Finiatur,*" he croaked, and the light winked out. He staggered and collapsed into one of the wooden chairs.

Maia understood how he felt. Tears rained down her cheeks,

and she didn't even care. Becket, still standing frozen by the door, had both his hands covering his face, while his shoulders shook.

"It worked," she said, unable to fully believe it. "Goodness me, it *worked*."

* * *

It took rather a long time for the three of them to compose themselves again, understandably enough. Part of Maia wanted to flee, give her raw emotions a chance to settle and give Len a chance to adjust to this new hope. The other part of her couldn't bear the thought of leaving *now*.

Luckily, when courtesy made her half-heartedly suggest she leave Len to himself, he disagreed so vehemently she had to stay instead. At last, they returned to the sitting room, where Becket, himself again, if with a new lightness in his step, made them a fresh pot of tea and they attempted to hold a reasonable conversation.

"What will you do now?" Maia asked.

"I hardly know," Len said. He spread his hands on his knees and watched his still-shaking fingers. "An hour ago I thought I was magic-less for life. Now that I'm not … I don't know."

"Will you want to return to Intelligence, do you think?" she pressed. It wasn't polite, but she had a reason for asking.

"No!" he said, startling them both with his vehemence. "No," he said more quietly, but with no less emphasis. "That chapter is done. I'm tired of it, Maia. The scheming, the plotting, the dubious morality, the constant justification of petty evils as for the greater good. It was wearing me down before, only I couldn't see it. Harrison was right. I'd been in the field too long."

"I see."

"Besides, I'm tired of working for others. I want to be my own man for a change. D'you know, since I was a journeyman I was part of Intelligence? Even before then, unofficially." He smiled. "It had its grand moments, and I'm proud of what I've done for England and for magic, but it's done now. It's time for something new. I only wish I knew what." He rubbed his chin for a moment. "What about you? Have you decided where to focus your talents?"

Maia's heartbeat sped up. This was it.

"I have, actually," she said. "I realized it at the Magicians' Ball, only there was no time to think about it. Aunt Amelia thinks I'm a fool, but she told me if I wanted to waste my talent it was up to me. The thing is, I don't believe it will be wasted. I think this is the most important thing I can do with my magic. The only thing, really."

"What?" Len asked. "What is it?"

She forced herself to meet his eyes. This wasn't easy for her. She wasn't accustomed to relying on other people, to asking for things, to opening herself up for rejection.

But this was Len. He was dearer to her than a brother, the closest friend she'd ever had. And she had realized, in all this mess, that she didn't want to do anything with her magic that didn't have him as an integral part. "Actually, I'd hoped you might be interested in joining me," she said. "Because you care. You care about justice for everyone, not merely the 'important' people. And that's what I want. I want to use my magic to seek out truth, and to find justice for those who can't get it from others." She half smiled. "I'm not so different from my little sister Merry, I suppose, except her passion for equality and justice has turned toward politics. I could never be a Socialist, I don't think politicians will ever set aright the world's ills.

"I like puzzles, and adventures, and, and *making things right*. And it seems like a childish thing to do, a little girl who refuses to let go of nursery tales, but …" She spilled the next words out in a rush. "Len, I want to start a magical detective agency and I want to do it with you." She closed her mouth with a snap.

Len blinked as he tried to assimilate her words.

"I don't want you to feel guilty if you say no," she hurried to say. "I'll start it even without you." Oh dear, that didn't sound right at all. "I mean, I want you as a partner, but I'll do it on my own if I have to." She was making things worse. "You don't owe me anything for your magic. I would have done that no matter what, I hope you know that. And I understand if you want to take time to think about it. I know you were heading for Scotland. I can wait for your answer—"

Len leaned forward and rested one hand over hers. "Maia," he said, cutting her off.

She closed her mouth.

"Maia, I can't think of anything I would rather do than join you in opening a magical detective agency."

She released her breath. "Really?"

He squeezed her hand and then let go and sat back. "Absolutely. I never would have thought of it on my own, but hearing it from you, I can't think of anything more perfect. It is the right thing to do. Whitney and Davies, private investigators."

She wrinkled her nose at that. "I don't know, that sounds like a couple of undertakers rather than a detective agency."

"Davies and Whitney, then," he said promptly.

Now that it was settled, Maia was herself again. She laughed aloud. "Nonsense! Whitney and Davies it is."

"Becket!" Len called. "How would you like to be a private detective instead of a junior Intelligence agent?"

"Splendid, sir," Becket replied from the kitchen. Len looked at Maia.

"You've no objection to Becket, I trust?"

Maia rolled her eyes. "If ever I tried to separate the two of you I should shudder for the consequences. Besides, how do you know I didn't ask you simply for the sake of gaining Becket?"

Len smirked. "We might want one or two others," he said, tapping his fingers on his knee. Maia noted that they shook no more. "Helen, do you think?"

Maia shook her head. "Helen is starting her own fashion design company. Her dream has come true. She is the first master magician in the field of fashion glamours. She already has half a dozen students begging to apprentice to her! Even her mother is almost resigned. Helen will be far too busy to take up detecting as anything more than an amusing side hobby."

This was not the end of their friendship, despite the different paths their magic was taking them on. Maia was not going to live any longer with Aunt Amelia now she had the freedom to leave, and Helen felt that her new business required a measure of independence not to be gained under her parents' roof. The two young ladies had taken a flat in Bloomsbury, and Aunt Amelia's housemaid Elsie had jumped at the chance to come along and take care of the cooking and cleaning.

"Cor, that'll be a proper challenge, that will," she'd said when Maia awkwardly proposed it. The flat was tiny and the kitchen a disgrace, but Elsie seemed to think that made it all the more interesting. "And it'll get me out from under Mr. Lorde's thumb!" she'd finished gleefully.

"I do have another person in mind," Maia said now to Len. "You remember Gwen Zhang, from Basingstoke?"

"Of course," he said.

"I spoke to her recently, to let her know how the case turned out. Your Harrison Eastwood told us to not spread gossip, but since Gwen had been part of the case, I thought it only right she hear the end. Turns out she's not happy in Domestic Protection. She wants, as we do, to see justice done for all England's magicians, but the lackadaisical way everyone treats Deep, including Deep themselves, is frustrating her no end. She had thought about asking to transfer to MI when she'd gained enough experience, but hearing about Driver, and of Agent Barry's ruthlessness and eventual disgrace, made her rethink that. So I thought, maybe we could ask her. She's clever, innovative, and sharp-witted. Her time at St. Dorothea's means that she's not as bound to tradition as someone coming up from apprentice to journeyman, as we did. And she's likable enough, which is also important. I think we could all work together rather well. What do you say?"

"Perfect," he agreed, to her relief. Maia had been afraid she was being too overbearing. "And four is enough to be starting with, don't you think? At least until we are so famous and successful that we need a whole host of underlings."

"At which point we will simply take over Domestic Protection and run it the way we like," she agreed.

"I'd give us three months," Len said.

They laughed together. Len picked up his teacup and held it out.

"To Whitney and Davies Investigations," he said.

"To friendship and new dreams," Maia said.

"To us."

"To us."

They clinked their cups together and drank.

The fire crackled before them. Maia could hear the soft sound of Becket puttering in the kitchen. In the chair beside hers, Len sipped his tea and absently hummed under his breath, an amiable bumblebee. The armchair was comfortable, the books lining the walls cozy. She didn't think she'd ever felt such peace in all her life.

"Maia," Len said, breaking the silence. "Thank you."

That was all, but she understood. "You're welcome," she replied, and it was enough.

That moment, with the two of them together, was more than enough.

THE END

Acknowledgments & Author's Note

It's been six years since I published the first edition of Glamours and Gunshots. Not much has changed between then and now—I would still be utterly lost without my editor and dear friend A.M. Offenwanger. Amanda McCrina is still designing the best covers imaginable for the Whitney & Davies series. My husband Carl Ayers is still assisting me with Latin translations. I am as grateful now to the beta readers and proofreaders from the first edition as I was then: Heather Elliott, Cimone Watson, and Heather Belleguelle.

I am, if possible, even more grateful to the readers of the Whitney & Davies series now than I was six years ago. They have patiently stuck with the series through the very long waiting periods between books, they have sent me notes of encouragement, and have championed Maia and Len (and their friends-and-relations) for the last ten years. Without you, the readers, there wouldn't even be an ongoing series, much less a need for new editions.

On that note, a word about this edition: there isn't much that's changed between the first edition and this one. Most of the changes have been at a distribution level, in order to make it as easy as possible for booksellers to find and order copies of the books in this series to carry in store. However, astute readers may note that a few errors in-text have been cleaned up, and a few changes made to bring Maia and Len's recollections of the events of Magic Most Deadly more in line with the current edition of that story. The heart of the story, however, has remained the same. If you are an old reader, I hope you enjoy it just as much now as you did earlier. If you are a new reader, welcome—I hope you feel at home here. Stick around—we'd love to be able to call you friend.

About the Author

A storyteller from the time she could talk, as soon as E.L. Bates learned to write she began putting her stories down on paper and inflicting them on the general public. Stories of magic and derring-do have been her favorites from almost as young. She is a firm believer in Lloyd Alexander's maxim that "fantasy is not an escape from reality; it is a way of understanding reality." Also, it's a lot of fun both to write and to read.

When not writing, Bates works as a freelance editor and an office admin, and recently returned to school for Information and Library Science. In her spare time (what's that?) she enjoys knitting, reading, and hiking with her family.

You can find out more about E.L. Bates via her website, where you can also sign up for her newsletter for exclusive looks at new books and upcoming sales.

You can connect with me on:

🌐 http://www.stardancepress.com

Also by E.L. Bates

Whitney and Davies
  Magic Most Deadly
  Glamours and Gunshots
  Death by Disguise
  Magic & Mayhem (short story collection)
  While Shepherds Watch (a Christmas novella)

From the Shadows (a cozy space adventure)

Writing as Louise Bates
  Pauline Gray Investigates

www.ingramcontent.com/pod-product-compliance
Lightning Source LLC
Chambersburg PA
CBHW061245310726

48971CB00007B/2223